"We Have to Talk," Jase Said.

"Ti, what happened between us shouldn't have. I'm sorry. I fell in love with you—"

"You're sorry you fell in love with me?"

"No. I'm sorry I have to say this. I work for your grandfather. He gave me his trust when he asked me to come talk with you. I violated that trust."

"You can't be serious. Loving someone isn't a violation of trust."

"In this case it is. Ti, there are rules about people like us. Rules that cannot be broken. I work for your grandfather," he repeated. "There are unwritten rules that prevent the mixing between . . ." He paused.

"Between what? The classes? No, Jase. If you love me, nothing else matters."

"Because I love you, it does."

Dear Reader:

Silhouette has always tried to give you exactly what you want. When you asked for increased realism, deeper characterization and greater length, we brought you Silhouette Special Editions. When you asked for increased sensuality, we brought you Silhouette Desire. Now you ask for books with the length and depth of Special Editions, the sensuality of Desire, but with something else besides, something that no one else offers. Now we bring you SILHOUETTE INTIMATE MOMENTS, true romance novels, longer than the usual, with all the depth that length requires. More sensuous than the usual, with characters whose maturity matches that sensuality. Books with the ingredient no one else has tapped: excitement.

There is an electricity between two people in love that makes everything they do magic, larger than life—and this is what we bring you in SILHOUETTE INTIMATE MOMENTS. Look for them wherever you buy books.

These books are for the woman who wants more than she has ever had before. These books are for you. As always, we look forward to your comments and suggestions. You can write to me at the address below:

Karen Solem
Editor-in-Chief
Silhouette Books
P.O. Box 769
New York, N.Y. 10019

The Gentle Winds

Monica Barrie

Silhouette Intimate Moments
Published by Silhouette Books New York

America's Publisher of Contemporary Romance

Other Silhouette Books by Monica Barrie

Cry Mercy, Cry Love
Island Heritage

 SILHOUETTE BOOKS, a Division of Simon & Schuster, Inc.
1230 Avenue of the Americas, New York, N.Y. 10020

Copyright © 1983 by Monica Barrie

Distributed by Pocket Books

All rights reserved, including the right to reproduce
this book or portions thereof in any form whatsoever.
For information address Silhouette Books, 1230
Avenue of the Americas, New York, N.Y. 10020

ISBN: 0-671-46948-7

First Silhouette Books printing September, 1983

10 9 8 7 6 5 4 3 2 1

All of the characters in this book are fictitious. Any resemblance to actual persons, living or dead, is purely coincidental.

SILHOUETTE and colophon are registered trademarks
of Simon & Schuster, Inc.

SILHOUETTE INTIMATE MOMENTS is a trademark
of Simon & Schuster, Inc.

America's Publisher of Contemporary Romance

Printed in the U.S.A.

For Lucian Zachery Wind

I would like to thank those people who made the research on this novel possible:

the Gundlach-Bundschu Winery, in California's Sonoma Valley, and especially Mr. Lance Cutler, their dramatic, enthusiastic and extremely knowledgeable winemaker;

Bridgette Plummer and Alyce Dea of the Chateau and Estate Wines Company of San Francisco;

Joseph Seagram and Sons, Inc.;

the Hi-Tor winery in New York.

M.B.
Pomona, N.Y.
February 1983

Chapter 1

THE KEY MADE A CLICKING SOUND AS IT ENTERED THE lock. With a final turn, the door opened and Ti Caissen sighed and turned around.

"Thank you for a pleasant dinner," she said with a smile.

"The evening's not over yet," the man replied, his own smile firmly fixed in place.

"For me it is. Dinner was wonderful, Tom. Again, thank you," she repeated, trying to keep the irritation from her voice as she maintained her smile.

"C'mon Ti, I told you I can help you. I don't give up easily."

"Tom, please. We have to work together," she pleaded, trying to avoid any further mistakes with the man. She realized her error in accepting the dinner invitation with her boss, and didn't want to compound it further.

"Don't be stupid!" he said, a sneer curling the outer edges of his lips as he looked at her.

Ti pushed back the tide of anger that was fast rising within her and held back her biting retort.

"You've worked for me for four months. I think you're smart enough to understand that besides my being the head of the department, I have a lot of power in many areas of the company. Whatever I say goes. You're my assistant. Either you're nice to me, and go places in the company, or I find an assistant who will!" he threatened, his eyes hardening as he leaned over her.

"Then," Ti replied as she exhaled slowly, disliking the acidic taste in her mouth brought on by his words, "I guess I won't be in tomorrow."

"Ti, I want you," he whispered as his mouth closed on hers. Ducking her head, she tried to evade his groping hand, but could not. Her light anger turned to rage as she stiffened under his pawing.

Suddenly she was free.

"The lady said she wasn't interested," came a deep voice.

"Butt out, fella," Tom Hutchings replied with a sneer. Instantly, he was jerked backward by the collar of his coat.

"I can't do that." The newcomer, who towered over Hutchings by three inches and outweighed him by thirty pounds, spoke in a low, steel-tinged voice.

Ti watched, fascinated by what was happening, and strangely unafraid of her circumstances. She saw her now ex-boss dragged backward. His face was a sagging, grotesque mask of confusion and anger. Time ground to a halt, and, when her eyes found the stranger's, her breath caught in her throat. His wavy dark hair glistened under the hallway light, and the shadowed planes of his face seemed to glow. High cheekbones, full lips, a powerful chin, and a straight, aquiline nose fitted his rugged features to perfection. The bountiful mustache above his mouth matched his hair, and the crow's-feet at the corners of his eyes told Ti that he and the outdoors were friends. All of this scrutiny happened in less than a second as Tom Hutchings was pulled from her.

"Mister, get your hands off of me!" Hutchings yelled.

"Ma'am, shall I escort him to the elevator?" inquired the stranger, ignoring Hutchings's ineffectual threats.

"Please," Ti replied.

"You're going to regret this," Hutchings warned her.

"No, I don't think so. I think *you're* the one who'll have regrets. Make sure my check is in the mail, tomorrow!" she answered. Leaning against the door, she watched her unknown savior forcefully escort Hutchings to the elevator.

She knew she should be upset. She was watching the first step of her long-sought-after career going down the drain. But it wasn't bothering her at all. Her eyes stayed on the man's broad back, watching until the elevator door opened and he gave Hutchings a gentle but firm push. When the door closed, and the panel set into the wall above it showed the elevator was indeed going down, the man turned and looked at her.

He walked toward her, and again strange sensations filled Ti. He strode with a rolling gait that was graceful and commanding at the same time. He was tall, at least six feet one, and even beneath the bulk of his coat she knew his body would be as powerful as his walk.

"I can't tell you how much I appreciate what you did," Ti said as she offered her hand. "Thank you, Mr. . . . ?"

His hand grasped hers and held it tightly as he shook it. "Patten. Jase Patten," he told her as his dark umber eyes locked with hers.

Ti ignored the electric shock that raced along her arm

the moment their hands met. "Do you live on this floor?" she asked. She'd moved to this building after finishing graduate school, and, as was the pattern in cities like Philadelphia, she'd met only a few of her neighbors.

"No," he answered. Ti accepted his penetrating gaze, and at the same time decided not to pursue her questioning.

"Well, again, I must thank you."

"You're welcome, and I think you should choose a better class of man next time."

"I believe you're right," she agreed as she turned and opened the door. "Good night, Mr. Patten."

"Miss Barkley?" he called.

Ti froze. No one in Philadelphia ever called her Miss Barkley. No one she knew had ever heard of that name. Ti whirled around to stare at Jase Patten.

"What did you call me?" she whispered.

"Barkley. Ti Barkley," he repeated.

"How . . . ?"

"Your grandfather sent me," Jase informed her.

"My grandfather sent you?" she asked incredulously.

"Yes ma'am, and I think it was just in time."

"Mr. Patten, I don't know my grandfather. I've never seen him, or spoken to him, and I have no desire to do so now."

"I know. He thought you would react that way. All I can say is that he asked me to come here, and to bring you home."

"This is my home!" she retorted fiercely, her body trembling with forced restraint.

"Miss Barkley—"

"Caissen!" Ti snapped, cutting him off. "My name is Ti Caissen. Now, Mr. Patten, if you'll excuse me, I've had a long day and want to go to sleep." With that, Ti stepped into her apartment and closed the door. But she couldn't close it all the way; the toe of Jase's boot effectively blocked the door three inches from the frame. Angrily, she whipped the door open again.

"Do I have to call the police? Just tell my *grandfather* that I would not go."

"I'll be back in the morning to see if you've changed your mind. In the meantime, he wants you to read this." Jase withdrew an envelope from his inner pocket and handed it to her. A split second later he was gone.

Ti closed the door, slamming it loudly as she held the envelope. But all she saw was his smiling face, and she felt surrounded by the aura of his powerful presence that still hung in the air. Slowly, drawing in a deep breath, Ti turned on the apartment lights, took off her coat and sat on the only chair of her almost-unfurnished living room.

She waited several seconds before opening the letter, and thought about Jase Patten. She could not rid herself of the man's face, of his ruggedly masculine features and deep eyes. He was a man such as she'd never met before, and she was very much afraid of her instant attraction to him. *But that will not be a problem,* she told herself. She would not be seeing him again.

The envelope in her hand was forgotten as the thought of Jase, calling her by her mother's maiden name, brought out the secret memories she had buried long ago.

Ti tried desperately to stop herself from remembering. Her eyes swept the bare living room, and stopped when they fell on the mantel of the fireplace. Sitting by itself was an old stuffed teddy bear. Again, memories assaulted her and she could not prevent them from filling her thoughts.

They were the memories she had always kept private, hidden in a corner of her mind, refusing to dwell on them or on any facet of her mother's early life before she had been born. But she did know the entire story. She knew her family background as well as the subjects she'd mastered to attain her MBA.

Ti Barkley Caissen had been born twenty-four years before to Jenna Barkley. She had been born out of wedlock, so it had been said. Ti shivered as the memories grew strong. While she stared at the old teddy bear, she could see her mother's face, ten years ago, when Ti was fourteen years old and Jenna had told her the story of her birth.

They were sitting at the kitchen table, and had just finished eating their dinner. It was a Friday night; there was no school for Ti and no work for Jenna the next day. They were relaxing in the comfort of each other's company, and Ti, not for the first time, wondered why her relationship with her mother was so different from her friends'. She got along with her mother almost all the time, while her friends seemed to do nothing but fight with their parents. *Perhaps*, thought Ti, *it's because my father died so long ago that mother and I are close.* And because of that closeness, Ti ventured to ask her mother about it.

At first Jenna looked startled, then smiled softly. "I think we have something special because we work at it," Jenna said.

"No, Mom, we don't. That's the point. We get along so well because we don't work at it. I think it's because there's just you and I."

"You and *me*," she corrected gently. "I don't know, perhaps you're right." Jenna looked at Ti and the smile left her face. She reached across the table and took her daughter's hand. Ti felt the callouses on her mother's fingertips from her typewriter, and winced, but did not comment. "Ti, I think it's time we talked."

—

"We always talk," Ti replied, but the tone of her mother's voice told her this would be different.

"You've never asked about your father. Why?"

"I don't know. I guess because I never knew him, and what you told me about him was enough. Maybe because I know how much you miss him, and I don't want you to be hurt by talking about him."

"I love you," Jenna said in a choked voice. Then, gaining control over her emotions, she stood. "I have to get something, I'll be right back." Ti watched her mother leave the table, and return a moment later with something furry in her hand. She smiled, and placed the teddy bear on the table. Then she took Ti's hand again and began to talk.

"Ti, I . . . I better start at the beginning. As you know, I grew up in California. But what you don't know is that my father, your grandfather, is the owner of a prestigious winery in the Napa Valley. He is a wealthy, powerful man. Things might have been different if my mother had lived, but she died two years before you were born."

Ti stared uncomprehendingly at her mother. The words she was hearing were so alien to her, she did not really understand them. But, wisely, she held back the thousands of questions that were on the tip of her tongue as she waited for her mother to continue.

"Your father was a wonderful man. He was kind, gentle and handsome. He worked for my father, Samuel Barkley, as his general manager. Jamie, your father, was a tall, slender, quiet man. He loved his work, and he loved me. But my father did not approve of any man he had not hand-picked for me to date, and his attitude whenever I brought anyone home was one of instant dismissal."

Ti noticed then that her mother was trying very hard

to control her voice and not let any emotion show through in her words.

"It got worse after Mother died. Father seemed to become a dictator. We were fighting, arguing and barely talking to each other. He always told me the men I was going out with were fortune hunters, only after the money, the property and the winery I would one day inherit. He always disapproved, unless he chose my escorts. Life became more difficult with each passing week, and I used to take refuge in the fields, walking through the vineyards and talking to the vines. One day, after a particularly nasty fight with Father, I was in the fields and met Jamie there. He looked at me and saw how upset I was. We talked for a long time, and soon I felt something new come over me."

Jenna paused for a moment and smiled warmly at Ti. "I didn't realize it at the time, but I must have fallen in love with Jamie long before that day. But at that very instant, I recognized what was happening to me. I didn't say anything, but rather I just enjoyed his company.

"Soon our meetings became a regular thing, and as we talked, we realized that we enjoyed each other's company immensely, and looked forward to our times together. But I was afraid because of two things. Jamie was fifteen years older than I. Oh, he was so handsome! His hair was dark, like yours, and there was just a touch of silver beginning to appear at his temples. I'd known him for ten of my twenty years. The other problem that scared me was my father. He'd made it plain enough, on several occasions, that he did not condone the mixing of owners and employees.

"So, as each day passed and I fell more and more in love with Jamie, I grew more and more afraid of being found out, although nothing had yet happened between us to warrant that fear.

"Then a special day came. I still remember every detail of it," Jenna said as her eyes came back into focus and she smiled at Ti. "I remember it as if it were this morning. I was out in the fields, walking, when I met Jamie. We didn't speak, we just looked at each other and knew it could not be hidden. Within moments we were in each other's arms, kissing, crying and admitting the love we shared.

"For a year we met secretly, never letting anyone guess our feelings. For a year we tried to think of a way to make our love work." Jenna paused for a moment and her hand tightened around Ti's. "I realize you're only fourteen, but in many ways you're much older than your friends. I hope what I have to say will not harm you, but now that I've begun I won't stop."

"Nothing you can ever say will hurt me. Mother, I love you," Ti whispered.

"Jamie and I knew we were in a bad situation. We loved one another deeply, but could not show it to the world. One night, under a beautiful silver moon, we stood in the vineyards and exchanged vows. There was no minister officiating, no witnesses to say yea or nay, only the two of us and our love. That night, to ourselves, we married. That night, you were conceived under that very moon."

Ti's silence was suited to a much older woman as she watched the tears fall from her mother's eyes. She could not speak, but instead pressed her mother's hand tight and waited.

"We were married, as far as we were concerned. But we still could not say anything. First, Jamie had to look for another job far away from our home. If we told my father about us, he would have locked me away and fired Jamie. No one in the Valley or the surrounding area would hire Jamie if Father blacklisted him, and that would be only a small part of what my father was capable of. So we waited, and two months later Jamie took several days off and went to be interviewed for a promising position in a winery in Mexico.

"He called me one night, very excited. They liked him and had offered him the job. He would be driving back the next day, and when he returned we would tell my father, then leave to be married in a church and start a new life.

"He called me on the very day that I had received important news from my doctor. I was pregnant with you. I didn't tell Jamie on the phone, I wanted to wait until he was with me so I could see his face. I knew how happy he'd be.

"The next day, the day your father was due to arrive, the county sheriff drove up to the house. I watched from my window as he spoke to my father. A few minutes later I came downstairs and heard Father on the phone. He was speaking to Jamie's mother. I listened, horrified, while he told Jamie's mother that Jamie had been killed in an automobile accident, ten miles from our home. I don't remember everything that happened. I fainted, and when I awoke my father and the doctor were there."

"Oh, Mother," Ti whispered as she, too, began to cry. Ti saw Jenna fighting back the pain of her memories as she continued to speak.

"After a few minutes my father left the room and I asked the doctor if he'd said anything about my pregnancy. He hadn't, and I asked him not to. He agreed after I told him who the father was. The doctor was shaken—Jamie had been a patient of his, also.

"That terrible day finally passed. As the weeks turned into months, I could no longer hide my condition. I had no choice left, I had to tell my father. He was incensed. He ranted and raved and carried on, insisting that I get an abortion. I refused. Then he insisted I go to a 'special home' until you were born, and afterward put you up for adoption. I refused," Jenna said, as her hazel eyes looked deep into the matching eyes of her daughter.

"Then he gave me an ultimatum. The great Samuel Barkley told me that either I do as he said, or leave! I chose to leave. I moved to Philadelphia to be as far from California as possible, found a job, and continued with my life.

"When you were born, my reason for living returned. In you I saw your father, and my love for him stayed strong within me. Since the day I left my home in California, I have never spoken to my father. I never will."

Jenna smiled sadly at Ti, and shook her head. "I named you after your great-great-great-grandmother. She and her husband founded the vineyards and the winery. She was a strong, independent, hardheaded, beautiful woman. She was also a rebel and a magnificent person. Her father named her after a fort, because he was a general in the Union army. His wife objected, but he overruled her. He named her Ticonderoga. Ti, for short. I was named for her sister, Jenna. Your name is the only inheritance I can give you. Ti, after your ancestor Ti Bennett; Barkley, because you are a Barkley; and Caissen, after your father. You should be proud of those names and wear them well."

"I will," Ti promised.

Jenna smiled softly and released Ti's hand. She picked up the teddy bear, looked at it, and then looked back at Ti. "Your father won this for me at a fair. I've had it for fifteen years, it was the only thing of his I had until you were born." Jenna lifted the bear and held it out to Ti. "It's time you had it," she whispered.

Ti took the bear silently, and felt a warmth flow

through her as she held the furry stuffed animal. Blinking back tears, Ti gave the teddy bear back to her mother. "No," she murmured, "it's yours." Mother and daughter remained silent for several long seconds before Jenna nodded slowly with the understanding of what her daughter had just done.

"Now I need to know something," Jenna said.

"Mom?"

"How do you feel?"

"Loved, happy and glad you told me," Ti answered truthfully as she stood and went to her mother's arms. "I love you," she whispered against the comfort of Jenna Caissen's warm bosom.

Suddenly Ti returned to the present as another memory hit her like a stone. Her mother's funeral, three years ago. *No more,* she told herself, fighting away the tears her too-vivid memory had brought on. She blinked several times before looking at the thick envelope in her hands. With a sigh, she opened it, taking out several handwritten pages. Slowly, she focused on the first words.

Granddaughter,

Yes, granddaughter. It is time we met. It is time for you to know who you are, and to . . .

Jase Patten stood on the darkened corner outside Ti's building and pulled his collar up against the chill breeze whistling along the avenue. He looked up in a vain effort to pick out her window.

Shrugging his shoulders, Jase began to walk. His mind whirled in confusion. He'd stood in the hallway outside her apartment for two hours waiting for her. When she'd gotten out of the elevator, he'd seen she had someone with her and had stepped into the hidden shelter of a doorway.

Without Ti or her companion seeing him, he'd started toward the elevator but had not been able to avoid hearing them talk. A warning chill had raced along his spine as the man spoke, and he found himself unable to leave.

When the man's voice had turned ugly, Jase started toward them. As Ti tried to avoid the other's groping, Jase had moved quickly and pulled the man from her.

After he'd taken Hutchings and put him in the elevator, he'd turned and taken a good long look at Ti Barkley. She was beautiful. In fact, she was probably the prettiest woman he'd ever seen.

Her coal-black hair gleamed in the low hallway light, and fell in waves to frame a face of ivory skin. Her lips, although unsmiling, were shaped in the double arches of a bow. Her small nose set off two large, almost iridescent hazel eyes. Green flecks glowed from them, and, as he stepped next to her, he was almost lost in them. Her hand, as he shook it, had felt like soft, delicate velvet.

The look she gave him when he had spoken of her grandfather would have shaken him if he'd been less prepared, but Sam had forewarned him.

Jase crossed a dark street and shook his head as he looked around, wondering who would want to live in a city when there was so much magnificent land available to live on. Jase Patten didn't like cities, he didn't like the confinement, or the dirt in the air. But he would stay here until he accomplished what he'd come here for—until he brought Ti Barkley home.

Again, her face floated before him. He couldn't rid himself of the way she looked. Forcing himself to think of something else, Jase's thoughts focused on Barkley

Vineyards, and the meeting between Sam Barkley and himself.

"Jase, I want her here," Sam had said. "I want her to live here and to see what is hers. It's time . . ."

Jase had looked at his boss and shook his head. "Sam, she's your granddaughter. You have to be the one to ask her."

"I will, with this," replied the older man as he'd handed Jase an envelope. "But I need you to deliver it. Jase, if I go there she'll throw it in my face!"

"You don't know that."

"Yes I do. I made a mistake a long time ago when I made an enemy out of my daughter. Up to the day she died, she would not talk to me. Our last words were spoken twenty-five years ago, in anger. She wouldn't answer a single letter. Ti must know the story and she'll feel the same way. She's a Barkley, and we're known for being stubborn." Sam Barkley had paused for a moment as he'd lifted the glass in his hand and sniffed the fragrance of the wine that rose to greet him. Instead of drinking it, he'd lowered the glass to gaze at Jase. "I've watched her grow from three thousand miles away, and I've followed her life and her mother's. No, she won't talk to me. Jase, I'm counting on you."

And Jase saw now that Sam had been right. She hated the grandfather she'd never met. As soon as he'd mentioned Sam Barkley, Jase had been aware of the instant hatred that had filled her eyes.

He took a deep breath, crossed the final street and walked into the lobby of his hotel. There, he went into the partially filled bar and sat on a stool away from other people. He ordered a drink, and when the bartender served it he took a long swallow.

He owed a lot to Sam Barkley, and he would do everything he could to get Ti to California. Then he smiled. Even if he didn't care for the old man, now that he'd met Ti Barkley he knew he wouldn't give up until she was on the plane with him.

Ti woke suddenly, her body reacting to the stimulus of the alarm. Reaching over to the end table, she shut it off and lay back again.

The alarm had been preset, and she'd forgotten to turn it off last night. She had no reason to get up at six o'clock, with no job to go to. Ti exhaled slowly and tried to go back to sleep.

Five minutes later she gave up. Everything that had happened to her yesterday kept flashing violently in her mind, from Tom Hutchings's treatment of her and the loss of her job, to the meeting with Jase Patten and—topping it all off—her grandfather's letter.

A flood of warmth filled her as she remembered the way Jase Patten had handled her boss. A fluttering in the pit of her stomach accompanied thoughts of his rugged face and flashing smile. Then a spurt of anger wiped away the newfound feeling as she thought about Tom Hutchings. She had wanted this job with Matheson and Company. She had worked hard all through graduate school, and even harder during the summer's apprenticeship program at Allied, in her efforts to prove she would make a good financial analyst.

She'd beaten out three other candidates, all men, but she realized, after last night's experience, it had been because Tom Hutchings had wanted a plaything as his assistant.

"Damn it!" she yelled to the empty apartment. She had played everything very close, choosing to use her mother's life insurance money to finish school instead of working full-time and going to night school. She knew her savings would only be enough to last another few months, if that long.

She'd rented this apartment just before graduation,

planning to furnish it slowly as she earned her money. If she didn't get a new job soon, she didn't know what would happen. *No,* she corrected herself, *I will get a job, and everything will work out.*

Ti left the bed quickly and went to the bathroom. She showered and washed her hair, trying as she did to wash the negative thoughts from her mind. When she finished drying her long waves, she picked out a gray herringbone-tweed business suit and an antique ivory blouse to go with it.

Ti had no intention of waiting. Today she would start to look for a new job. She dressed, putting on only a minimum of makeup, just enough to add a bit of maturity to her face, and then twisted her hair into a bun centered at the nape of her neck.

She liked the feel of her long hair, but when it hung loosely it made her look too much like a student. The bun and the unnecessary makeup gave the illusion of adding a few years to her age, which made her look like a serious job applicant.

When she was dressed, and had checked herself over in the full-length mirror, she nodded and stepped into black low-heeled shoes. Then she went into the living room, and froze.

On the floor in front of the chair was her grandfather's letter. *Why now?* she asked herself. *Why not years ago when Mother was alive?* She went to the chair, bent, and picked up the pages of the letter she had angrily flung away last night.

The letter itself had been simple and direct. Samuel Barkley wanted Ti to visit him. He expressed concern for her, and a desire for them to meet. He had written that there would be no obligations, only that it was time she learned about her family.

While hatred for him burned within her, fired by the

memories of her mother's life, she realized she was also
torn and curious to know about Samuel Barkley and
her family.

Ti had always been somewhat interested in learning
about her roots. In college, everyone around her
always spoke of their parents, grandparents and other
relatives. But at the same time, Ti had purposely not
tried to find out anything about her family. The only
thing she had ever known had been what she'd learned
that one night when she was fourteen. After that her
mother never spoke of it, and Ti couldn't bring herself
to ask. She knew how much pain that one night of
memories had brought on. When her mother died, Ti
no longer had the time to think about her family
background. She had to work hard in school, and also
work a few hours a night to make sure she would not go
through the money she had too quickly.

Ti folded the pages of the letter and returned them to
the envelope as she went into the kitchen to make her
breakfast. Just then, the doorbell rang.

"Now what?" she muttered, changing direction and
walking to the front door. Her breath caught the
moment she opened it and gazed into the dark eyes of
Jase Patten. Her head spun as she stared at him. Her
anger rose almost as fast as her heart suddenly started
racing. The memory of the burning feel of her hand in
his last night added to the confusion running rampant
in her mind. *What's happening? Why is he here?* Then
she remembered his words; he'd said he would talk to
her this morning.

"You could be polite and invite me in," Jase said.

"Why?" Ti replied, finding her voice at last.

"For breakfast."

"Mr. Patten—"

"Jase."

"Mr. Patten, go away."

"Miss Caissen, I've brought you breakfast," Jase countered as he lifted a large brown bag.

"Why?" she repeated again, acutely aware he had called her Caissen, not Barkley.

"Maybe because I have a job, and you don't."

For some reason his words struck her in a funny way. "Oh, I thought your job was to take me to California?"

"No—" Before he could finish, Ti cut him off.

"Then you don't have a job, either?" she asked him sarcastically.

"Yes, I have a job, but taking you to California is a favor to your grandfather, not my job."

"I don't understand. . . . Wait! You've brought me breakfast to ease your guilty conscience because you helped me lose my job!"

"Did you want the job *that* badly?" Jase teased, unable to hold back a smile. Not one word she'd spoken had bothered him—in fact, he was enjoying this banter.

Ti stared coldly at him but couldn't maintain the look . . . or the anger. When he smiled, two cutting lines etched deep grooves from his cheekbones to his jawline, and sent a tingle racing through her body. Without speaking, Ti stepped back and held the door for him.

"I'm afraid I don't have a dining table yet," Ti explained while Jase stood in the living room, looking for a place to put the food down. She watched his back, her heart still beating too fast as she took in his appearance. He wore a tweed sports jacket, tailored to fit him perfectly, with soft leather elbow patches and pocket trim that matched. The collar of a light blue shirt rested atop the jacket's collar, and the rust-colored slacks matched the rest of the outfit. The same tan boots he'd worn last night were on his feet.

"How about a tablecloth?" he suggested.

"That I have," Ti said. She went to the linen closet in the hallway and took out a white linen cloth. When she came into the living room, Jase was still holding the bag. He put it down and took the tablecloth from her.

"Right here," he decided as he stepped to the center of the room. Unfolding the linen, he shook it out and let it settle on the floor. "Knives, forks and spoons," he commanded.

"Yes, sir!" Ti said with a salute. By the time she returned from the kitchen, Jase had the food out and was sitting down.

"You do like bacon and eggs, don't you?" he asked.

"On occasion."

"Is morning enough of an occasion?" Jase shot back.

"We'll let it be this time," Ti replied, sitting and smiling at the same time.

"That's better."

"What?"

"Your smile."

Ti knew she was blushing and tried to ignore it. She sensed the tension in the air, and wondered if it was only in her mind. She watched Jase open his coffee and lift the white container to his lips. He flashed another dazzling smile before taking a sip and looking around.

"Nice place," he observed in a solemn voice. Ti almost spit out the coffee she had sipped as she saw his eyes speed around the almost-empty room. Her laugh was a half-choke which she quickly controlled, but lost again as Jase joined in.

"'Course it could use a bit more furnishing," he added.

"Just a few little things to make it homey?" Ti queried.

"Little things," Jase agreed. "A couch, some carpeting, a stereo, maybe even a coffee table."

"As a matter of fact, I was going to Macy's tomorrow to buy a few of those 'little' things."

"Was?"

"I need a job first," she reminded him.

"No you don't."

"Really? What do I need?" she asked, holding his eyes in a steady gaze.

"To eat."

"We are."

"No, we're talking. Let's eat," Jase said as he arched his eyebrows, "then I'll tell you what you can do."

Ti held back a biting response about his level of confidence, and instead nodded her head. They ate the rest of their breakfast in silence. When they were done, and the aluminum plates and styrofoam cups were piled neatly into the bag, Ti looked at him.

"Tell me," she commanded.

Jase nodded slowly. He didn't want to say what he had to. The mood they were sharing was too good, too relaxed to spoil, but he knew he had no choice. Gazing into her eyes, he lost himself for a moment before he spoke. "Don't bother with the furniture or looking for a job yet. Come to California with me and meet your grandfather."

"No." Ti said the single word quickly and firmly. She would not go, nor would she be seduced into going by Jase Patten's charm. She had a sudden feeling that Jase used his personality to its best advantage, whenever he could—he had that look about him.

"Ti, I have to be honest with you. I don't like this city; the smells, the dirt and the crowds bother me. No one should have to live like this, least of all me. But I'm not going to California without you."

Ti held her breath as he spoke. She watched his eyes, and saw he was telling the truth. "In that case, I hope you like living in Philly!"

"Have you ever been any place other than here?" Jase asked suddenly.

"What difference does that make?"

"Have you ever seen the Napa Valley?" he persisted.

"No, and I have no intention of doing so."

"It's beautiful. The colors are magnificent. The land is powerful, and the people are real, not cardboard imitations of the person next to them on the bus. Ti, you belong there. You're not like the people around here. You'll thrive there, you're too beautiful not to," Jase said with more emotion than he intended.

Ti could feel his words as if they were a part of her. The way he talked, and the way his features softened when he spoke, made her want to go and see the Valley for herself. But she pushed the vision away as she shook her head.

"No. Now if you'll excuse me, I have to find a job, and since you seem to be so determined, you'd better find an apartment to live in, because I will not be going to California with you."

"Ti . . ." Jase began, but stopped as he gazed at the hard set of her face. He rose slowly. "I enjoyed having breakfast with you," he said. Then, without waiting for Ti to stand, he strode quickly across the room.

He opened the door, and Ti watched Jase walk through it and close it softly behind him. "Good-bye," Ti whispered. A strange sense of loss weighed down on her, but it was not enough that she disregarded the other sensations coursing through her.

What was it about Jase Patten that made her feel the way she did? Still trying to understand, she stood, picked up the tablecloth and garbage bag and cleaned up. She still had to find a job, now even more than before, or she might find herself giving in to the handsome man with whom she'd just shared her floor and breakfast.

Chapter 2

THE ELEVATOR DOOR CLOSED WITH A HISS. TI'S LOW exhalation matched the sound. Her finger pressed the button for the fifth floor, and, as the elevator began its ascent, her eyes unfocused as she reviewed her day.

She'd had three interviews. All of them promising, all of them worthless in the end. Ti had never been one to waste time, and when she'd left the apartment this morning, she'd already had her day planned. She did not go to the employment agencies that abounded in the city; rather, she went directly to the personnel departments of several major financial corporations.

The first had been a large international banking firm, similar to the one she'd been working at the past months. She'd gotten through the initial stage when the question had been asked.

"Your application states it was a personal reason for leaving Matheson and Company, but after so short a time I must have a more encompassing answer," the personnel director had informed her.

"I'm sorry, but it was a personal reason," Ti protested. The look in the man's eyes had told her that her answer would not be good enough. Yet, intuitively, she also knew that if she told this man the truth, he would not believe her. Tom Hutchings's reputation as a straightforward businessman was strong within the financial community.

"All right, Miss Caissen, I'll keep your application on file and if there are any openings, we'll give you a call. But I think I should warn you that the job market is tight at present, and in the last two years we've been flooded with applicants whose backgrounds are more fully developed than yours."

Ti recognized the dismissal in his voice and shrugged her shoulders. She left the interview, not disheartened, but saddened that a personal reason for leaving a job was not enough of an explanation.

The next interview had gone the same as the first, but the third interview, for a large international conglomerate, had been very different. The head of personnel had been a woman, and during the interview, Ti had felt she could speak her mind to her.

She'd been right, yet it still hadn't mattered.

"Miss Caissen, you're in the real world now, not college. The situation you were in happens all the time. Men like Tom Hutchings think they can do whatever they want. Sadly enough, they get away with it. But you learned a very valuable lesson. Don't play unless you're willing to pay the price."

"I wasn't playing," Ti had tried to explain. "We'd been working late and Tom had offered me dinner to compensate for the hours. I didn't see anything wrong with that. At least," Ti had admitted, "until we were almost through eating."

"It usually works that way. But times are tight. Jobs of all types are extremely hard to find. There's nothing available right now, unless you want to be a secretary," the woman had said. "However, there is one possibility . . ." Ti gazed at her, and had seen her eyes grow distant.

"Yes?" Ti had prompted.

"It won't be pleasant, but job hunting and trying to explain your reason for leaving your last job isn't exactly the nicest experience, either. Start legal action against Matheson and Company for sexual harassment, which caused you to leave your job. File suit not only for damages, but for the return of your job."

"I . . ." Ti had begun.

"Think it out. Not only will they have to recognize your side, but they would be forced to rehire you and to put you in a different and probably better position. The public's attention would be focused on you and Matheson and Company, and Matheson would have to face the courts and the public and explain why they condoned Hutchings's behavior." Ti had nodded at the woman's words, and felt the excitement of a confrontation coming on.

"It would be a hell of a fight," the personnel director had cautioned as she wrote something on a piece of paper, and extended it to Ti. "This is the name of a friend of mine. She's a good lawyer, especially for this sort of thing. See her. She'll help."

"And what about a job?" Ti had asked.

"I'll put your application at the head of my list. You've impressed me. But, as I said earlier, there's nothing available in the area of your specialization, and it may be a while."

Ti shook her head as the elevator door opened. She was not looking forward to the night ahead, or the weekend, either. But she had already determined that on Monday she would continue with her job hunt. Ti strode purposefully toward her door, but stopped halfway. She sighed loudly. "Not again," she whispered raggedly, feeling her temper flare as she saw Jase Patten leaning carelessly against her door. But even as she worked to control her feelings of frustration, the sight of his handsome face sent a sudden thrill through her body. Ti fought and won a small skirmish with herself and didn't let the sudden warmth she felt show on her face.

"What do you want now?" she asked sharply.

"Dinner," Jase replied with a smile.

"I'm not broke!"

"Yet . . ." he said in a low voice as their eyes sparked in a clash of wills. His smile grew wider. "I don't want to take you to dinner because of that. I want your company."

"So you can talk to me about my grandfather?" she challenged.

"So I can look at you. Ti, I want to be with you for a while, for myself," Jase admitted as his eyes swept the soft slopes of her face. It was true, and he meant every word. Ever since this morning, when he'd left the apartment, he'd been haunted by her face.

"Jase . . ." she began, but stopped and shook her head. "Come inside for a minute," she said as she tried to sort out the confusion in her mind.

Once in the apartment, she turned and gazed at his face. A chill raced through her when she found herself unable to pull her eyes from his.

"Why me?" she asked.

"I'll pick you up at seven," he said.

"I haven't agreed yet."

"Please."

"You are conceited, aren't you?"

"No," Jase said with a shake of his head.

"All right," Ti agreed.

"Thank you." He flashed another brief smile and

went to the door. "I'll see you later," he told her as his large hand reached for the doorknob. A breath later he was gone, and Ti was again looking at a closed door.

"Enough!" Ti cautioned herself as she hummed a tune while brushing her hair. Ever since Jase had left, her mood had changed. She was feeling good. She knew she shouldn't be, but she was, just the same. She was looking forward to tonight—to talking with Jase, to being near him.

What am I doing? she asked herself. *That man is here for only one reason. He wants to take me to California any way he can, and I won't go!* But Ti couldn't prevent the troubling thoughts, and, try as she might, the confusion in her mind stopped her from being able to sort out her emotions. She knew she was facing a crisis, and Jase Patten's seductive presence was a major part of it.

Ti sat on the edge of her bed and bent her head over, flipping her hair so it hung toward the floor. She brushed the black mane vigorously, enjoying the feel of the bristles as they pushed through the thickness of her hair and stroked the nape of her neck. When she finished, she sat up and flipped her hair back. She could feel the blood rushing from her face as her hair settled around her shoulders.

Standing, she went to the bathroom mirror where she examined her hair and nodded. The shining waves framed her face nicely. Reaching down, Ti chose a pale green eye shadow and brushed it on her lids. When she finished, she applied some mascara, a small amount of blush, and finished off the look with a light coral shade of lipstick. Satisfied with the way she looked, she returned to the bedroom and went to the closet.

Her eyes roamed along the rack, choosing and discarding each item until she reached the end. Ti sighed loudly. Dating had never been easy for her, and at present she went out infrequently.

After two disastrous affairs, she'd consciously arranged her schedule so she would be too busy studying and working to become involved with another man. As Ti looked at her clothes, the truth of her thoughts struck hard. She realized her entire wardrobe was designed solely for business. With a shrug, she picked out the least professional outfit and began to dress.

Ti slipped a simple black jersey dress over her head. She belted it, put on a pair of black pumps, and walked to the mirror on the bedroom door. There, she gazed critically at herself. The dress fit her smoothly; its blouson bodice was form-fitting, showing off her slim waist yet minimizing her full breasts. She turned sideways and again nodded approvingly at the way the skirt of the dress hugged and flattered her rear before falling in a straight line just below her knees, allowing the trimness of her calves to show. The sleeves were full and cuffed at the wrists. *Yes,* Ti thought, *this will do.*

With a few final pats to smooth the dress, Ti turned and picked up her purse. As she entered the living room, the doorbell rang. She opened the door and again, her breath caught dangerously in her throat.

Jase stood silently, framed in the doorway. He was dressed in a navy-blue pin-striped suit, with a pale yellow shirt and a matching blue tie. His broad shoulders seemed even wider, and the two cutting grooves in his cheeks dug deeper as the corners of his mouth turned slowly upward.

"You look lovely," he declared as he stepped inside.

"So do you," she replied, her voice huskier than she'd wanted it to be.

"I'll take that as a compliment."

"You should, I don't say that to many men," Ti

bantered, aware of the heat that had quickly spread through her body as she gazed at him. *Stop it!* she ordered herself.

"Ready?" he asked.

Ti nodded and opened the small closet in the hallway. She took out a light sweater and put it over her arm. Then, with a smile, she left the apartment with Jase.

Ti lifted the white porcelain coffee cup, embossed with the symbol of the hotel's restaurant. "Dinner was very good," she told Jase. He nodded, but didn't speak. "Is something wrong?" she asked, concern filling her voice and drawing Jase's eyes to hers.

"No, as a matter of fact, everything is right," he admitted. It was the truth, but at the same time Jase's sense of responsibility weighed heavily on his conscience. He had an obligation to fulfill, one that was becoming increasingly difficult. He knew he should not allow his feelings to control him; he must maintain a distance from the beautiful creature sitting across from him. Yet, for the first time in his life, he couldn't. He'd never before felt anything that compared to his feelings for Ti.

"You're a strange man, Jase Patten."

"Not really, just different from what you're used to."

Ti stiffened, and then forced herself to relax. No one, except for herself, knew how infrequently she dated. Most people just took it for granted that she saw a lot of men. She knew she attracted men, but did not fully understand why.

"I don't think you know what I'm used to," she informed him tersely.

"No, I probably don't."

Ti shook her head at this new admission, again

confused by his directness. "Is Jase your real name, or a nickname?"

"Jason is my real name."

"Jason," she repeated. "I like your name."

"Thank you."

"You're welcome. Tell me about yourself, Jason Patten."

Jase looked at her for a long, drawn-out moment before he spoke, and when he did, another chill stiffened her spine. "My life started eight years ago, when I went to work for Sam Barkley—" Jase stopped himself. He hadn't meant to say that and didn't know why he had.

"Jason . . . ?" Ti prompted him hesitantly, sensing the strange depths behind his abbreviated words.

"Sorry, I guess this city is getting to me." Jason paused for a moment to sip his coffee. "Let's see. I'm thirty-three years old, the general manager of Barkley Vineyards, healthy, male, and I hate cities!"

"So I've noticed. Tell me about vineyards."

"If you've never seen the Napa Valley, I can't tell you about them. They are magnificent. They're powerful, beautiful and they can steal your soul."

"Have they stolen yours?" she asked.

"They tried. Ti, come to California," he urged.

"You promised—"

"I promised not to talk about your grandfather. I said nothing about California," he declared with a smile. But Ti couldn't help feeling a sense of betrayal.

Jase saw the tension in her eyes but did not allow it to stop him. His hand reached across the table and took hers, holding it firmly and pressing just enough to make her look at him.

"I know this sounds foolish, but from the minute I saw you, I knew you belonged there, not here. I can't explain what it is, but you must believe me. Ti, come back with me, see for yourself what I'm talking about. Throw away your business suits and put on a pair of jeans and walk barefoot on the soft, fertile ground. There's nothing like it in the world."

Ti shook her head slowly. She wasn't saying no, she was trying to chase away the vibrating hum that filled her mind with the visions his words evoked. His hand was a burning ember on hers as he spoke, and her heart was beating painfully. Slowly, Ti forced herself to control her runaway emotions.

"Do you know what he did to my mother?" she asked in a low voice. Jase nodded slowly. She sighed, relieved that she wouldn't have to explain why she felt as she did.

"That was twenty-five years ago. People change."

"Not everyone."

"You don't know whether Samuel Barkley changed!"

"I don't want to," Ti cried as she pulled her hand free.

"It won't cost you anything to go, you're not working now, why not give it a chance?" Jase asked somberly.

"It will cost a lot! And I won't go," she declared angrily, "because I hate him!"

"You can't hate him. You don't even know him."

"Yes I do!" Ti spat out, her vision turning red with anger.

"Just think about it. It can't hurt, and it might help you more than you think."

Through the misty haze of anger filming her eyes, Ti began to form her next retort. But Jase's hand covered hers again, and he smiled a gentle, warm smile. Her irrational anger diminished as he held her hand, and when it had almost gone, Jase spoke.

"Let's not talk about it. Let's dance," he suggested. "You do dance, don't you?"

"Not in a hotel dining room!"

"To a band in their lounge?"

"Possibly, but I'm not into disco," she said, suddenly nervous. She hadn't danced very often, and when she had, it had been at formal occasions such as weddings.

With a wave of his hand, Jase called for the check. After he signed it, he stood and drew Ti to her feet. They walked through the elegant dining room, and into a softly lit cocktail lounge. Once they were seated in a velvet-cushioned booth, and their drinks were served, Jason's hand again covered hers and his dark eyes gazed deeply at her.

Ti was very aware of the soft, rhythmical music. A quartet played in the background as she smiled hesitantly up at Jase.

Slowly, without his eyes leaving her face, and without a single word, he drew Ti to her feet and guided her to the dance floor. Once they were on the parquet tile, he pulled her to him, lightly placing one hand at the small of her back as his other hand reached for hers. The heat from his hand on the sensitive skin at the small of her back penetrated the thin material of her dress in a maddeningly wonderful way. He moved gracefully with the music, and soon Ti was lost within the soft call of the song and the strong feel of the man.

They danced, barely moving yet flowing smoothly within the confines of the music. Ti was totally aware of Jase, of his heady masculine scent, and the raw, sensual heat radiating from every part of his body. She gazed at him momentarily, only to melt under his smoldering eyes. Desperately, she drew her eyes from his and rested her cheek on his shoulder and chest.

Jase was extremely conscious of the woman he held as he looked at her dark-capped head, the top of which reached barely above his shoulder. He could feel the softness of her body against his, and tried unsuccessfully to quell the sparks of a desire he'd not felt in years.

They moved well together, blending their bodies as if they were one. Again, Jase's resolutions vacilated, and he knew he was caught in a dangerous game.

By the time the song ended, neither Ti nor Jase could speak. They stood in the middle of the dance floor, holding each other, waiting for the next number to start. When it did, they danced again, slowly, comfortably fitted to each other. The rest of the evening was filled with a lot of dancing and very little conversation.

By midnight, Jase knew he could handle no more of her closeness. Inside his mind a warning bell rang, and he made himself heed it. Carefully, as he sipped wine from a glass, he looked at her. "It's late."

"I know," Ti responded languidly. Silently, as if there were no need for words, they both rose. Jase helped her with her sweater, and when they left the hotel he signaled a cab.

"I'd rather walk," Ti said. She was pleased at his look of understanding and slipped her arm through his. As they walked through the almost-empty streets, she enjoyed the security of Jase's company. When the seven blocks had passed and they stood in front of her building, she didn't want the evening to end.

The elevator ride was over too fast, and suddenly they were standing before her door. The night was over. Ti turned to Jase and smiled. "Thank you," she murmured.

She watched Jase come closer. She could see every line in his face, and was even able to see herself reflected in his eyes. Her heart almost stopped when she realized he was going to kiss her. Her mouth was dry, and she moistened her lips with the tip of her tongue. Slowly, maddeningly, Jase's mouth neared hers.

Then his lips were on hers, and a flare exploded suddenly inside her. Fire seared her heart and her breathing turned shallow. His mouth covered hers as his arms went around her, drawing her close in a hard and passionate embrace. They stayed locked together for a long time. The only sound in Ti's ears was the rushing of her blood; her only awareness was the hardness of his chest and thighs against hers.

Then, without wanting it to end, they parted. Silently, Jase turned and walked to the elevator. She ignored the heavy rise and fall of her chest as she watched him go, and tried in vain to extinguish the fire still burning her lips. The key in her trembling fingers was forgotten as her eyes misted with confused emotions. She wanted to cry out to him but could not. At the elevator, she watched him turn and face her.

"Jason," she whispered.

"I'll call you Monday. That will give you two days to think about everything. I'll need your answer then."

Ti stared at him until she nodded her acceptance. When the elevator arrived, and Jase stepped inside it, Ti turned and tried to unlock her door. Her fingers shook, and she fought to steady them. When at last she flipped the lock and entered the safety of her apartment, she was still in a state of shock.

What had happened to her? Without her knowledge, Jase had created hundreds of new feelings inside her. Predominant among them was a new, unfulfilled ache, ebbing and flowing from her feet to her face in great, churning waves.

Once again Jase walked along the avenue, fighting the growing depths of his feelings, and battling also his need to do what he was sent to do.

Ti's green-flecked eyes haunted him. Her small mouth cried out to him, and the memory of her soft breasts crushed against his chest sent lances of desire piercing through him. Forcefully, Jase thrust these thoughts aside.

Sam Barkley had been good to him. He'd taken him from the wasteland his life had become, and helped him find a new life. When Jase had wanted only oblivion, Barkley had forced him to face the world again, to return to it and to grow stronger.

How could he let his emotions get so out of control? How could he repay everything Barkley had done for him by letting himself fall for the man's granddaughter? There were many potentially dangerous circumstances on the horizon, and Jase knew he could not let himself become more involved than he already was.

Yes, he knew the story of Jenna Barkley and her daughter. That, too, was part of why he was here. His heart had gone out to Samuel Barkley because he knew exactly what the old man had gone through for the past twenty-five years.

Jase had almost said too much at dinner tonight, but he'd been able to divert the conversation. Yes, he and Sam Barkley had many things in common. Unable to stop the memories, Jase became lost in them, even as he entered the hotel and continued to his room.

His life had fallen apart nine years ago. He had been twenty-four, out of college for two years, married, and the father of a two-month-old daughter. He had been working for a small, independent vineyard in the Napa Valley. One evening a cold, hard rain had swept across the Valley, and he, along with all the other men, had been out in the vineyards trying to save the crop by using plastic and heaters to protect the grapes.

The unseasonal chill had also forced them to use

propane heaters in the very old, small houses they lived in, in order to keep their families warm.

It had been late when one of the men had yanked Jase's arm and pointed excitedly toward the workers' houses. In the distance a sheet of orange flame blazed skyward.

"Let's go," he cried, dragging the other man with him. As he ran toward the fire, something deep inside told him it was his house. The certainty, and the fear, had lent an inhuman speed to his legs, and soon he was standing in front of the blazing inferno.

Without thinking he charged inside, ignoring the frenzied shouts coming from all directions. With sirens ringing in his ears, smoke burning his eyes, and flames scorching his lungs, Jase fought his way through the fire. Before he could reach the bedroom, and the screaming within, a beam fell from the ceiling and crashed down on his head. His last thoughts, as he fell inside a darkening whirlpool, were of his wife's voice crying out, and the knowledge that they would die together.

He awoke a long time later, swimming through a haze of smoke and pain. When he opened his eyes, he knew he was in the hospital. He turned his head, and needles of pain shot through it.

"Easy," came the voice of Jack Bullock, the owner of the vineyard.

"Susan?" Jase whispered, coughing as he spoke.

"We'll talk later," Jack assured him. "You sleep."

"They're dead, aren't they," Jase said, more a statement than a question.

"Jase, we couldn't get to them in time. . . ."

Jase didn't hear any more; he passed out again. But when he woke, he remembered the talk.

Two days later the hospital released him. He'd been burned on his back, but that was all. He was alive, and his wife and daughter were dead.

The next day he stood in the cemetery as they lowered the single coffin that held Susan and Claudia Patten. He stayed long after everyone left. He remained until darkness came and he could no longer see the grave.

Back home, he stared at the blackened cinders that had been his life. He remembered all the good times, and the bad, and especially how much he had loved Susan. He thought of the hard times, when his wife had worked selflessly to put him through the final two years of college, refusing to let him work, telling him he needed the time to study. He remembered how he had been awed by Claudia, his beautiful new daughter. Now they were gone, and Jase Patten had died that day, too.

During the next year, Jase moved from job to job. Like a sleepwalker, he existed numbly through each day, working himself to sheer exhaustion, hoping to sleep at night without the haunting dreams of flames and the helpless screams of his dying family.

Eventually, as he drifted from job to job, never staying long enough to allow a friendship to grow, he came to Barkley Vineyards. He worked there for several months, a loner in the fields, doing the work of two men so that he could sleep at night.

One evening as he was finishing work, Samuel Barkley came up to him in the northeast fields. "Jase, I'd like a word with you," the old man had said. Jase stopped what he was doing and looked at him. "You're a hard worker. I like what I see, and I'd like you to think about leaving the fields and working in the winery."

"Thank you, but I'm happy here," Jase answered.

"You're too good a man to be out here, Jase. I need young men like you."

"Sorry."

"Are you going to waste your life out here? Jase, you can't hide from the world."

"I don't know what you're talking about," Jase said, avoiding Barkley's eyes.

"The hell you don't. I don't hire anyone without knowing about them. I've spent my entire life in this valley. I know everyone and everything that happens. When it's something as tragic as the deaths of two people, everyone learns about it sooner or later."

"Then you also know I don't want to talk about it!"

"You have to, sometime."

"No I don't!"

"Jase, you're a young man, and you've got a hell of a future ahead of you. You've got the education that's needed nowadays to be in this business. Yes, I know all about you," Barkley admitted. "I know where you were born, and who your parents were. I know where you went to school and what you did after that." Barkley paused for a moment as his hazel, green-flecked eyes locked with Jase's.

"Son, you're not the first person who's been hurt, and you won't be the last, either. Now, what's done is done, and you have to keep going. Breaking your back every day, with the brains and education you have, is not only stupid, but a sin. Do you think your wife would have believed you were capable of this self-pity?"

"What the hell do you know about it!" Jase screamed, unable to hold back the pain Barkley's words brought out. "I lost everything!"

"No you didn't. You have your memories, and your life!"

"Maybe that's not enough," Jase said quietly.

"I'm afraid it's all anyone has. Jase, it's time to come back into the world. You think about it. Let me know in the morning."

Jase watched Barkley walk away. He sat and thought about his boss's words for a long time. It was well after midnight when he returned to his room. Slowly, he packed his single bag and slipped outside into the night.

Walking along the road, Jase began to think again. He stopped and turned when he was three hundred yards away, and stared endlessly at the single glowing light in the large main house.

Sam Barkley's words kept haunting him, and all Jase wanted to do was get away from the man, and ease his tormented memories. But even as these thoughts filled his mind, his feet carried him toward the main house.

He knocked on the mahogany door, and a few moments later footsteps echoed in the night. When the door opened, Jase faced Samuel Barkley.

"All right," he said.

"Good. I'll expect you in my office at eight." Barkley smiled as he closed the door.

That night, for the first time in a year, Jason slept dreamlessly. The next morning he began his new job as the assistant general manager, putting his background, experience and education to work. Two years later the general manager left, and at the age of twenty-seven, Jase Patten became the new general manager of Barkley Vineyards.

Ti gazed out over the illuminated darkness of Philadelphia. She'd been sitting in the living room chair since arriving home, her every thought centered on Jason Patten. She was confused and frightened by her emotional response to him. And that, she knew, was compounded by the very fact he was here to try and bring her to California, to meet the man she knew she should hate more than anyone in the world.

Suddenly Ti blinked. She drew in a deep breath, and tried to straighten out her thoughts. Jason filled them. His face floated before her, and her stomach fluttered in response. It was then that she made her first important decision. Come what may, she knew she didn't want to lose what might happen between her and Jase. Although she wasn't sure what it was, she knew instinctively that it was too important to chance ruining.

Ti turned on a lamp, and light flooded the living room as she walked to her phone. She dialed information, and got the number she wanted. When the hotel switchboard answered, she asked for Jase's room. A moment later his voice sounded in her ear. Again, she felt the need to moisten her lips.

"Jason . . ."

"Is something wrong?" he asked immediately.

Ti took another deep breath and spoke. "No. But weekends in Philadelphia can get very boring. Would you like to take in the sights tomorrow?" she asked.

"I can't think of a single thing I would rather do, Ti. Thank you."

"You're welcome," Ti murmured as she hung up the phone.

Chapter 3

HESITANTLY, TI OPENED HER EYES. BUT THE GRAYISH light of an overcast morning filtering through her curtains made her want to close them again.

Reluctantly, she forced herself from the bed, and as she stood she glanced quickly at the clock. On cue, her phone rang. She lifted the receiver, and spoke in the husky voice that morning always lent her.

"Did I wake you?" Jase asked.

"Good morning is the appropriate greeting, especially since at this point it can't possibly matter whether you've woken someone or not. And, no, I was already awake."

"Sorry, I wasn't expecting a foghorn to answer your phone," Jase teased. "Shall I pick you up for breakfast?"

"Why don't you give me an hour? I'll meet you in the coffee shop at your hotel," she suggested.

"Fine, see you then," Jase said and hung up the phone.

Ti shook her head. "Foghorn!" Then she smiled softly. She knew she could sing bass in a barbershop quartet when she woke each morning.

After she showered and washed and dried her hair, she clipped it smoothly back with a barrette and applied the barest hint of makeup before going to her closet. Ti remembered Jason's remarks about the way she dressed, and searched through her closet to find something casual. But again, the problem of her conservative, formal clothes presented itself.

It wasn't that she didn't like to dress casually, it had been a matter of economy. She'd bought what she could use efficiently in both her work and off hours. The problem was that her life had always centered around work and school.

As she moved the hangers around, she saw an old, forgotten pair of jeans half hidden under a pair of beige slacks. She smiled as she took them from the hanger. They weren't designer jeans, just an old pair of faded Levi's.

Ti took off her robe and put on a beige bra, panties and socks, before stepping into the jeans. When they were on, she went to the mirror behind the door and looked at herself. The faded blue jeans fit perfectly, hugging her hips and rear, and accenting her smooth, flat stomach.

Nodding, Ti went to her dresser and pulled out a lightweight wool sweater and camisole. Once the camisole was on, she slipped the sweater over her head, and lifted her hair free from the confines of the turtleneck. Before returning to the mirror, she put on brown loafers.

Turning in a circle before the mirror, Ti caught every part of her reflection. She was very conscious of the way the blue sweater emphasized the swell of her breasts, and in an effort to decrease the contrast between her slim waist and her breasts, she let the bottom of the sweater hug her waist, and hang loosely about her torso. When she was finished with her inspection, she smiled.

Jase Patten was getting his wish; he would see her in casual clothes. Glancing at the clock, Ti saw she had only fifteen minutes before she was to meet Jase. She left the bedroom quickly, scooping up her purse on the way out. From the hall closet she took a cotton-lined Windbreaker, put it on and went to meet Jason, a strange flurry of anticipation tingling her nerves.

"Did you know that?" Ti asked as they walked outside after viewing the Liberty Bell.

"What? That it got its name from the time of the Civil War, rather than the Revolution?" Jase smiled at her while he squinted against the slanting sun.

"Yes."

"Yes."

Ti shook her head and walked in the direction of Independence Hall, across the street from the Liberty Pavillion. She glanced quickly at Jase to make sure he was staying near her in the crowd of tourists, and at the same time felt another small tremor pass through her.

He was dressed as casually as she was. A pair of faded jeans hugged his hips, and a cinnamon shirt stood out proudly under a western-cut beige jacket.

They entered Independence Hall and joined a large group of people who were already seated and waiting for the tour guide. Ti chose two seats and motioned Jase to them. Just after they were seated, the National Park tour guide stepped into the room. As he spoke, Ti's thoughts returned to breakfast.

She had entered the coffee shop and paused to look for Jase. Spotting him off to the side, she had smiled and moved toward his table. When she'd reached it,

Jase stood and held a chair for her. After he'd sat again, Ti couldn't dim the smile on her face. She had been glad to see him. Really glad.

"Thank you," Jase had said.

"For what?" Ti had asked uncertainly.

"For looking so good today."

"Oh . . . my jeans?"

"No, but they're nice too. Ti," Jase had said, his voice as serious as his umber eyes had suddenly become, "there's nothing wrong with accepting a compliment. Don't look for a reason, just accept it and say thank you."

"Thank you," she'd murmured. Then she'd picked up her coffee cup, needing something to break the hold his eyes had on her.

"What is our agenda for today?" he had inquired.

"Being tourists in what was once the second largest English-speaking city in the world."

"Good enough," he had replied as he'd lifted his coffee cup and drunk from it. But all the while, his eyes had remained fixed on hers.

"If you will follow me . . ." The tour guide's voice broke Ti free of her thoughts. She stood, and as they moved with the crowd, she was very aware of Jase's hand holding hers.

They spent the next twenty-five minutes listening to the history of Independence Hall and looking at the different chambers of the building that had played such a vast and important part in the history of the country.

By the time the tour was over, Ti's stomach was rumbling and she suggested lunch. They ate in a small restaurant, and when they had finished, they visited one of the restored historical homes. It was there that Ti learned something very new, and her dormant, half-forgotten thoughts about her family history once again surfaced.

She was reading a plaque on the wall when she came across a familiar name. She gazed at it for a long moment, and a funny feeling of half-recognition tugged at her mind. Slowly, as she read the other names, she knew she had to find out if her hunch was correct.

With Jase in tow, she returned to the woman who sat at the greeting desk by the entrance.

"Where can I find more information about the people who played important parts in Philadelphia's history?" she asked.

The woman, perhaps sixty, looked up at Ti in close scrutiny. "Do you have a particular person in mind?"

Ti nodded, her eyes wide as she spoke. "I may be mistaken, but on the plaque in the library I saw the name Samuel Bennett. Is there someplace I could look him up, some reference book where he'd be listed?"

"I've seen that look before," the woman replied with a knowing smile. "From the expression on your face, young lady, you look like you've found a long-lost relative."

"I just may have done that. I remember my mother telling me that our ancestors were pre-Revolutionary settlers of Philadelphia," Ti explained, unable to control the excitement in her voice at the unexpected discovery.

"I would suggest the Historical Society of Pennsylvania. They have records that predate the Revolution," the woman informed her, and gave her directions to get there.

Once outside the building, Ti breathed deeply. Then, turning to Jase, she smiled. "Do you mind?"

"Do I have a choice?" he teased as he took her hand again. "Of course I don't mind."

Ti tried to ignore the heat of his touch as their eyes locked again in the insane way they had been doing all day. Then, dismissing the tension that radiated between them, she led the way toward the Historical Society building.

As they walked, Ti's mind battled several emotions at once. This new desire to learn about her family roots, and the almost overpowering feeling of being near Jason Patten overwhelmed her. She liked both the feeling and the man more with each minute they spent together. Finally, unable to sort out the confusion, Ti gave up and let her mind relax as best she could.

Once inside the Historical Society, and having explained what she was looking for, a matronly clerk led her and Jase to a table, and set an old, large ledger-type book upon it. She opened it to the section that contained the name Bennett, and left Ti and Jase alone.

"What are you looking for?" Jase asked in a low voice.

"My family," Ti replied.

"No, what particulars about your family are you looking for?"

Ti turned to him and gazed into his eyes for a long, silent moment. "I don't know," she admitted before returning her eyes to the book. Carefully, she began to read.

Ten minutes later she found the name Samuel Bennett; however, Ti realized it was not the same Samuel Bennett she was looking for, but his grandfather. She sighed audibly as she began to read about the origins of what she suspected was her family.

The Samuel Bennett she was searching for was among the second generation of Bennetts born in America. Samuel Bennett was born in 1820 and was the only son of John Bennett, one of three children of the original settler, Samuel Bennett, who had arrived in Philadelphia in 1755 with his wife Amanda.

The first Samuel Bennett fought in the Revolution,

and afterward had become a member of Congress. His grandson, named after him, was a general in the Civil War.

General Samuel Bennett had been the last of the Bennetts to live in Philadelphia, having moved west several years before the Civil War. His wife had died on the journey to Texas, leaving him to oversee the raising of his three daughters, Ticonderoga, Jenna, and Kay. General Bennett was distinguished in the Army, and credited as one of President Lincoln's most trusted military advisers.

"Look," Ti cried as she tugged on Jase's sleeve. Her other hand hovered over the page, her index finger pointing to the name of her great-great-great-grand-mother.

"I always wondered what it stood for," Jase said.

"What what stood for?"

"Ti."

"Now you know. And no comments, please," she added quickly as she closed the book. Her face was flushed with the excitement of her find, and her body churned with a restless energy that the knowledge seemed to impart to her.

"Would you mind if we walked back?" Ti asked. "Or do you want to keep on sightseeing?"

Jase looked at his watch and then back at Ti. "It all depends."

"On what?" she asked, her eyes flashing in a sudden challenge.

"On whether you're having dinner with me tonight."

Ti's stomach fluttered in warning, and she drew in her breath slowly. She knew what she wanted to say, but was afraid at the same time. "Aren't you getting bored with my company?"

"For someone who has beauty, brains, and the ability to use both intelligently, I'd appreciate it if you didn't answer my question with another question, especially a stupid one." Ti bit her lower lip as she looked at him. She should be angry at his words, but he'd stated the truth, simply and directly. That scared her, too.

"Sorry. Yes, I'd like to dine with you."

"Ti . . ." Jase gazed down into her eyes. He hadn't meant to be so brusque, but at the same time he wouldn't compromise his own ways. His hand reached up and gently caressed her cheek. "I'm not a city businessman who plays games with words. What I have to say, I say. And I hope whomever I'm speaking with will give me the same courtesy."

Ti couldn't speak. The soft touch of his fingers as they stroked her cheek unnerved her. The gentle cupping of his hand beneath her chin, making her meet his eyes, further stopped her reply. Instead, she nodded her head slowly.

Ti stood in front of the bedroom mirror, looking at herself and hoping the dress she was wearing would suit wherever Jase was taking her to dinner.

For a change, tonight's dress had not been a torturous choice for her; she'd solved the problem of her wardrobe in an unusual and impulsive way. That afternoon, after Jase had dropped her at home, she'd gone to a small boutique down the block. There she'd chosen a new dress, a somewhat expensive one, which would strain her checking account and could not possibly be worn to work. Even though she couldn't really afford this luxury, she had felt a need to wear something special tonight.

It was a soft, pale green dress that clung to her, yet fell in smooth lines. Its bodice, held by two triple-strand spaghetti straps, was cut low enough to reveal the creamy skin of the tops of her breasts, while at the same time maintaining an edge of modesty. The waist was cinched by a narrow leather belt, and the skirt of the dress flowed over her hips before dropping to her knees.

Why am I doing this? she asked herself. *What hold does Jase Patten have over me?*

Her bell rang at exactly eight-thirty. Ti flipped back a random strand of hair and nervously smoothed out her dress before answering the door. When she opened it, her breath almost left her. Jase stood there, a smile on his lips, the hall light glinting daringly off his shiny dark hair and mustache, as the twin grooves in his cheeks accented his masculine strength. The skin around his eyes crinkled as he looked at her, and Ti's heart beat faster.

Jase was dressed in a single-breasted blue suit, with a lighter blue shirt and tie. She glanced quickly down his length and noticed he was wearing shoes, not boots. Her stare must have been apparent, because his smile grew wider as he nodded.

"I do wear shoes on special occasions," he said dryly.

Ti's face was burning, and she knew her light makeup couldn't possibly hide the scarlet flush of her skin. "I . . . I never doubted it for a moment," she responded lamely.

"Ready?" he asked.

Ti nodded, and Jase took her arm and guided her along the hallway to the elevator. "You look lovely tonight. Green suits you."

"Thank you." She smiled shyly.

Outside, the night air cooled Ti's skin, causing goose bumps to form. "Where are we having dinner?" she asked as she crossed her arms over her breasts. Jase reacted by slipping the sweater she had taken with her over her shoulders.

"Top of Centre Square," he answered as he waved his hand in the air.

From the corner of her eye, Ti saw a strange shape approach. She caught her breath and looked up at him for a quick second. Coming up the block was a horse-drawn carriage, one of many that took tourists through the historical section of Philadelphia.

"You didn't!" she exclaimed.

"Of course I didn't," he replied as he took her arm and guided her to the carriage. "This is but a figment of your imagination." He helped her into the carriage.

Without a word, the driver lifted the reins and started the carriage forward. Ti smiled as she sat back and leaned comfortably against Jase's arm.

"This is very nice," she murmured. Conscious of his intense stare, Ti turned and saw his face shadowed by the street lamps. Her heart raced again, and her breath was labored.

Slowly, taking an eternity, Jase leaned down. His lips brushed hers gently, and darting needles danced through her body at the moment of the kiss. It was over as fast as it had begun. Ti just stared at him.

"Sometimes I can't help myself," Jase said.

"Sometimes," Ti faltered, willing her voice to be steady, "you have to try to help yourself."

"I think that's what I did."

"That's not what I meant."

"Are you sure about that?"

"Why are you doing this?" Ti demanded, pointedly avoiding his question and the insight it showed him capable of. Her throat was tight and her words were forced. There was no longer a smile on her lips, nor on Jase's as he answered her.

"Because I have to."

"For my grandfather?" she whispered.

"For me."

Ti couldn't respond. Instead, she closed her eyes and tried to calm her mind and ease the pounding of her heart. When she opened them again, the carriage was turning onto Market Street. They rode the rest of the way in silence, both aware of the other's closeness.

Dinner, high above the flickering lights of the city, was marvelous. Ti loved lobster, and tonight she feasted on it. The restaurant's featured dish was excellent, and the tender, broiled lobster had been stuffed with finely chopped crabmeat and more lobster.

Jase had chosen a Chenin Blanc, a lovely dry white wine that suited the shellfish perfectly. As she sipped the first glass, she nodded appreciatively.

"I knew you'd like it," he announced.

"And just how did you know that?"

"It's in your blood."

"No more riddles please, wine *is not* in my blood," she informed him.

"This one is. It's a Barkley wine."

"Jase . . . please," she pleaded softly, but was unable to stop her eyes from going to the bottle and reading its label.

"I'm just stating a fact. Ti, you were meant for more than this city. A lot more. Damnit, hold up that glass. Look in it! Can't you see the sunshine? Can't you smell the earth? Can't you taste the country when you drink it? It's part of you. It's in your blood!"

Ti gazed at him, almost falling into the swirling, fathomless pools of his eyes. She felt a sudden chill run through her when he spoke, and could almost see what he was saying.

"No," she murmured. "No more talk about my family."

"Ti, this afternoon you were very excited when you learned about your ancestors. For well over a hundred years they've cultivated the land. It's a part of you. You were born with it, and you must not deny it."

"Jason, you promised."

Jase's eyes held hers for a long moment before he finally nodded. Ti's breath escaped in a low sigh.

They ate slowly, and after a few minutes the tension eased. When they started talking again, Jase asked questions about Ti's life, and they both made every effort to avoid the earlier mistake of talking about her family.

Halfway through dinner, Ti finally relaxed enough to enjoy herself. The Top of Centre Square was an elegant, romantic and expensive restaurant, which hummed with subdued conversations. It vibrated with life, and Ti loved it. She gazed at the variety of people and the way they dressed. She laughed silently at some, while admiring others.

But overshadowing it all was the handsome man across the candlelit table from her. His very presence seemed to have myriad effects on her, and her emotions vacillated randomly. His smile made her smile His dark eyes made her feel protected, vulnerable, wanted and . . . Ti wasn't sure what the "and" was, yet.

By the time they finished their coffee, three and a half hours had flown by. The city's lights still shimmered below them romantically and, Ti realized again, she must be very careful of the man she was with. *No,* she corrected, *I must be careful of myself.*

When they returned to the street, Ti saw the same horse and carriage waiting at the curb. "You didn't."

"I thought we already went through that tonight," Jase responded as he guided her to the carriage. He covered their laps with the soft blanket the driver had provided, and again, without instructions, the carriage began to move.

"Where are we going?" Ti asked.

"Does it matter?"

"No," she whispered and leaned her head back on his arm.

The carriage moved slowly, and its rocking movements lulled Ti into a state of acceptance. The stars were barely visible through the haze of city lights, but she did see them.

As the carriage moved along the streets, the echoes of the horse's shoes played a quiet tattoo in her ears. Ti's eyes closed and she drifted into a pleasant state of half-consciousness. The closeness and heat from Jase, the coolness of the night, and the warmth from the blanket all seemed to caress and lull her in a magical way. For endless minutes in time, Ti rested against Jase. The sounds of traffic were blocked from her ears by his nearness. She was vaguely aware of the scent of water, and knew they must be near the Delaware. But through it all, Ti remained relaxed and comfortable next to Jase.

Suddenly, she sensed a lack of movement. They'd stopped, and as she breathed the air, the scent of the river was gone and Ti realized she'd fallen asleep for a few minutes.

"We're here," Jase whispered into her ear.

"Here?"

"Your building."

Ti opened her eyes and looked around. She felt a quick wave of sadness that the night had ended. Then she sat up and smiled at Jase.

"It was a wonderful evening," she said.

"It was," Jase agreed as he took the blanket off them and stepped down from the carriage. He walked her inside, and went with her up to her apartment.

When she opened her door she turned to him, a firm smile fixed on her face. She hoped it hid the way her body and mind were reacting. She hoped, but wasn't sure.

"Jason, I—" Before she could thank him again, his arms reached out and gripped her. He drew her close, pressing her tightly against him. She was acutely aware of the hardness of his chest against her breasts, and of the unexpected flaring of heat that passed through their clothing at the close contact. Then his lips were on hers, burning in their intensity, drawing her into the kiss in a way she'd never experienced before. The tip of his tongue entered her mouth, and a moan echoed deep in her throat.

Ti's arms wound around his back, her hands pressed him to her. Flames erupted deep within her, and her heart seemed to explode in a series of staccato bursts. Then he pulled back.

Ti gazed at him, wondering why he'd stopped, but glad he had. Her chest rose and fell, and she saw, suddenly, that his chest was also straining forcefully against the thin fabric of his shirt.

"Ti . . ." Jase began, but stopped as his expression softened, easing the sharp edge of desire that had held it. "Good night," he murmured in a hoarse voice. Then, with Ti still unable to speak, he turned and strode quickly to the elevator. Five seconds later he was gone.

The sun burned brilliantly down upon the lush fields, illuminating the emerald vines. Jase wiped the sweat from his brow, and breathed deeply of the sweetly scented air.

The soft, rolling hills of brown earth, the green vines and their precious, sweet fruit, mixed in splendor with the mountains that rose so majestically in the background. It was a beautiful day, filled with life. Then he heard his name and turned quickly. The sun bounced off the long, coal-black waves of Susan's hair. Her face held a smile as she waved to him. In her other arm she carried Claudia, who snuggled against her shoulder, her dark eyes wide with curiosity.

Jase began to run toward her. He couldn't understand why they were here, at Barkley Vineyards. But he didn't care, it had been so long. . . . Then he stopped suddenly. Something was *very* wrong. Susan had auburn hair, not black. Susan was dead. So was Claudia. . . .

"No!" Jason screamed and sat up suddenly. His body was covered with perspiration, and he was breathing in sharp gasps. Slowly, calming himself, he reached out and turned on a lamp.

Soft yellow light flooded the room, and Jase lay back on the bed. He stared at the ceiling for a long time as he tried to unravel his thoughts. It had been several years since he'd dreamed of Susan. It had taken a lot of time to heal the wound.

He remembered clearly that Susan's hair had been a rich, midnight color. Now, as he thought about the dream, he realized her hair color and even the shimmering waves themselves, had been Ti's.

Jase had known, from the first moment he'd seen Ti, that she was different from any other woman he'd known. The desires that had filled him, the emotions that had grown within him, all told him the truth.

Was it because he wanted her that he'd had this dream? Did he feel guilty because he was alive and Susan dead? Or was it because he found himself attracted to another woman for the first time since he'd fallen in love with Susan? Jase wasn't sure of the answers, and even more, he didn't want to know.

With his mind in turmoil, Jase rose from the bed,

dressed, and left the hotel room. He needed to be outside, to walk in the night and to think.

Ti lay in bed, unable to sleep, powerless to still the runaway thoughts that had been holding her in thrall since Jason had dropped her off. She shivered at the memory of his unexpected yet wanted kiss and willed the empty aching within her to leave.

Ti shifted on the bed, trying to find a comfortable position. She couldn't; she couldn't sleep, nor could she stop her mind from picturing Jason, remembering his passionate kiss and her body's startling reaction to him. Never had she known such instant response to a man. Never before had she desired someone as she did Jason.

But she couldn't have him. She knew that. How could she? He was her grandfather's man. He was here for only one purpose, to make her return with him to meet the one person she hated more than any other living soul.

"Why?" she whispered in the darkness.

Ti willed herself to blot out all thoughts, to think of nothing and to ignore her body's internal cry. Slowly, the tautness that held her eased, and without realizing it, she began to drift off to sleep. Just before the gentle curtain of darkness descended, Jason Patten's face floated before her and she felt something stir deep within her very core.

Chapter 4

"SAM, I'M TRYING," JASE SAID. HE HELD THE RECEIVER tightly, disliking the fact that he was unable to tell Sam Barkley what the man wanted to hear.

"I'll know tomorrow," he promised as he hung up. Jase shook his head and stared at the black instrument. He felt Sam's pain sharply, and wanted desperately to help him.

He wanted to have Ti return with him, wanted it for more reasons than he was willing to admit. But he also knew he would not force her, would not use any means other than honesty to get her to California.

Jase stood and walked to the window. His hotel room was high above the city. The shining monolith was a modern miracle of architecture, and one that made him feel trapped within its sealed environment. He wanted out—out of the hotel and the city. He needed to smell the clean air of the Napa Valley, and to walk on its soft surface.

Jase's eyes searched below, picking out the varied buildings, and seeking the clear spaces of green grass that signaled small parks. He shook his head and turned. Purposefully, he strode across the room and picked up the phone. He dialed the number from memory, and waited patiently for his call to be answered. After the tenth ring, he replaced the receiver in its cradle and stared at it.

Ti sat in the lone chair in her living room, reading the Help Wanted section of the paper. Her eyes scanned each column in a fruitless search for a job opening.

She shook her head sadly each time something interesting caught her attention. By the time she finished reading each of the job descriptions, she knew none were for her.

"There has to be something!" she declared angrily. Ti knew she would find something, she just didn't know when and that's what bothered her. She had enough confidence in her abilities to know she would get a job. But at the same time, she wanted a job that would further the goals she'd set for herself long ago. She would accept nothing less, even if it meant going out of her field until something came up that suited her.

Damn him! she thought, as a picture of her ex-boss rose in her mind. *Why can't men treat women as their equals in work? Why do they have to look at us differently from the way they would another man?*

The sudden ringing of her phone jarred her thoughts and refocused her attention to the room. Shaking her head, Ti reached for the receiver. Her hand stopped in midair. Intuitively, she knew who was calling.

She gazed at the phone, her heart beating loudly. *I can't talk to him now,* she told herself. *I can't take that chance.* The ache that had grown so strong last night returned, sending arrows of tender-sweet pain rippling through her insides. She wanted, more than anything, to pick up the phone and hear Jason's voice.

"No!" she cried as she stood, ignoring the incessant call of the phone. From the moment she'd awakened today she'd thought about Jason. He'd been with her all morning, his umber eyes caressing her as she moved about the apartment. Only her ability to focus on the newspaper had banished his image. That, and her angry thoughts about losing her job, had enabled her to force his image away.

But she knew she couldn't talk to him. His gentle voice would send a wave of longing through her. He would ask her out tonight and she couldn't go. She was too afraid that if she did, she would weaken and give in.

She didn't want to go to California. She didn't want to be attracted to Jason Patten. Finally the phone stopped ringing and Ti breathed deeply in relief. But even as she reached for the paper, the phone rang again.

"Leave me alone!" Ti yelled suddenly. Then she stood and went to the closet. Grabbing a jacket, she stormed out of the apartment. In the hallway, the muffled sound of the phone still called to her, its plaintive ringing following her to the elevator. Only after the elevator door closed, and she was dropping toward the ground floor, did the ringing cease.

Ti spent the rest of the afternoon walking aimlessly through the streets, her mind a confused maze, her eyes seeing everything around her, but registering little. By late afternoon she was sitting on a park bench watching small children play with their parents. Everywhere she turned, couples and families walked. It was a pleasant Sunday afternoon, a time when people relaxed and enjoyed themselves with the ones they cared about.

But Ti was alone. It had never bothered her before,

but today that very fact became excruciatingly clear. *It's because of him,* she thought. *I was happy until two days ago. Then* he *came along, and everything changed.*

Suddenly Ti knew what was happening to her. "No," she whispered. "No," she prayed. Slowly, as if in a trance, she rose from the bench and walked out of the park.

She walked unerringly for fifteen blocks, until she reached the gleaming glass-and-steel structure that was her destination. Taking a deep breath, she entered, barely nodding to the red-uniformed doorman who opened the hotel's main doors for her.

Striding to the bank of telephones, Ti reached for one and lifted it.

"May I help you?" asked the hotel operator.

"Mr. Patten's room, please," Ti instructed. A few seconds later she heard his voice.

"Jason . . ."

"Where are you? I've been calling all day."

"Downstairs," she informed him, conscious of the tightness in her voice.

"Here?" he asked incredulously.

"Here," she replied as she hung up.

Five minutes later she saw him cross the lobby toward her, dressed in jeans, a long-sleeved shirt, and his cowboy boots. Her chest constricted painfully as she gazed at him. He moved gracefully, his powerful strides carrying him quickly toward her. His eyes were fixed on hers and his mouth was set in a tight, serious line.

"What's wrong?" His eyes, filled with concern, swept across her face.

"You!"

"Me?" he asked, drawing his head slightly back and squinting at her.

"Yes, you!" she repeated, unaware that her voice had risen sharply and several people were openly staring at them. "Why did you have to come here? My life was fine. Everything was just fine until you showed up."

"Ti—"

"Don't interrupt me. I had my life planned out. I knew who I was, and where I was going. Then you showed up like a knight in shining armor to save the poor maiden from the clutches of evil. You came with soft words, and tried to seduce me into thinking about my family. You want me to leave here and go to California with you. You want me to do something I don't want to do. Leave me alone!"

"Do you know what you're saying?" Jase asked as he gazed at her. His eyes moved across her face, looking at her delicately curved mouth, her small nose, until finally they stopped and met her large green-flecked eyes. Tentatively, Jase raised a hand and placed it on her shoulder.

Ti shook his hand away as she glared at him. "Don't touch me. Yes, I know damn well what I'm saying!"

"Then explain it to me, because I don't."

Suddenly Ti's eyes widened. Everything she was thinking and feeling welled up within her. She was dizzy with his physical aura, which surrounded her with mysterious power. She wanted him to hold her, but she couldn't let that happen. "I wish I'd never met you," she whispered.

"Why?" Jase asked.

"Because then"—she took a deep breath—"I wouldn't have fallen in love with you."

"Ti . . ." Jase began as he stepped closer to her, reaching out to hold her.

"No!" Ti cried, avoiding his arms. "Leave me alone. Don't make my life any harder than it is!" With that, she turned and ran from the hotel. The tears that stung her eyes were disregarded in the wake of the terrifying truth she'd just admitted.

Three blocks later Ti slowed to a walk. She was unnerved by what she'd done, but in a way she now hoped she'd freed herself to think and act like a normal person again.

As the blocks passed, and she neared her apartment building, Ti came to the realization that she'd accomplished nothing. In fact, she had added only more to the muddled haze her mind was fast becoming. She could still feel the way Jason's kisses burned on her lips. The empty ache had deepened instead of abated, and the tears that had begun in the hotel lobby returned to trace their way down her cheeks.

How could I have said that to him? she asked herself. At the park, as she'd watched the couples around her, she had begun to realize the truth. But it had taken Jason's presence to bring voice to her thoughts.

In her misery, she ignored the curious glances of the people who stared at her tear-streaked face. Even when she reached her building, the turmoil in her mind controlled her. It was maddening, and humiliation haunted her like a dark shadow.

Riding up in the elevator, she could still see Jason's shocked expression as she had spoken to him. *I told him I loved him,* she thought again. *How could I have been so stupid?*

Before the elevator door opened, Ti wiped her eyes and took a deep breath. She reached into her pocket for her keys, and suddenly remembered that she'd run out earlier without her purse or her keys.

With a sad shake of her head, Ti walked to her door. She could only hope she'd left it unlocked. The superintendent was off on Sundays and if the door was locked she'd have to call a locksmith. Her foolishness would be very expensive.

Slowly, Ti turned the doorknob and breathed a sigh of relief as it moved freely. The door opened, and she stepped inside.

After she took off her jacket, she walked toward the living room and froze.

Jase watched Ti's receding back. He ignored the people around him who were staring as a slow smile spread across his face. When she'd told him she loved him, he was stunned, not by the words, but by their suddenness. Even as her admission echoed in the chambers of his mind, he was aware of a new warmth coursing through him and a vague feeling that this wasn't supposed to happen to him anymore.

When Ti disappeared through the doors, he went after her. He needed to talk to her now! Once outside, he saw her almost a block away. She was still running, and he too began to run, but he made sure he stayed on the opposite side of the street.

When she slowed to a walk, he did the same. Jase saw that she was headed home and he picked up his pace. Three blocks from her building he passed her without turning to look at her again. His long strides made the remaining blocks disappear, and by the time he reached her building, he had a full block lead. He went to the elevator and rode it to her floor.

In the hallway Jase tried to decide where to wait for Ti. *At her door,* he told himself. *She won't be able to run away from me then.* He went to her door and leaned against it to wait for her. Without warning, it swung open and he stumbled into her apartment. Nimbly regaining his balance, Jase stared around. He was inside. She'd not only left the door unlocked, but hadn't closed it completely.

Jase smiled as he closed the door. He went to the

living room and turned its single chair to face the hallway and front door. Then he sat down to await Ti's arrival.

He didn't have long to wait. Two minutes later the door opened. He watched as Ti entered and reveled in the sight of her. He smiled as she took off her jacket and hung it in the closet. His smile was still firmly in place when she turned and walked toward him.

"What—"

"Do you always leave your door open?" Jase asked in a low voice.

"What are you doing here?" Ti demanded angrily. The tears of moments before were forgotten as she stared unbelieving at him.

"Did you expect me to stand in the hotel lobby and wait for you to come back?"

"I expected you to pack your suitcase and go back to my grandfather," she told him truthfully. *Please go,* she pleaded silently. *I can't face you now.*

"I'm sorry, but I can't do that."

"Get out of my life!" Ti ordered, her voice rising as she glowered at him. But her mind and body were betraying her and making lies of her words even as she spoke them. A warmth permeated her as she caught her breath. Her heart thudded painfully against her ribs, and a slight tremor ran along the inside of her left thigh.

"I can't," Jase confessed as he stood and walked toward her. When he was only inches away he stopped. His eyes locked with hers and the warmth of his breath washed across her cheek.

"Leave me . . ." Ti whispered, fighting against the longing and need that swelled within her.

Jase lifted his hand and cupped her chin. Ti felt his fingers burn her skin. The tremor in her thigh spread upward to her stomach. Slowly, Jase lowered his mouth until it touched hers. His lips scorched hers, and tears spilled from her eyes.

Her mind dissolved as he pulled her to him. His mouth crushed hers, and Ti sank against him. His tongue entered her mouth and she accepted it avidly. She could not fight him, or the desire spreading rampantly through her body.

His hands were like steel, pressing her to him; his mouth was molten, igniting the suppressed flames within her. The ache that had filled her body since last night deepened painfully, and not even the wanton pressing of her hips against his eased the throbbing need she now slowly recognized.

Then Jason's mouth was gone. She gazed into his eyes, saw the desire within them and knew they mirrored her own.

Jase held her tightly as his eyes searched her face. Through the rising tide of his desire, he tried to control himself. He couldn't let his body rule him. He tried to stop himself and tear his eyes from her. But he could not ignore the soft warmth of her breasts against his chest, or the searing heat that flowed from his thighs to his chest.

He knew that to give in would hurt them both, but he could not speak the words or expect her to understand them. Instead, he closed his eyes and lowered his mouth once again to hers.

Ti tasted the sweetness of his lips, felt the tickling tease of his mustache on the soft skin above her lip and suddenly was luxuriating in the sensation. Her hands were on his back, trying to pull him harder against her. The strong muscles of his thighs pressed into hers, and through their clothing, her sensitive breasts were crushed against the taut muscle and bone of his massive chest.

Caught within the whirlpool of her desire, and aided by the knowledge that she had unwillingly fallen in love with Jason, Ti closed her eyes. She couldn't bring herself to open them. She could only feel him against her.

He tore his mouth from hers again. "Ti, I want you," he whispered huskily.

He released her suddenly and stepped back. The wrenching separation forced Ti to open her eyes at last. She searched his face, waiting for him to say something. But then, as she looked at him, she knew he didn't have to speak. What he felt was etched on his face, and she knew it as well as she knew her own mind.

Silently, she reached out to take Jason's hand. Together, they walked into her bedroom.

The last vestiges of daylight filtered through the window, softly illuminating the room. Ti turned to Jason and smiled tentatively. Her throat was dry, and she swallowed several times before she was able to speak. "When you called this afternoon, I couldn't answer the phone. I was afraid."

"Are you still afraid?" he asked.

Ti nodded. "But not of you. Of what will happen later," she explained honestly.

"Ti—"

"No more words Jason, please. Just kiss me," she pleaded.

Jase nodded slowly and pulled her back into his arms. He kissed her deeply, a kiss filled with passion yet ruled by tenderness.

They stayed together for endless moments, each drawing the most from the kiss. Ti felt secure in his grasp, while a floating sensation captured her in a dizzying wave. Her breasts grew heavy with desire, her stomach tightened in a combination of passion and fear.

Breathlessly, Ti pulled her lips from his and burrowed her face into his neck to taste the pliant skin beneath his ear, and breathe deeply of his masculine scent.

Jase's hand wound through her long coal-black hair and lifted her head. He kissed her lips, tasting them fully before drawing slightly away. Slowly his mouth traveled upward, lavishing the softness of her skin with tender kisses for an eternity before returning to the warmth of her lips.

Ti surrendered to him. His lips were passionate and demanding as his hands roamed along her length, touching, caressing, drawing her closer.

Although her clothing separated his hand from her skin, his very touch burned her. Ti moaned as his hand slid upward from her hip, until finally he cupped her breast and little shocks tunneled deeply within her. Her breath grew harsh as her hands caressed his back and neck.

Slowly, he began to undress her.

Ti's legs trembled and she was afraid she would fall. It was like a dream. Everything was hazy as Jase undressed her. Ti felt helpless, unable to assist him, but even when she tried, Jase firmly took her hands away.

"Let me," he begged as he caught her hands in his and gazed into her eyes. He lifted one hand to his lips, and turned it over. His mouth seared her palm. His tongue caressed the joining of her fingers as his eyes stayed locked with hers.

Through a fog of desire, Ti nodded as all resistance fled. Jase released her hands and kissed her neck as he unbuttoned her top. She caught her lower lip between her teeth as the warmth of his breath brushed across the newly exposed skin.

Button after button was released, and with each one,

another of Ti's inhibitions departed. Time stood still for her; it could have been minutes or hours later when her top was fully open and his mouth pressed dizzyingly to the base of her throat. His lips scorched her skin as his hands slipped the material from her shoulders.

Ti kept her eyes closed. She was afraid to look at him, afraid of what she would see in his eyes. The sharp intake of his breath startled her. Her eyes fluttered open and she saw him gazing at her.

"You're beautiful," he whispered in a husky voice as he kissed her lips again. Ti wanted to cry out her need, but his mouth prevented her. Then her mind stopped its tumultuous wanderings as his lips traced a sensual path downward from her neck. When his mouth reached into the depths of the valley between her breasts, his fingers unsnapped the bra clip, and her breasts came free.

The sound of her breathing was loud in her ears. Jase cupped her breasts gently, his hands almost large enough to cover them, and Ti bit down on her lip in sudden reaction to the excruciating pleasure of his touch. She moaned as his mouth traversed the top of one breast, and then the other. She moaned again, deep in the back of her throat, when he took one peach-colored nipple into his mouth and caressed it endlessly, before leaving it to grace the other. Ti's breasts vibrated with the sensations of his hands and lips.

Another cry was torn from her as Jase left her breasts, and let his mouth trail across her stomach. Ti's legs were trembling so badly that she could barely stand. His mouth traveled endless new paths along her breasts and stomach, and her hands wound into his hair as she cried out again.

Jase lowered himself to his knees and pressed his

cheek against the warmth of her abdomen. His hands dug into the flesh of her rear, and he felt the tightness of her muscles through her pants.

Swiftly, he undid them and drew them down. Then he stood and, in one quick motion, lifted her from the floor. Her arms went around his back, and she pressed herself to him. She was looking at him as he placed her gently on the bed.

Her eyes stayed open as Jase stepped back. He held her gaze with his own, and slowly began to undress.

Ti watched him, her mind whirling with emotions that were new to her. The fiery brand of his lips and hands still burned her. The aching need for him still throbbed, unfulfilled, deep within her. Her fingers trembled, matching the vibrating warmth that held her in thrall.

As Jase opened his shirt, Ti again felt as if she were part of some strange dream and willed herself not to wake up. The gentle, fading light was enough to see by, and its hazy, ethereal quality made her breathing even more labored.

She watched him take off his shirt to reveal a broad chest, covered with a fine mat of dark, curly hair. Her eyes followed his hands, and as they undid his belt, she saw the finely etched lines of well-developed muscle outlined on his flat stomach. He had the lean, smooth form of a perfectly proportioned athlete; his wide chest tapered to a slim waist, and even as he lowered his pants, Ti knew she would see sleek hips and powerful thighs.

Suddenly she was gazing into his eyes again and he was standing over her. Her arms moved of their own volition, lifting and opening in invitation to him.

"Jason," she moaned as he joined her on the bed. She came to him as he covered her lips with his. A volcano erupted inside her. Another low moan floated above them, unheard as they were lost within each other.

Jason kissed Ti deeply, his desire now unrestrained as he held her tightly. His tongue joined hers in a dance of passion, his breathing forced as the length of her body pressed against his. The soft, velvety texture of her skin sent a shower of sparks shooting through his mind.

He pulled his mouth from hers, only to bring it back as he trailed his lips along her neck. His hands caressed her full breasts, lavishing them with attention, softly at first, and then with more passion. Soon his mouth followed his hands. He tasted and caressed each breast lovingly. The softness of her flesh was like an endless expanse of beauty to him. He drew first one nipple, and then the other into his mouth. Teasing, tasting, touching and caressing until both peaks stood hard and pointing.

Then his face was only inches from hers and his eyes bored into hers. "You're exquisite," he said wonderingly before returning to the soft beauty beneath him.

Ti's body was alive with newly awakened passion. Jase's gentle caresses stoked the coals within the furnace of her body and drove her upward in wild, maddening bursts of desire. His lips on her nipples sent shock waves coursing through her. Her hands pressed his mouth to her breasts, and she moaned again at his touch. His lips, tongue and hands drew out every response possible from her. She was weak with desire and filled with the strongest need she'd ever known. His lips teased her stomach, and then his hands were in the waistband of her panties. Slowly Jase drew them down across her thighs.

As he freed her of her last garment, his mouth moved upward from her calf. "Jason," she murmured throatily.

He shifted and lay next to her, but his hands did not stop their exploration. Ti felt the tips of his fingers as his hands ran along the downy covering of her femininity. "Please," she whispered as his fingers caressed her, making her moist for him.

Jason forced himself to be still. Glancing into her eyes, he saw passion and love floating within their hazel depths. Slowly, gracefully, his mouth covered hers and his arms went around her.

Ti was conscious only of the sweet taste of his demanding lips and the hot tip of his tongue as it met hers. Then she felt the hardness of his masculinity pressing against her thigh. Tentatively, shyly, she slid her hand along him and moved her leg. His low groan gave her the full evidence of his desire.

Their minds seemed to blend together and they moved as one until Jase was poised above her. His lips crushed hers, but neither closed their eyes. Slowly, Ti guided him into her.

The first fiery contact surprised her. She tensed for a moment but relaxed when she saw the tenderness in his gaze. And then he was in her, filling her with himself.

They merged together and Ti could no longer think. He was deep inside her, and she was overwhelmed by his physical power. Her legs wrapped around his hips, and her arms fastened his chest to hers. His lips burned along her ears as tiny pulsing shocks raced through her. The aching need that had filled her earlier was easing, caressed by his manhood, and tended by their desires.

Ti moved with him, unifying, complementing, and knowing that they were becoming one. Every inch of her skin was covered by his. The strength of his body flowed into hers, giving her more strength with which to make love to him. Then another tremor began to shake her, building in intensity as it shot upward. Sparks shot through her mind again and again, until she could no longer maintain any hold on reality. Suddenly, before she realized what was happening, Ti bit into Jase's shoulder. She could feel him fill her to her very core. Then she was helpless. She could do nothing except be carried forward by Jason on this flight of love until she reached the pinnacle of their loving.

Unexpectedly, she exploded with Jase as she felt him filling her with molten fire. Then, as their mingled cries ceased, and their labored breathing eased, Ti relaxed within Jase's arms.

"Jason," she whispered as a rainbow of colors seemed to descend in the room to bathe them in beauty and peace.

"Shhh." He kissed her tenderly. They stayed together for a long time, until finally Jase moved and gently slid his weight from her without releasing her completely.

"Jason," she whispered again as she rested her head on his chest, content for the moment to listen to the strong, rhythmic beat of his heart. His hand was around her shoulders, cupping her breast comfortably. A few moments later she lifted her face and gazed into his eyes.

"I didn't mean for this to happen," he said.

"I know. I didn't mean to fall in love with you either, but I did," she admitted. She saw Jase try to smile, and also saw the intensity of his emotions in his eyes.

"It's all right Jason, I'm a big girl. No law says you have to love me because I love you."

Jase smiled softly as he lifted his head and kissed her. "As I've already told you, you're a beautiful, intelligent girl. Stop saying silly things. There's a law that governs what happens to people. Sometimes it's fair, sometimes it's not."

"Why did it have to happen?" she asked him.

"What? My falling in love with you?" he replied in a low, firm voice.

Ti stared at him, her breath catching in her throat as she tried to deny the words he'd just spoken.

"No Jason, don't say that . . . You can't . . . Oh, Jason, no . . ." Suddenly, tears were falling from her eyes.

Jase pulled her against him, confused for a moment by her reaction. Then he understood.

"Just accept it for now," Jase told her, his voice firm but still soft in the silence of the bedroom. "Stop fighting everything and everybody, and accept what is freely given!"

He kissed her then, pulling her to him and feeling the intensity of their earlier lovemaking return in full force. Her soft, pliant skin sent renewed passion coursing through his body. The satin of her lips eagerly responded to his and again they came together into another, more powerful and gripping flight of love that let them soar above the world in each other's arms.

Chapter 5

JASE LOOKED AT THE GLOWING RED NUMBERS OF THE clock on the bed table. It was six in the morning. He turned to gaze at Ti. *She's beautiful even in sleep,* he thought as his eyes roamed across her shadowed features, barely illuminated by the first faint glow of the coming day.

Carefully, so as not to disturb her, he got out of bed. He couldn't sleep any longer. Too many thoughts were crowding his mind. Last night he had created a problem, and he held himself responsible because he had known better.

Jase silently crossed the bedroom, closed the door, and went into the living room. His mind recalled all the events since his arrival here in Philadelphia, and came especially alive with the memory of last night's lovemaking.

It had been a long time since he had been with anyone he cared about. Only necessity and loneliness had allowed him to be with other women, and then it had been as infrequently as possible. But that had suddenly changed since his arrival in Philadelphia. And he wasn't sure he really wanted the change.

How could he explain the realities of his life to Ti? How could he tell her what his position and status meant to their relationship? How could he tell her he loved her, and then, if she returned to California with him, tell her they couldn't be together?

How would he be able to face Sam Barkley after making love to his granddaughter? Jase walked to the window and looked out. Although it was early, the gray light of dawn mingled with a blue sky, signaling to the city's residents that it was Monday morning and the beginning of another work week.

Monday, Jase thought as he shook his head. Today was the day he'd set as Ti's deadline. She would have to give him her decision. Jase knew two things with a dreaded certainty. The first, that he must return to California soon. The second, that he didn't want to go without her. But even if she did go, she was lost to him. Either way, Jase knew that what had happened between them was destined never be repeated.

On top of those unhappy thoughts sprang another clear and brilliant picture—the memory of Ti's skin, of her warm and gentle caresses as they had explored each other's bodies.

Ti stirred and reached out. Her eyes snapped open and she looked across the bed. Jason was gone. She glanced at the clock and saw it was six A.M. She heard a sound and recognized her bedroom door being closed. As she lay alone in the bed a slow smile spread across her face. *I love you.* She had never spoken those words to anyone, except her mother. Last night she'd told Jason those very words, screamed them over and over as he held her close, kissing and loving her passionately.

She knew she had been ashamed and shameless at the same time. Last night had left Ti feeling alternately shaken, loved, scared and relieved. It had been a range of emotions she'd never known before. This morning she knew there was only love.

She thought about last night and a delicious shiver rippled along the length of her body. It had been dark when they'd gotten around to eating a take-out Chinese dinner on her living-room floor. They'd spoken about many things and yet said very little. But regardless of the words, she had been able to see the depths of his emotion and the truth of his feelings in his eyes. She had seen, in those open pools of umber, everything she had needed.

Although they had made love twice before dinner, their desires had not abated. In fact, the air around them had crackled with the electricity of their passion. Ti had never wanted anyone as much as she did Jason, and without words her wants had been transmitted to him.

They had made love again, but it had been vastly different from before. It had been a slow, beautiful and intensely satisfying time in which they had explored each other intimately and shared a magical journey of awakened pleasure.

Lying in bed alone, with the heat of Jason's body still fresh on the sheets, Ti remembered every last detail, from the touch of his hands on her breasts, to the taste of his nipples in her mouth. His hands had aroused her, and she in turn had aroused him. They had joined together finally, moving in perfect unison, rising high above reality, to float in a multicolored universe that she sensed only a very special few have ever viewed.

They were carried aloft by the intensity and depth of

their lovemaking, and returned, satiated and complete, to fall asleep in each other's arms.

Yes, complete, Ti thought. *For the first time in my life I can understand what some of my friends have told me about love. Yes, I feel complete.*

As slowly as Jase had moved earlier, Ti moved now as she left her bed and went to the bathroom. A few moments later she emerged with drops of water sparkling on her forehead. The bedroom was still empty, and she went into the living room and found Jase staring out the window.

"I didn't want to wake you," he said after turning and seeing Ti standing near him. His blood pounded as he gazed at her naked beauty.

"You didn't. I get up early, remember?" she reminded him.

"Yes." He put his arms around her and drew her to him. The twin points of her breasts were like two burning needles on his chest, but he ignored their call as he looked into her eyes.

"Did I tell you how lovely you are?" he asked.

Ti nodded silently, unable to speak.

"Then let me show you," he whispered as he lifted her and carried her back to the bedroom.

"Jason," she called as he lowered her to the bed.

"Hush," he ordered. "I told you foghorns are too noisy in the morning. Close your eyes and stop giggling."

Ti tried, but it wasn't his order that stopped the giggling, it was his lips as they traced a maddening path along the top of her thigh. Suddenly her blood was roaring uncontrollably, and her breathing grew forced and shallow. The inside of her thigh tremored in added response to his lips. Her hands reached out for him suddenly, but he evaded them.

"Let me make love to you," he ordered in a husky whisper. "Lie back and close your eyes."

Again, the searing touch of his lips on her thigh sent excruciating waves of instant desire through her body. His hands joined in the exploration of her thighs, dropping occasionally to tease her calves and gently stroke the tender, sensitive skin. Staccato pulses generated upward in fiery tentacles of desire, filling her body with need, and making her ache with desire.

Then his lips were crossing the soft covering of her womanhood, and his fingers followed. The tip of Jase's tongue lightly caressed the silken folds guarding the entrance to her most feminine treasures. Pinpricks of light and heat assaulted her and her body tensed. Within seconds she melted under his glorious mouth, the tension fleeing as her body arched in response to his gentle, passionate, tender and abandoned lovemaking.

Years passed in seconds as his fingers moved and his hands kneaded her skin, while his lips and tongue tore cries of desperation and love from her throat. Then, slowly, his mouth began to move upward, trailing maddeningly across her stomach, pausing every inch to kiss the satin smoothness of her skin before continuing on.

When Jase's mouth reached the now oversensitive skin of her breast, he drew one stiffly pointed nipple into his mouth. Ti cried out and her hands went to Jase's hair, her fingers entwined within the thick mass as wave after wave of incredible pleasure shook her body. Her skin was glowing, and her insides trembled and flamed with need for him.

His mouth left her breast and Ti opened her eyes to see Jase staring at her. His eyes had deepened with desire, and she could feel the electricity flow between them. With her hands still wound tightly in his hair, she pulled him to her. He slid sensually along her body and she could almost feel each of the individual hairs of his chest, stomach and legs rub excitingly along her body. Her entire being trembled with anticipation.

"Now Jason, please, now," she pleaded, her normally husky morning voice made deeper with desire as she met his lips hungrily and darted her tongue into the warm recesses of his mouth.

But Jase held back against her demand. Suddenly Ti turned, forcing Jason to follow her until he was on his back. He opened his eyes and looked deeply into hers. She smiled as she drew her lips away, conscious of the way their chests were straining against each other. Slowly, teasingly, she slid her hand from his back to his chest and her fingers began to stroke his muscles and hair as she lifted herself up from him.

But even as Ti's fingers caressed him, her eyes bored into his. "I love you," she crooned. Before he could speak in return, her mouth sealed his, and her body pressed down heatedly upon him. Moving with feline grace, Ti slid along his powerful torso until her thighs were pressed against his. She rose up and guided him to her.

It was a sight Jase would never forget. Her beauty alone made his heart cry out. The feel of her around him was incredibly warm and soft. Her large breasts, so perfectly formed, moved in rhythm with the rest of her body. Her hands on his chest, caressing and pleading at the same time, were like the fingers of a magician, giving him more and more power and pleasure, until finally he could no longer watch or control himself. He gave in to the ageless call of her femininity, her aura, and the love she was so abundantly offering and showering on him, and released himself to her in a mighty crescendo of fulfillment.

Ti was lost as she joined with her lover. He filled her

with every inch of himself, penetrating upward in a searing path toward the very center of her being. The deep, pulsating rhythm they shared took all thought from her. There were only she and Jason in the world now. Her body was no longer controlled by her mind, but rather by her love and desire for the handsome man beneath her. She tried to see him, but could not open her eyes. She could only feel him. For the first time in her life, she surrendered the tight reins and freed her body, mind, soul and heart—a gift to the man who had awakened her womanhood.

"Oh," she cried as she realized the end was nearing. Then it didn't matter as they peaked together in a searing flash of love and completion that left Ti weak and happy, falling on top of Jason and trying vainly to catch her breath.

"I love you, Ti. Remember that, believe that," Jase said intensely.

The depth of his words forced Ti to lift her head and gaze at him through moist eyes. "I know," she whispered, wondering if it was a trick of the morning light, or her own imagination that showed his eyes to be as misty as hers.

They lay together for a long, silent time before Ti moved again. She slid from him and nestled into the crook of his arm. She was comfortable there, and safe, she realized happily. Then the quiet of the room was broken by a gurgling echo and Ti blushed.

"Hungry?" Jase asked.

"No, but I think my stomach is," she acknowledged.

"Good, because I'm starved. Woman, you sure worked me hard!" he told her with a wide smile.

Again, warmth flooded Ti as she basked in the glow of his smile. The crow's-feet crinkled once again at the corners of his eyes, making him look even more handsome.

"You're beautiful," she said as she traced the pattern of the lines with her fingers.

"When two people make love, and they lie together afterward the way we are, it's the man who is supposed to tell the woman she's beautiful, not the other way around."

"Does it matter?" Ti asked.

"No," Jase said as he kissed her.

"I like Jason better than Jase," she informed him.

"Yes?"

"Yes. And, I've made my decision." As she finished speaking, she felt Jase's body stiffen for a fraction of a second before he relaxed. Her eyes met his openly, and saw the question in them. "I'm coming with you," she finished.

"Why?" Jase asked.

Ti stared at him for a moment, surprised by his response. She'd thought he'd be happy, but his face showed nothing at all. "Why?" he repeated.

"Because of everything that's happened in the past few days. Because of myself, you—"

"No!" Jase interrupted vehemently as he sat up, dislodging Ti from his arm and shoulder. "No, I didn't make love to you in order to get you to come with me—"

"But most importantly, because I believe I owe it to myself to see what my grandfather is like," she finished as if she had not been interrupted.

"Are you sure?" Jase asked.

"I don't know," Ti replied honestly, "but I'll never be sure of anything until I've found out about *him.*"

A slow smile spread across Jase's face, and Ti smiled with him. "I'd like to leave today," he said.

"It will have to be late, I've an appointment with a lawyer," she told him. Then she explained what had happened on Friday, when she'd been interviewing for jobs.

"That could be dangerous. It could hurt your future if you lose."

"I won't lose. I don't think it's fair that just because I'm a woman I'm looked down on," she said through clenched teeth.

"Easy, I'm on your side. Remember, I'm the one who pulled him off you."

"I remember," Ti said with a smile as she pulled herself up and pecked his cheek. "But I'm still hungry."

"Then I shall feed you!" Jase declared.

They showered together, slowly and languorously, enjoying the feeling of washing and caressing each other beneath the stream of hot water. Twenty minutes later they were walking toward a restaurant.

By the time they ordered breakfast they had finalized their plans. After Ti's appointment, she would meet him at her apartment. From there, they would go to the airport and catch the late afternoon flight to San Francisco. Although she was apprehensive about what would happen in California, she was also confident that with Jason beside her, she would be able to face her grandfather and survive.

Ti glanced around the lawyer's modern reception area. It was antiseptic in appearance, with gleaming chrome-and-leather fixtures. The receptionist sat behind a large desk, typing a letter and answering the endless stream of calls that entered through her switchboard.

The walls were light blue, and abstract paintings and modern posters enhanced the impersonal feeling. But Ti also noted the decor's lack of gender—this could be the office of a man or a woman. Although she disliked the cold reception area, she agreed with the reasons for it.

A buzzer rang at the desk, and a moment later the receptionist called Ti's name. "Ms. Daley will be right out," she announced.

Before Ti could reply, a door at the far end of the reception area opened, and a tall, well-dressed woman of about forty walked directly toward her. The woman's blonde hair was streaked with fine strands of gray, and she carried herself with an air of total assurance.

"Ms. Caissen?" she asked as she extended her hand.

Ti nodded as she stood and took the woman's hand in hers. Ann Daley had the kind of strong grip that Ti liked; it inspired confidence.

"Shall we go to my office?" the lawyer suggested as she turned and motioned for Ti to walk with her. Two minutes later Ti was seated next to the attorney on a tweed couch.

"Coffee?" Ann Daley offered.

"No, thank you," Ti replied as she sat back on the couch and looked at her.

"I had dinner with Sondra Marks last night," Ann Daley said as she looked steadily at Ti. "And we discussed your problem. Do you have any idea what you're getting yourself involved in?"

"I don't understand. It was Mrs. Marks who suggested I contact you," Ti explained defensively.

"I know that. Ms. Caissen, what you're going to do can affect the rest of your life. It can possibly destroy any chance for you to become a successful businesswoman, as well as besmirch the reputation of a well-respected man and the company he works for."

Ti's body tensed as she digested the woman's warning. Her mind exploded angrily and she was unable to control the words of indignation that spat like bullets from her mouth. "What you're saying is that I should forget what happened, find another job, and then let some poor girl who is half scared to death be manipulated and used by the man who tried to do the same thing to me?" Ti stood angrily. "I think I made a mistake in coming here," she stated.

"Please, have a seat and hear me out," the lawyer said in a soothing voice.

Ti sat back down on the edge of the couch and waited, noting that a half smile had suddenly appeared on the lawyer's face.

"If you had answered my question with one ounce less anger I would have asked you to leave," Ann Daley said bluntly. "The action you are about to take will not be easy. If you didn't have the guts to speak out now, you wouldn't make it halfway through the trial. But Sondra said she sensed you were a fighter. I think so, too."

"I don't know whether to thank you or not," Ti admitted.

"You can thank me when we win this case. Now, I want every detail, every single fact and incident you can think of from the moment you began work at Matheson," she instructed as she sat back and waited for Ti to speak.

An hour later Ti finished. The lawyer had been scrutinizing her carefully throughout the meeting, but now Ti saw a vague, faraway look in the woman's eyes and waited patiently. A moment later Ann Daley's blue eyes sparkled with life.

"Let me tell you what we'll have to do from this point. I will file suit in Federal court. The suit will be an action against Matheson and Company for sexual harassment in violation of Federal statutes, and against

Tom Hutchings for the same thing. We will seek financial damages for their treatment of you, and sue for the return of your job at the same pay, plus the loss of pay from the time you quit until the suit is settled." The lawyer paused for a moment as she gazed at Ti.

"In order for this suit to be successful, you will not be able to look for a position that will be equal to what you had at Matheson."

"Why?" Ti asked.

"One reason is that if you are working in a position of equal stature, they may be able to avoid paying damages by stating that your leaving their company in no way interfered with your ability to obtain gainful employment at the same level; however, the real reason is that once we file suit, it will be extremely difficult for you to find a job. Not many companies will be willing to hire a person who is involved in a controversial employment suit."

"I'll be blacklisted?" Ti asked, horrified at the thought.

"Not exactly, but you can look at it like that. However, if, as you say, you don't want anyone else hurt the way you were, then you're going to have to play the game the way I tell you to."

"Ms. Daley—"

"Ann."

"Ann, I'll do whatever's necessary," Ti stated calmly.

"Good. Now, there are some other things you should be aware of. There are certain ramifications involved in this suit . . ." The lawyer went on to outline the problems they would face. The defense would be out to discredit Ti in any way they could. She would have to face a summary of her background, and be able to dispute any charges of immorality they would bring up.

"I have nothing to hide or be ashamed of," Ti told her.

"For some reason I don't doubt that. I'll have the papers drawn up for your signature."

"I'm leaving for California today, could the papers be done now?" Ti asked.

"How long will you be gone?"

"I'm not sure," Ti answered truthfully. "I'm . . . I'm going to visit my grandfather."

"That may be for the best. Could you stay there until the hearing?"

"When will that be?"

"I don't know. The court calendar is pretty full, but I can use whatever influence I have and if there's a cancellation of a case, we could get in. I would say anywhere from a month to six months."

"I . . . Ann, I really can't say how long I'll be in California. I'm not going just for a visit. You see, I've never met my grandfather." The open, honest invitation in the lawyer's eyes seemed to demand that Ti explain herself fully. For the first time, she found herself telling someone of her personal background. When she finished, she took a deep breath and waited for some response.

"For someone as young as you are, you've got an extremely interesting background, Ti. I'm at a loss for words. You do what you must in California, but my basic concern is for your ability to support yourself until the case is heard," Ann said.

"I'll find a way, either here or in California."

"I think you will," the lawyer admitted as she looked into Ti's face. "And, I think a little publicity will help, also. Since the legal papers will take a little time to get drawn up, will you join me for lunch?"

"Thank you."

"Don't thank me yet. I have an idea that may help you," she said and pressed the intercom. "Susan, get me Cybil Ashe."

"The political reporter from the *Philadelphia Inquirer?*" Ti asked.

"The same," Ann responded. A moment later her phone rang. Two minutes later she hung up the phone, a triumphant smile on her face. "Lunch will be very interesting," she pronounced. "You're going to give Cybil an exclusive interview."

"Why?"

"Strategy," she stated simply.

Ti closed the suitcase and locked it. Then she shook her head. It had been a busy day. Lunch had taken longer than she'd expected, almost two hours, and during that time, Cybil Ashe had listened, asked and dug deeply into Ti's mind. Then, when lunch was finished, the political reporter had shaken Ti's hand and smiled.

"I've been waiting for a story like this for a long time, Miss Caissen. Thank you."

Ti had smiled warmly, gaining confidence from the woman. "You're welcome."

When they'd returned to the lawyer's office, Ti had signed the multitude of papers. Then she'd promised to call Ann from California and give her an address where she could be reached. On the way home she'd stopped at the telephone company and arranged for her phone to be temporarily disconnected until her return.

In her apartment she packed the clothes she thought appropriate, and made sure she included the jeans she'd worn the other day. With the suitcases packed and sitting by the front door, Ti closed down the apartment and called the superintendent to let him know she would be gone for a while.

When everything was done, she dialed Jason's hotel and asked for his room. When she was told he'd checked out already, she hung up the phone and sat in the living room chair to wait for him.

Her mind began to wander, and for the first time that day she had a chance to think undisturbed. *What am I doing?* she wondered. Everything had happened so quickly her mind was still filled with turmoil.

Was she doing the right thing in going to California? What was her grandfather like? She sighed, knowing that she would find out in a little while.

And Jason? She'd never felt this way about another man. Ti knew she was inexperienced with men, and not even the two men she had dated seriously could be counted. And then she suddenly recalled the lawyer's words. She remembered Ann warning her that her ex-employers would delve into her background. Ti wondered what they would find.

She questioned whether the two times she'd been involved with men would affect anything. *No,* she reasoned, *they couldn't possibly.* Those affairs had been so one-sided, she remembered; she had been used, and poorly. She had felt little for them and hadn't even understood why she'd let herself become involved.

Yes, she could understand, she thought sadly. It had been peer pressure. She hadn't wanted to be the one left out of everything. But she had been wrong. She was different from her friends. She couldn't have casual affairs, or pretend to have emotions she didn't feel. Ti learned that lesson with hard facts.

When she was eighteen, she'd met Jerry, and had thought she was in love. It had been in her first year of college, and they'd dated steadily for almost three months. She had thought herself in love with him, and had finally given in to his insistent demands. But when he'd had his way, quickly satisfying himself without regard to her feelings, he wouldn't even look at her. When Ti had waited by the phone the next day, expecting the call he'd promised, she'd sat for nothing. It had taken Jerry a week to call her, and when he did, he had nothing to say. Ti had been unable to talk about it with her mother because of the shame she'd felt.

A year later, Ti had met Arthur. She thought he was different. He was filled with life, a happy-go-lucky post-graduate student who seemed so wise. Because she was so naive, and believed what he'd told her, she'd lowered her defenses and they had become lovers. But Ti had soon learned that she was only one of many. She had broken their relationship off quickly, and had sworn she would not be used again, that she would devote all her energies to reaching her goal of success.

Ti opened her eyes. No, those two incidents wouldn't harm her case. Suddenly she could feel Jason's presence surround her. He was different. She knew that intuitively. He was good and he was not using her. The feeling she had for him was so vast and far from any she'd known that even now, alone, she felt secure in the knowledge of her love for him, and what lay ahead in their future.

It was nice, Ti thought, remembering last night, and the first time they had made love. No words had been needed. They had both wanted each other desperately. When it was over, and he'd told her he loved her, she had been shocked. She hadn't wanted to hear his words. She only wanted to love him. Now she understood why. It was safer if she loved him. She could be in control. But he'd stopped that from happening. And Ti didn't care.

The ring of her doorbell startled her. She rose

quickly and went to the door. Opening it, she saw Jason's smiling face. He was dressed similarly to the first time she'd seen him. He wore a suede jacket, corduroy slacks and brown boots. His cocky smile and the way his mustache reflected light made her heart quicken.

She smiled and met him halfway. Her arms went around him as he drew her close. They kissed, deeply, lovingly, for a long while. Then, reluctantly, they separated.

"Ready?" he asked.

"Almost. Jason, there's one more thing we have to discuss," she said in a tightly controlled voice as the reality of what was about to happen struck her fully.

Jase lifted one eyebrow, and his dark eyes ordered her to speak.

Ti took a deep, anticipatory breath before she spoke. "I want you to promise me something."

"What?" he asked as his hands caressed her shoulders. Gentle heat emanated from his fingers, penetrating the material of her top, and spread soothingly across her skin.

Ti searched his face, drinking in its handsomeness. "After we're at my grandfather's winery, if there comes a time when I feel I must leave, I want you to promise you won't argue with me. You'll accept my decision and take me away from there."

Jase was silent for a moment as he listened to her words; her shoulders, under his hands, were tense. He could feel the doubts that filled her mind, and in her eyes he could see the trust she was offering him. His stomach knotted painfully as he looked at her, but he kept his emotions from showing on his face. "You have my word," he promised.

"I think I'm ready now," she replied.

Jase nodded as he released her and went to the two suitcases. "The cab is waiting, we've got barely an hour until the flight."

Together, they left the apartment, and Ti wondered again what would now happen to her life.

Chapter 6

THE HUM OF THE 747'S ENGINES COMBINED WITH THE meal she'd just finished lulled Ti into a light sleep. They had been in the air for over four hours already, and would be landing in another hour or so.

Ti let her thoughts replay the flight. When they had boarded the wide-bodied airplane in Philadelphia, Ti had been nervous but had tried not to show it. This was her first time in an airplane.

They had made the flight just in time, and were the last two people to board. Ti had remarked on the size of the seats the stewardess had taken them to, and Jason had smiled quietly in response.

The first-class section of the jet was smaller than she'd pictured, but it was well-appointed. The large seats were comfortable, and minutes after they'd taken off a stewardess was preparing to serve them drinks. Ti had also hoped that the vibrations from the jet's large engines had masked the trembling of her hands.

She had watched in fascination as another stewardess instructed them in the use of the oxygen masks and life preservers, and had whispered a question to Jason that had made him laugh.

"If we're flying over land all the way, why do we have to worry about life preservers?"

Jason had shaken his head and grasped Ti's hand in his. He'd gazed into her eyes and spoken.

"Those are the rules. Have you ever flown?" he'd asked.

"Only in my mind," Ti had replied as she'd flashed a nervous smile at him.

"It's safe, and you'll get used to it quickly."

"How high are we going?"

"Very high," Jase had responded with another smile and had squeezed her hand comfortingly.

Before anything else could be said, the plane had leveled off and the stewardess had served them champagne.

Ti had sipped the cold, bubbling wine and followed the cool path it traced to her stomach. Then, closing her eyes for a moment, she'd leaned her head on his shoulder.

"What can I expect when we get there?" she'd asked.

"Whatever you make it," Jase had answered honestly.

Her hand, no longer trembling, was still within his, and he had pressed it tightly. "Tell me about the winery," she'd suggested.

Jase had complied eagerly. As he spoke, Ti had been able to picture everything. The rolling green hills of vines, and the soft earth which gave life to the grapes that grew on them. She had listened as he'd described the winery itself, and the layout of Barkley Vineyards.

The main house had been built in 1868, by Arren Barkley, two years after he founded the vineyards. It was a large structure, modeled after the earlier Spanish homes of Southern California, but built for the cooler climate of the Napa Valley.

Jase's words had evoked beautiful pictures, and Ti had found herself longing to see the area. The only thing that kept her from showing her enthusiasm was the fact that when she finally did see it, she would also have to face her grandfather.

For an hour she had listened to Jase's varied descriptions. Jase, as general manager, had his own small house on the grounds. There were many other structures on the property, including quarters for the rest of the vineyard's workers.

Jase's description of the winery had been interrupted by the stewardess informing them that dinner would soon be served. Ti had been once again amazed at the service and the choices for dinner. Dinner itself had been slow and languorous, accompanied by two different wines. By the time she'd finished eating, she'd felt a bit light-headed.

"I don't understand why so many people complain about the food and service on airplanes," she'd commented to Jase over coffee.

Again, Jase had laughed at her naivete. Then he had explained the class structure of airplanes, and also the fact that the elaborate meal they'd just finished had reflected the price of the ticket.

"There couldn't be that much of a difference, could there?"

"Just a few hundred dollars a person over the tourist fare," he'd responded, amused.

Ti had been shocked to realize that this flight, and the seat she was in, cost more than she took home after three weeks of work. Even though she had two business degrees, she'd never flown, nor had she had any reason to check on the prices.

The stewardess had come down the aisle, offering headsets for a movie. Both Ti and Jase had declined, and within the now-darkened cabin they had become silent. Without realizing it, Ti had begun to doze lightly.

Jase looked at Ti and knew he'd made a mistake. He gazed at her face, relaxed in sleep, and watched for a moment. Then he lifted his head and gazed out the window. The sky told him they were nearing their destination. Purple-and-blue bands proliferated behind them, chasing the pink-and-crimson shades toward the west. When they landed in San Francisco, it would be nighttime.

Jase took a deep breath and tried to organize his thoughts. What had happened between them in Phila-delphia was his fault completely, and he'd have to pay the price for what he'd done. He knew he must explain it all to Ti before they reached the winery. The words would hurt her, but if he didn't tell her now it would be too late. He had to tell her what she was about to face, and explain the way she must act toward him.

"Ti?" Jase murmured as he stroked her hair gently.

She heard her name called as if from a distance. Slowly, as she forced herself to become aware of her surroundings, she opened her eyes.

The cabin was dark and the movie was over. Most of the passengers were asleep and the overhead lights were low. She turned and gazed up at Jase.

"Sleep well?" he asked.

"I wasn't really asleep, just thinking," she replied.

"We have to talk," he said in a low, intense voice.

"What is it, Jason?" Ti asked as she took his hand.

"Do you believe I love you?" he asked as he gazed into her eyes.

Ti nodded slowly as she searched the shadowed contours of his face to look for clues to what he was trying to say. All she saw was a sad longing reflected in his expressive eyes.

"Ti, what happened to us in Philadelphia should not have occurred."

Ti's sharp intake of breath was audible in the silent cabin. The shock of his words numbed her mind and paralyzed her tongue. She stared at him, trying to comprehend what he was saying.

"Ti, I'm sorry. I fell in love with you—"

"You're sorry you fell in love with me?" she asked, cutting him off as she found her voice.

"No. I'm sorry I have to say what I must, not sorry that I fell in love with you. What happened between us is impossible under the circumstances. I work for your grandfather. He gave me his trust when he asked me to come east and talk with you. I violated that trust."

"Jason, you can't be serious? Loving someone is not a violation of trust," she declared adamantly, fighting the dizzying wave his words caused.

"In this case it is. Ti, there are rules for people like you and me. Rules that cannot be broken. You are a Barkley, heir to one of the oldest and most prestigious wineries in California."

"My name is Caissen, not Barkley," Ti hissed angrily.

"You can call yourself whatever you want, but it doesn't change a thing. I've known you for only a few days, and no matter what you say, everything you do, every gesture you make, even the way you look at things, analyze them, and make your decisions, reminds me of your grandfather. Whether you like it or not, you're a Barkley."

"What difference does it make who I am?" Ti

whispered. But intuitively, she knew that no argument on this subject could be won.

"I work for your grandfather. I'm an employee. There are unwritten rules that prevent the mixing between . . ." Jase paused then, unable to continue as Ti stared at him.

"The mixing between what? The classes? The blood? The mixing of love and desire? Tell me, the mixing of what?" Ti demanded in a seething, rage-filled whisper.

"All of it," Jase replied.

"No, Jason, if you love me, nothing else matters."

"Because I love you it does. Ti, you must also understand that I love and respect your grandfather," Jase continued, forcing himself to speak calmly and not show his torn emotions. "I can't hurt him to satisfy myself."

"And what of me? You seem to be able to hurt me without any qualms," Ti said through clenched teeth. The earlier, numbing shock of his words was gone, replaced by hurt, rejection and a growing, uncontrollable fury.

"I was wrong, but I couldn't help myself," Jase began, his eyes still locked with hers, his large hand tight around her smaller one. "The minute I saw you something happened to me. Feelings and emotions I thought long gone, came alive. Everything I had been brought up to believe in disappeared, and all I could think of was you. That was wrong. I realized it a little while ago. I wasn't thinking about you, I was thinking about me. I hope that one day you'll forgive me." As he gazed at her, he saw her eyes turn hard and cold and knew he was losing her.

"You're lying," Ti cried as she pulled her hand free from his. "You seduced me, you made love to me for only one reason."

"No—"

"Yes, damn you! You did it all to bring me to California."

"Ti, I made love to you because I had to. Because more than anything else, I wanted and needed you."

Ti shook her head, trying to deny his words, but sensed their truth even as she refused to listen to them. "If you love me, these ridiculous rules you're telling me about can't matter."

"They do. It's because I love you I have to tell you about the rules. I love you, and I won't see you hurt and torn apart by what I've done to you. You're coming to a new road in your life, and you can't afford any complications."

"I can afford whatever I want. Jason, don't do this to me," she pleaded. Then she took another deep breath as she tried to fight the onslaught of oppressive feelings claiming her. "Why did you have to tell me you loved me? Why, damn you?" she whispered as she turned away from him.

"I've never lied in my life, I wasn't about to then or now."

Ti whipped her head around to stare openly at him. Although her voice was still low, hurt and rage sent her words flying like missiles. "Haven't you ever heard that there are times when a lie is kinder and less painful than the truth? I could have managed loving you without your giving me the same in return, but you had to tell me you loved me. Jason, how can you love me and tell me it was wrong all in one breath?"

"Ti, it isn't our love that's wrong, it's the violation of a trust given to me. I have obligations to your grandfather that go far beyond the employee relationship. I owe my life to him, and I won't stab him in the back!"

They sat in silence for several long, agonizing minutes, and finally, through the heavy curtain of betrayal that had formed around her, an icy shroud settled into her mind. "What obligations could possibly be so important that they force you to deny your own emotions and needs?"

"It doesn't matter what's important to you or me, it's the way of the Valley, and you have to learn that, now!" he said in a tight voice. But for all his brave words, he was lost in the sad depths of her green-flecked eyes, and found himself fighting against the memories that her words evoked.

In a far compartment of his mind, he could hear his wife and daughter scream in terror as the flames engulfed their home. He saw himself wandering aimlessly along the highway. And he relived, briefly, the year he'd spent as an itinerant, mindless worker before Sam Barkley had jolted him from his grief. Slowly, Jase shook his head. He couldn't tell her about that, either.

"Ti, I'm sorry. I love you, but it can't be."

"You told me you knew the story about my mother, isn't that right?" She snapped the question at him quickly and waited for his nod. "Don't you think it's a little strange that I'm suddenly going to meet my grandfather, and at the same time I'm about to repeat my mother's life?"

"No, you're not living your mother's life, you're barely beginning your own."

"How could you do this to me? How could you put me in this position?" she demanded. Her eyes bored into his as her mind screamed. She wanted to invoke his promise, and make him put her on the next plane back to Philadelphia.

But, in a remote and sane corner of her mind, logic spoke to her. She had committed herself to coming to California, and when she'd made the decision it hadn't been because of Jason Patten, it had been because she wanted to know her grandfather. She wanted to stare at the monster who had haunted and hurt her mother so unfeelingly.

"I hate you, Jason Patten. You deceived me, lied to me and tricked me," she hissed as she turned from him and closed her eyes. The hopes that had been growing in her for the last days died. Anger welled up like a red, flaming wall, and suddenly she knew she had made the same mistake she had made in the past. She had given her trust to someone, and had been rewarded by the betrayal of that very trust.

Again, she was reminded of the promise she'd made to herself long ago. She was all she had. She could only trust herself, no one else.

"Last call for champagne, we'll be landing in ten minutes," announced the stewardess as she came to their seats. She heard Jase decline and was about to herself, but when she opened her eyes and saw the towel-wrapped bottle in the woman's hands, she changed her mind.

"Is that domestic or imported champagne?" she asked.

"Domestic, California," replied the stewardess.

"I'll have a glass, thank you," Ti said, keeping her voice as level and unemotional as Jase's had been.

The stewardess poured the sparkling liquid into a new glass, handed it to Ti, and moved on to the next seats.

"Ti—" Jase began, but the look Ti flashed him stopped any further words.

"I really am glad this is not *good* French champagne, I would so hate to waste it," Ti said as she smiled sweetly at Jase and flicked her wrist, expertly emptying the contents of the glass into his unsuspecting face.

She watched as the sparkling liquid ran down his face in rivulets of foam, and, as he silently wiped it from his face, she spoke venomously. "That's for being such an

unfeeling, unemotional, obsequious son of a bitch!"
she whispered in a cold, harsh voice before turning
away from him.

The flashing of the overhead seat belt sign reflecting
on the window broke through her churning thoughts,
and her ears popped as the plane began its descent. Ti
took a deep breath as she gazed down at the twinkling
lights of San Francisco. Her now-unavoidable destination was below her.

The icy silence that had fallen between Jase and Ti as
the airplane had landed, continued as they sat as far
from each other as possible in the back seat of the large
limousine that sped along the darkened highway.

Ti stared out the window, gazing at the dwindling
proliferation of motels, restaurants and signs that
marked the freeway leading from the airport. Soft
music floated in the air, effectively shutting off any
sounds that came into the car from the outside.

Finally, Jase's voice broke the silence, startling Ti
and making her tense. "We'll be leaving the freeway in
a few minutes. I wish it were daytime so you could see
the beauty of this valley."

"I prefer it this way," Ti said in an icy voice, refusing
to turn her head to acknowledge his words. It was true,
she preferred to arrive in the darkness that matched her
mood. She did not want to see beauty, not while she
was so filled with the ugliness of his betrayal.

"Damn it, Ti," Jase cried as his hand grasped her
shoulder tightly, his fingers digging into her flesh as he
swung her around to face him. She stared at him,
unconscious of the pain, unflinching against the hardness in his face.

"Take your hand off me," she hissed.

"I did it for you," he insisted.

"No, I think you did it for yourself, to ease your own guilty conscience."

Jase reeled at her words, and the blood drained from his face. Without her knowing it, she had spoken the truth.

She stared at his ashen face, and suddenly her heart sank. She had hurt him deeply, yet at the same time she didn't want to believe the words she'd just uttered had been the truth. She had wanted him to deny them, but he had not.

Stop torturing yourself, she commanded. *Stop being a fool.* Slowly, she drew her eyes from his and once again stared out the window; the loss of love left a bitter taste in her mouth.

Soon the limousine left the freeway. Ti tried to see the landscape through the darkness. As the limousine picked up speed, Ti saw they were on a smaller, well-paved road.

Twenty minutes later the car slowed and turned. This time they were on a single-lane drive. She knew they had arrived even before she saw the bold wooden sign ominously illuminated by the vehicle's headlights. Carefully, as if she were imprinting it in her memory for all time, Ti read the sign.

BARKLEY VINEYARDS

FOUNDED IN 1866 BY ARREN AND TI BARKLEY

NAPA, CALIFORNIA

Ti's breath caught as she read the sign. For a moment she had trouble adjusting herself to the fact she was here, and then the limousine moved on. Closing her eyes, Ti forced her nerves to settle down and concentrated on what lay ahead. She would see *him* in a few minutes. After twenty-four years of life, she would meet her grandfather.

Ti lowered the window and breathed in the sweet, fragrant air of the Napa Valley. Her senses were assaulted by the unidentifiable scents carried to her.

Then she saw the house. Even in the dark it was an imposing sight. Light shone through a multitude of windows in a warm, beckoning way. The front of the house rose two stories, and was topped with a dark tile roof. Wood pillars ran upward, breaking the whiteness of the Spanish stucco. The windows were also framed in wood.

For some reason, Ti had already known the house would look as magnificent as it did. Suddenly her heart was pounding and her hands trembled. With all the determination she was capable of, Ti stopped the trembling, chased away the trepidations that rose within her and, as the chauffeur opened her door, regained complete control of her emotions.

Then, as the chauffeur went to the trunk of the limousine to get her luggage, Jase came around and faced her. Silently, he took her arm and guided her along the walk toward the two large mahogany doors. Before Jase rang the bell, he turned and gazed deeply into Ti's eyes.

"Don't hate me, don't hate your grandfather. Hold off making judgments about either of us until you've been here for a while. Learn about our ways, and our life here," he whispered. Then he rang the bell.

Before she could say anything, Jase turned again, bent quickly and brushed his lips across her forehead and without pausing, walked away. Ti turned to call to him, the feel of his lips still warm on her skin. But no words came, her hurt and anger stopped them.

The door opened, and Ti faced it.

"Miss Ti?" asked a soft, feminine voice, and Ti

found herself looking into the friendly, open face of a middle-aged woman.

"Yes," she managed to say.

With a smile, the woman stepped back and motioned Ti to come in. As she did, the chauffeur entered with her two bags and stood there looking at the women. A rapid dialogue in Spanish followed, and the chauffeur nodded his head and walked toward the stairs.

"Welcome. I am Angela, the housekeeper," she said to Ti. "George is taking your bags to your room," she added as she watched the chauffeur walk up the stairs.

As Ti listened to the housekeeper, she glanced around the hallway of the house. The floors were highly polished wood—oak, she thought. The walls were lined with many paintings, and the furnishings were all of dark, stained wood.

"I hope your flight was pleasant," Angela said with another smile.

"Yes, thank you," Ti replied, knowing the lie was necessary.

"If you will come with me, Señor Barkley is waiting in his library," she said as she turned and led Ti through the house.

The beauty of the house called to Ti with a longing she'd never experienced. As they walked through the living room, Ti gazed at it appreciatively. Two long couches faced each other and between them was a large, low table of the same dark wood as the rest of the furniture. A sculpted figure of a horse sat on the center of the table, and even as they walked by Ti could make out the perfection of the piece. A stone-and-marble fireplace dominated the far wall of the living room, and above the mantel hung a large portrait of two people. Instinctively, Ti knew they were her ancestors, Arren and Ti Barkley.

She paused for a moment to look at the portrait. The

man was exceedingly handsome. He had dark hair, blue eyes, a straight nose, and sharp, good looks. But the woman next to him was the one who cried out to Ti. Her face was familiar, very familiar, with large eyes and light hair. Suddenly Ti realized that her smile was the same as Ti's mother's.

A flash of sadness overwhelmed her, and Ti fought to banish it. "Miss Ti?" called Angela.

She nodded her head and took one more quick glance at the portrait before following Angela again. Soon they entered a long hallway and, walking halfway down, Angela stopped to knock on a door.

Without waiting for a reply, she opened the door and turned to Ti. "Please," she said as she motioned for Ti to enter.

Ti tried to smile, but could not. She tried to say thank you, but the words didn't come. Angela smiled softly and nodded her head in understanding. "I will bring tea, unless you prefer coffee," she said.

"Tea is fine," Ti whispered, and watched Angela nod, turn and walk back down the hallway.

With a deep, preparatory breath, Ti stepped into the room. The first thing she noticed was one long, book-lined wall. She was aware of the scents of leather, books and tobacco pervading the room. With her second step she saw her grandfather.

He was standing next to a large brown leather chair, smiling hesitantly as he gazed at her. Ti returned the frank gaze as she studied him through the beating of her heart, still unable to speak as she looked into her grandfather's hazel, green-flecked eyes for the first time.

His face was deeply etched, not with the wrinkles of age, but rather with the weathered lines created by the sun. He had a full head of neatly combed salt-and-pepper hair. A short, well-manicured beard and mustache of almost pure white contrasted handsomely against his tanned skin. Although she hadn't known what to expect, she hadn't pictured him looking quite as tall and distinguished as he did. Nor did he remotely show his sixty-odd years of age as he stood silently under her inspection.

Over his shoulder Ti noticed another portrait. As her eyes involuntarily flicked upward to it, she gasped.

"You are as beautiful as your mother," Samuel Barkley observed, breaking the tense silence as he followed the direction of his granddaughter's eyes.

"Thank you," Ti replied stiffly, shaken by the unexpected sight of her mother's likeness in this room.

"Please, have a seat," Samuel said, pointing to a leather couch against the far wall. When Ti walked toward it, Samuel Barkley did the same.

"Was your trip pleasant?" he asked as he seated himself a short distance from her.

"It was fine, thank you," Ti answered, unable to keep the nervousness from filtering into her voice.

"I'm very glad you decided to come," he said.

"Really? I was under the impression that *Mr. Patten* would have camped on my doorstep for the rest of my life if I had not agreed to fly here." Again, Ti was unable to prevent bitterness from mingling with her words.

"Jase takes his responsibilities very seriously," Samuel acknowledged as he studied Ti.

"So I've noticed. Why did you want me to come?" she asked suddenly, moving the subject away from Jason. Her eyes locked with his, and she stared at him in challenge.

"Because it was time. I wanted . . . no, I *needed* to meet you. You are my granddaughter."

"There were other times, when my mother was alive," she challenged.

Ti watched as her grandfather's eyes grew momentarily distant. Then he shook his head and his eyes were focused again on her. "No, there was no other time. Ti, I'm not your enemy. I don't want to fight with you, not now. Just let me look at you. I've been denied you for too long," he said in a low voice.

Before Ti could say anything, there was a knock on the door and Angela entered with a serving tray. She placed it on the low table by the couch, and put cups and saucers before Samuel and Ti. She poured the steaming tea into the cups, placed the milk and sugar between them and left without speaking a word.

"Ti, I won't pretend to believe I can understand what you're feeling. All I can ask is that you give me the next few days to let you learn a little about me."

In order to cover her confusion from his unexpected plea, Ti turned to the table and added a spoonful of sugar to the amber tea. She stirred it slowly, and when she finally lifted it, she looked at him.

"All right, no fighting," she agreed.

Samuel Barkley nodded his head, then smiled. The smile disappeared as Ti, unable to stop herself, yawned deeply.

"You're tired," Samuel stated.

"Sorry," she apologized. "I think everything that's happened today has caught up with me. What time is it?" she asked, suddenly aware of how close to exhaustion she was.

Her grandfather glanced at his wristwatch and then back at her. "Almost ten, but it's actually one o'clock for you. You have your mother's eyes," he said suddenly.

"So do you," Ti whispered in response.

"Tomorrow, after breakfast, I'll take you on a tour of the winery, but for now," he said as he stood and offered her his hand, "I think you should prepare for bed."

Ti stared at the hand he offered her. Ignoring it, she rose. "Thank you, I think I'll do that."

Samuel Barkley did not let her rejection show on his face as he nodded and led her from the room. They walked silently to the foot of the wide wood banister of the staircase. There he called for Angela, who appeared a moment later.

"Please show my granddaughter to her room," he said. Then he turned to Ti and smiled. "Sleep well, my dear."

Ti nodded silently. Then, conscious that Samuel's eyes were on her, she kept her shoulders straight as she followed Angela upstairs and down another long hallway to a door that was already open.

"This will be your room," Angela said as she guided Ti inside and turned on the lights.

Ti froze as she looked around. The room was large and beautiful. The walls were snow-white, and two large, curtained windows filled the far wall. As she gazed about, she realized that the highly polished furniture was antique. A high, seven-drawer chest and a long dresser with an oak-framed mirror were on the wall opposite the bed. And the bed itself almost took her breath away. It was a large four-poster bed with a canopy of cream material that showed off the oak to its best advantage. A small wrought-iron vanity, with a gilt-framed mirror and stool, were on the same wall as the bed.

"It is a truly magnificent room, no?" Angela asked.

"Yes," Ti whispered. "This is a guest room?"

"No. This was the room of one of your relatives, long before you were born."

"It has never been used since?" Ti asked, both awed and unbelieving at the same time.

"Not since I have been here, and that has been for thirty years," Angela explained.

"You knew my mother?" Ti asked.

"Sí, I knew her," the housekeeper responded in a sad voice which told Ti it was not the right time to ask questions. "The bathroom is through this door," Angela said as she opened another door and turned on the lights. Although the bathroom wasn't modern in the true sense of the word, it did have all the amenities of a present-day bathroom. As her eyes took in all the fixtures, she noticed the white porcelain tub with claw feet that dominated one side of the room. A continental shower was attached to it.

"Would you like me to run a bath?" Angela asked as she saw the direction Ti's eyes had taken.

"I have to unpack first," Ti replied.

"It is already done," Angela informed her. "When you were with your grandfather."

Ti couldn't stop the surge of anger that Angela's words brought on. "How dare he have someone go through my things!" she spat out, feeling the invasion of her property as if it were an invasion of herself.

"Miss Ti," Angela said, her face flushed with embarrassment, "I am sorry you feel this way, but it is the way things are done here. Nobody has looked through your belongings, I unpacked them myself."

Ti stared at Angela, as shame at her words replaced the anger of seconds ago. Suddenly she realized that the tension of the day had stretched her nerves to the breaking point. "I'm very tired, and I must apologize," she said to Angela in a formal tone.

Angela nodded her head knowingly, and without any further talk went to the tub and turned the gleaming brass faucet on. "What time shall I wake you?" Angela asked.

"Does the sun rise on this side of the house?"

"Yes."

"Then I won't need anyone to wake me," she said.

"Miss Ti?"

"Yes?"

"You have made your grandfather very happy. Thank you." Ti saw moisture forming in Angela's eyes, and realized the woman felt very strongly about Samuel Barkley. Wisely Ti chose to nod, rather than speak.

As soon as Angela left, Ti undressed and went into the bathroom. She turned the water off and stepped into the tub. As she sank into the soothing warmth of the bath, she closed her eyes and sighed.

She was here, in California, in her grandfather's house. Often, as she had grown up, she had wondered what it would be like. Now she knew.

While the hot water eased her muscles, her mind began to relax. Samuel Barkley had not been the ogre she'd expected. In fact, he seemed just the opposite. *At least on the outside,* Ti thought.

But then, she'd also thought Jason to be very different from what he'd revealed himself to be. "Why?" she whispered to the mustached face that filled her vision and gazed at her with umber eyes. "Why did you betray me?"

The night was cool and clear. The scent of grapes growing on the vines mingled with the fresh smells of the earth to wash over Jase soothingly as he walked through the garden of the main house. Next to him was Samuel Barkley.

"I want you to know how much I appreciate what you've done," Sam said.

"I think you'd better hold back on the thanks for a little while. Your granddaughter isn't thrilled to be here. Sam," Jase cautioned as he stopped and looked at his boss, "she has a lot of hatred trapped inside her. It will take a lot for you to win her over. You'll have to be patient."

"I've already had a sample tonight, but I've also had twenty-five years to learn patience. I think I can handle it," he said wryly.

"Be easy with her, Sam, she's been hurt and needs understanding."

"Everyone's been hurt, Jase. You of all people should know that."

"This is different. Don't rush it," Jase warned, aware of the close scrutiny with which Sam was favoring him. Jase turned and looked around him. "I never thought I'd miss this place so much in just a few days."

"It becomes a part of you," Samuel Barkley replied as he gazed at Jase. "I could do with a drink. Join me?"

"Not now, thank you. I'll just stay out here for a while."

"All right. Jase, again, thank you."

"You're welcome, Sam," Jase replied. *I hope,* he added silently to Samuel Barkley's retreating back as it disappeared in the darkness.

Chapter 7

TI WOKE TO STRANGE NOISES. STRUGGLING TO CONSCIOUS-ness, she tried to identify the sounds. Then a smile creased her face and she opened her eyes. She was hearing the soft calls of birds.

Turning, she looked at the windows. Daylight filtered through the gauze curtains that stirred softly in response to breezes entering the open windows. Ti took off the covers and slipped out of bed. As she walked across the room the hem of her long white nightgown grazed the cool wood floor.

With a smooth motion, Ti opened the curtains and looked out. The day was glorious and the sky was a color she'd seen only in pictures. A light, dreamy-blue cloudless sky went on for as far as she could see. *The sun must have just risen,* she realized, as she gazed at the yellow globe without having to blink. Beneath it, in the distant background, the high peaks of mountains were outlined, and, as she drew her eyes downward, she saw the terraced vineyards stretched out along the rolling emerald hills.

A large, stately tree stood near her windows, and Ti saw several brilliantly colored birds perched on its limbs. She smiled at them, enjoying their calls, and leaned on the windowsill to stare at them.

Other sounds drifted up to her, and Ti searched out their sources. Along a dark dirt path she saw five men walking. Each held an implement on his shoulders, and their jovial voices, although incomprehensible from that distance, reached Ti.

Then she heard a familiar voice and her body tensed. Turning her head and craning her neck as far as possible, she was able to make out Jase's form near the corner of the house. A combination of desire and anger mixed in an emotional whirlpool that forced her to continue watching him for several more minutes.

He was talking to another man when he suddenly looked up at her. He stopped speaking as his eyes met hers. Ti quickly drew her head into the room.

Breathing deeply, she turned and went to the bathroom. After she washed her face, she stared into the mirror. *I must be strong! I must not let him know!* Ti knew she loved Jason, and knew sadly that nothing further would ever come of it. She shook her head, but could not draw her eyes from her reflection as her thoughts continued. And her grandfather! He was so different from how she'd pictured him. She had expected a monster, and had met a dignified man. *No, wait and see. Don't jump to any conclusions,* she cautioned herself.

Ten minutes later she opened the closet door. In the cedar-lined closet, her three business suits hung next to two pairs of slacks and two skirts. One of the skirts caught her eye. It was a simple, Indian-print cotton skirt she felt would suffice for the day.

Ti took the skirt down and laid it on the bed, then she went to the dresser and took out a bra and panties, deciding against the panty hose as she breathed in the warm fall air of the Napa Valley. When these were on, she opened another drawer and took out a plain white scoop-necked blouse with a buttoned front. She put the blouse on and stepped into the skirt. When she was dressed, she looked at herself in the mirror.

The outfit looked fine; the Indian skirt showed off the flatness of her stomach, and sloped smoothly from her rear. Then Ti brushed her hair and, using two decorative combs, pulled the sides back and caught them above her ears. She returned to the closet and took out her old leather sandals and slipped them on. Knowing she couldn't delay any longer, she prepared to face the world.

Downstairs, Ti was uncertain which direction to take when she heard the voices of women. Following the sounds, she emerged in the kitchen. Angela stood there speaking in Spanish to a young dark-haired woman. The younger woman saw Ti and said something. Angela turned and flashed a welcoming smile.

"Good morning. You slept well?" she asked.

"Like a log," Ti replied, responding to the friendly warmth Angela radiated.

"Good. Would you like breakfast on the patio?" she asked. "It is very nice outside," she added.

"That sounds wonderful," Ti agreed as she followed the housekeeper through the kitchen.

They went through open double-glass doors and onto a cement walk. The garden was beautiful, filled with trees and shrubs, and an abundance of flowers seemed to call out to her. The air smelled clean and fresh.

"Here," Angela said as she stopped. Ti saw a glass-topped table with four white wrought-iron chairs around it. Two places were set, and in its center a copper carafe sat over a candle warmer. "Would you like breakfast now?" she asked.

"Just some toast, please," Ti replied.

"Hmmph," Angela snorted as Ti sat. The housekeeper lifted the carafe and poured steaming black coffee into one of the china cups.

"Is my . . . my grandfather up yet?" Ti asked.

"Yes, Señor Barkley is always up early. He will join you soon," she informed Ti. Then, with another warm smile, she left.

Ti sipped the coffee and sighed. It was strong, but good. Then she sat back and looked around. The garden was peaceful; the birds called out above her, and the sun reached down with warm fingers to gently caress her skin.

It was so different here from what she was used to—quiet, peaceful and unreal. *Why am I here?* she asked herself for the thousandth time. *To face my mother's father! To chase the devils that haunt my mind!*

"I don't think I've seen so lovely a sight in years." Sam Barkley's voice interrupted her thoughts. Ti jumped at the sound, and then forced a smile as her grandfather sat down. "Didn't mean to startle you," he said.

"This garden is conducive to losing yourself in thought," she admitted.

"Did you sleep well?"

"Very, thank you."

Angela appeared then and placed a napkin-covered basket and two earthenware jars on the table. She poured Samuel a cup of coffee and departed without a word.

"Ah, you're in for a treat," Samuel proclaimed as he reached out and uncovered the basket. Steam rose upward from the golden-brown biscuits within. "María, Angela's daughter, makes the most wonderful biscuits," he said as he pushed the basket toward Ti. "Butter and preserves," he added as he pointed to the brown jars.

Ti picked up a biscuit, opened it and spread butter across its surface. "You are having more than just that, aren't you?" Samuel asked.

"I don't eat much in the morning," Ti confessed.

"You should—" Sam started to say, but stopped himself as he saw a warning look rise up in her eyes and changed the subject. "I thought you might enjoy a tour of the winery today."

"That would be very nice," Ti admitted.

"Good. After you finish breakfast, we'll go."

"Aren't you having any?" Ti asked, forcing herself to be polite.

Her grandfather shook his head, and Ti saw sunlight reflect softly from his hair. "I had my breakfast several hours ago. I usually get up about five."

"So early?" Ti commented as she took a bite of the biscuit. "These are very good," she added.

"Try Angela's preserves," he suggested as he pointed to the other jar. "I've been getting up at five since I was twelve years old. It's a hard habit to break."

"But you don't work in the fields."

"No, but I still get up when my workers do. I like to be part of what happens here. Besides," he added as he looked around the garden, "I enjoy the early morning. It's a friendly, peaceful time."

"Angela told me the room I'm in hasn't been used in years Whose room was it?" she asked suddenly.

"My aunt Jenna's, my father's sister. Your mother was named after her," he said as his face turned serious and the smile disappeared.

"Did she live here all her life?" Ti asked.

"Yes." Samuel nodded.

"She never married?"

"No, when she was a child she fell from a horse. She was never able to walk after that."

"It must have been difficult for her," Ti said, feeling a strange, sudden empathy for a woman she'd never met.

"It was for a while, but she overcame it. The Barkleys are a stubborn breed, as you should be well aware of," Sam commented as he gazed into Ti's eyes.

Ti nodded her head slowly and took another bite of the biscuit.

"By the time Jenna turned twenty, she had decided to become a teacher."

"Really? I would think that at the time it would have been a very hard thing to do," Ti replied as she noted the warmth with which her grandfather spoke.

"As I said, we Barkleys are a stubborn lot. Jenna became a teacher, graduated from college back east, and then went on to teach handicapped people like herself."

"In the east?" Ti asked.

"No, here in the Valley. When I was fifteen, she died a well-respected, satisfied woman who had lived a fruitful life. But," Samuel continued in a lighter voice, "there will be plenty of time to tell you about our family. Right now I want to show you the winery, if you're ready."

Ti took one last sip of coffee and nodded her head. "I'm ready," she said aloud, but in her mind she wondered how true those words were.

Ti and Samuel walked away from the house, and although Ti didn't know it, he was watching her very carefully. He knew the pride he felt within him was justified. She held herself proudly, her head straight, her shoulders pulled back, but not unnaturally so. She was perhaps an inch taller than her mother had been, but her physical proportions were almost identical. The only difference between his daughter and her daughter was the color of her hair. Jenna had had soft blonde hair; Ti's was a rich coal-black.

Her stiff countenance was expected, and Samuel knew he would have to tread lightly. He'd lost his daughter, and he was determined not to lose Ti.

When Ti paused for a moment and wrinkled her brow at the strong scent of the breezes, Samuel smiled. "The last of the late harvest is being crushed," he explained as he pointed to a distant building that seemed to be carved into a hill.

"Crushed? I thought grapes were pressed," she said.

"That building is where the grapes are brought. There are two machines in it. One is a crusher-stemmer, the other is the grape press."

"Then you *do* press the grapes to make the wine," she persisted.

"Absolutely not!" Samuel Barkley declared.

"Then," she said as she stopped and locked her eyes with his, "I don't understand."

"There's a popular misconception about wine making. The best wines are made from the juice of grapes that are crushed, not pressed. When you press grapes, you get solids as a by-product from the grape itself.

"When the grapes are crushed, they are skinned and stemmed, and the juice that's extracted is pure, high in sugar content, natural, and also free of solids. For every ton of grapes crushed, we can extract about a hundred and eighty gallons of juice. The remainder is pressed, and another forty or so gallons can be gained," he concluded.

The analytical part of Ti's mind accepted the lesson she was being taught, savoring and examining everything she was told. When she had digested the information, she asked one question.

"What happens to the juice from the pressed grapes?" Ti asked.

"Good," Samuel encouraged, "you catch on quickly. The pressed juices are sold to other wineries."

"But if the crushing method produces the best juice for wine, why do they buy the pressed remains?"

"The wineries that buy it are commercial wineries that sell their products at a lower cost. They utilize the pressed by-products, and use extractors, centrifuges and chemicals to remove the solids and remains. They also use additives to enhance the flavor, but anyone familiar with wines can tell the difference just from smelling the wine."

"But if the wines aren't up to the standards of the buyers, how could they make money?" Ti asked, bothered by the logistics of what her grandfather had just explained.

Samuel smiled warmly at Ti. For the first time since her arrival, he let himself enjoy her. She had a good mind—quick, alert and inquisitive. He would have been very disappointed had she been any different.

"There are several standards for wines, and for the people who buy them. The large corporations who manufacture immense quantities of wine can't possibly take the time to process their product the way we do. They sell to the people who cannot afford the better wines, but still prefer wine over other drinks. Also, the consumers themselves have not been taught the differences between the qualities of wines."

"Then the Barkley wines are very expensive?"

"That's relative to the buyer. I have a Chardonnay that retails for seventy-five dollars, and another that retails for seven," Sam said. "But those people who are used to buying a half-gallon of wine for under six dollars find it hard to buy a smaller bottle at a higher cost, especially if it's a domestic wine."

"Why?"

"They are uneducated."

Ti felt an unreasonable stab of anger at his words and stared at him defiantly. "That's not fair. I don't know the difference between a good wine and a bad, and I'm well-educated!"

Her grandfather's gentle laugh caught her off-guard. "No, Ti, uneducated about wines."

Ti's anger drained from her body as she fought to hide an escaping smile. "Sorry," she murmured.

"Enough on the subject." He dismissed what they'd said with a wave of his hand. "Come, let me show you what has made the Barkley Vineyards among the best in the world."

With that, he opened the door to the winery and motioned Ti inside. The first thing she saw was an enormous wooden barrel standing eight feet high. The stained wood was held together by four metal straps; each strap met at the center and was held together by a long bolt and nut.

"This barrel is French white oak. It is over a hundred and twenty years old, and was imported from France by Arren Barkley. In it, the first wine ever produced by the vineyards was made. We don't use this barrel now, but it's kept here as a reminder of the origins of the vineyard."

Ti stared at the large barrel, and for some unknown reason felt a deep sense of *déjà vu*, brought on by her grandfather's words. Gazing at the oak barrel, Ti suddenly wondered what it had been like to be here in the 1860s.

"The first wines produced by the Barkley Vineyards

were aged in this barrel, in eighteen sixty-eight. Ti"—he pointed to a small brass plate near the bottom of the barrel—"the first Ticonderoga, Ti Barkley, named the wine The Year of The Gentle Winds."

"That's a strange name for a wine," Ti commented as she read the inscription on the plate.

"Your ancestor was a tough but sentimental woman. The wine earned its name because of the season. It was an almost-perfect growing season. It was warm, not overly hot; there were no heavy rainstorms, no tortuous winds and no hail. Just gentle breezes and winds that brought the crop to fulfillment."

"But," Ti said as she thought about Sam's words, "I thought you would want a lot of rain to grow the grapes?"

"Of course, but when the fruit is on the vine, and we have heavy rains and harsh winds, the grapes are damaged. A heavy windstorm or rainstorm will destroy much of the grape's juices before we can extract them. The first crop of the Barkley Vineyards grew in almost total perfection, hence the name 'Gentle Winds.'"

"I'd like to know more about Ticonderoga Barkley," Ti ventured.

"You shall," Sam promised with a hidden smile. "Now, shall we continue?" He took his granddaughter's elbow and led her deeper into the winery.

He spoke in an even voice, but Ti heard the passion contained within it as he told of the wine-making processes.

He showed her the large, stainless vats, and explained every step of wine making from the harvest to the bottling of the wines. She learned a great deal as Sam Barkley explained the different processes involved in making red and white wines, the way each was fermented, and the way each was cared for during the fermentation process.

By the time they were finished, Ti's inquisitive mind was clamoring for more information, but she held off her questions until they were standing at the last of the gleaming vats. "With all this modern equipment, why use the wooden barrels?"

"Ah . . ." Sam smiled and nodded his head. "To gain the correct balance between the acidic tannin and the fruitiness that makes for a perfect bouquet. When wine is left to ferment in oak, it draws from the wood and brings out a special balance. The winemaker is the one to judge how long it remains in the barrels. Then, as it ages in the bottle, and the heavy tannic taste lessens, the fruitiness of the wood smoothes it out. But if you go directly from vat to bottle, you will not have that important taste of velvet rolling across your tongue."

"I see," Ti replied, but she wasn't quite sure she did understand. "And that's what makes your wines more expensive also, right?"

"Not really. Look around. If you haven't noticed, this room is totally sterile. Every time someone comes in and touches any equipment, it must be sterilized again. Look up," he said, and Ti followed his orders. Above them was a large vent in the roof, and Ti realized that the low hum she'd been hearing had been a ventilator.

"Because we do not use bi-sulfate as a preservative, we must always protect the environment against bacteria. Without preservatives, any bacteria that gets into the wines will destroy them. That is one of our most expensive costs."

"I would think it unnecessary in this day and age," Ti commented.

"And that's what makes the difference between us

and them. I will not use any chemical additives! The Barkley wines have always been, and will always be, the purest.''

Ti was momentarily taken aback by the emotion in Sam's voice, and waited a moment before saying anything else. Then, as she gazed into his eyes, she realized she would have to be careful about which questions to ask.

Ti was almost overwhelmed with the information she'd learned, yet at the same time she felt a kinship with the winery she'd never imagined possible.

"What do you think of all of this?" Samuel asked as he once again took Ti's arm and led her toward the door and the outside.

"I never realized how fascinating it could be," she admitted truthfully. Ti felt his smile more than she saw it, and knew that what she'd said had made him feel good. A strange twinge of guilt assailed her, and she suddenly realized it was because she was beginning to like her grandfather. It was as if she were being disloyal to her mother.

"Would you like to see Napa?" Samuel asked.

"I thought we were in Napa," she replied quickly. She heard the traces of resentment in her voice and looked away for a moment.

Her grandfather ignored her tone as he looked around them. "I meant the town. I've an appointment at the bank after lunch. I thought you might enjoy the drive and the scenery."

"Thank you," Ti assented, now completely in control of her voice.

She and Samuel walked to the house, and Ti realized that the morning had already passed.

"Am I dressed properly for town?" she asked as they reached the walkway to the house.

"A trifle overdressed, but you'll survive. Most people just wear jeans during the day, but at night it's different. We like to dress a little fancier for dinner."

"Then I'd better pick up a few pair of jeans in town. I only brought one pair," Ti explained as Samuel opened the door for her.

She missed the smile that flashed momentarily across her grandfather's face as she spoke. By the time he closed the door the smile was gone, yet in his mind it still shone brightly. If Ti planned on buying several pairs of jeans, then she was also thinking about staying for a while. *Yes,* Samuel thought, *perhaps she will loosen up and learn about herself, too.*

Ti sank gratefully into the hot water of the bathtub. The day had been long and for the most part enjoyable. But there was something tugging at her mind, making her think and rethink everything that had happened today in an effort to pinpoint exactly what it was.

The morning tour of the winery had been an education in itself. She'd learned and retained a vast store of information she'd never before imagined. The way things were done, she'd learned, was almost the same as it had been since Arren Barkley had founded the winery. The small differences, which in actuality were major ones, were in the scientific areas, not in the methods of processing at all.

And this afternoon had also been an education of sorts. They'd driven into Napa, and Ti had been surprised by the small and pleasant town. It seemed to be a warm community. As the chauffeured limousine drove along, Ti listened to Samuel tell about the different stores and businesses they passed.

The vehicle slowed and Samuel pointed to a small but elegant-looking boutique and asked if she would like to stop there while he was in the bank. Ti had

agreed, and after the limousine had stopped Samuel
pointed down the block to the bank.

"I'll wait for you there," he told her as the chauffeur
opened the door.

Ti stood on the sidewalk for a moment and watched
the blue limousine continue on down the block. Then
she turned and entered the store. It was cool inside,
and as she glanced around she saw a wide variety of
items which she knew would be very expensive.

"May I help you?" asked a woman who emerged
from the rear of the shop. As she approached Ti, her
smile froze and a look of shock flitted quickly across her
features. Then the woman shook her head and came
closer to Ti.

"I'm sorry, but you startled me. For a moment I
thought you were someone else," she explained. "Are
you new in the area?"

"I'm just visiting," Ti answered, but she was acutely
aware of the woman's scrutiny.

The saleswoman shook her head again. "I really am
sorry, but you remind me of a friend of mine from high
school."

Ti studied the woman in turn, and guessed her to be
in her mid-forties. Suddenly she knew what was happening. "Jenna Barkley?" Ti asked in a hushed voice.

"Yes," the woman said as she nodded her head in
surprise.

"I'm her daughter."

"Oh my God. . . . You're Ti!" she cried and Ti saw
tears begin to form in the woman's eyes. "How is she?
Is she here with you?" she asked rapidly as she
searched Ti's face. "I'm sorry," the woman added
quickly, "but it's such a shock. I'm Melissa Daniels."

"Mother died several years ago," Ti told her. Melissa
nodded her head slowly.

"I'm terribly sorry," she said as she blinked away tears. "You must think me a perfect fool."

Ti shook her head slowly as she saw the sadness that filled the woman's face. "Not at all. You and my mother were very close?" she asked.

Melissa nodded and smiled. "Very. It broke my heart when she left. We wrote often at the beginning, but over the years . . ." She finished with a shrug. "But you didn't come to visit me, did you?" Melissa asked. Ti started to shake her head, but stopped as a new thought struck her.

"I think I may have been sent here purposely," she admitted.

"Sam?"

"Yes. He suggested this store to me."

"How is he?"

"I'm afraid I can't answer that. I have nothing to compare it to," Ti said truthfully.

"It took him many years to get over your mother's leaving," Melissa commented.

"Perhaps, but I don't think my mother ever got over going, either," Ti stated bluntly.

Melissa looked into Ti's face in reaction to the fierceness of her words. "Sam's had to pay for his mistakes many times over, just as your mother did," she said suddenly.

A deep silence fell over the women as they gazed at each other. It was Melissa who broke the silence with a smile and a shrug. "But that's history. Are you visiting your grandfather, or have you moved out here?"

"I'm just visiting," Ti told her.

"Perhaps we could get together one day before you leave and I can tell you all those terrible things that high school girls did thirty years ago."

"I'd like that," Ti agreed quickly.

"And now, what can I do for you?" Melissa asked.

A half hour later Ti had selected three pairs of jeans and three shirts. Melissa folded them neatly and put them in a bag before presenting Ti with the bill.

Ti glanced at it, and realized she didn't have enough cash to cover it. With a smile, she extracted her bank card and gave it to Melissa.

Melissa stared at the card and then shrugged her shoulders. "I'm sorry, but I don't accept credit cards. I'll send the bill to you at your grandfather's house," she offered.

"Don't you lose sales?" Ti asked.

"Only to tourists. Everyone who lives around here has a store account, or pays by check or cash. When shall we get together?"

"Call me at my grandfather's anytime," Ti suggested. "And thank you."

Melissa stepped around the counter and smiled. "May I?" she asked, her eyes misting again as she opened her arms. Ti nodded and stepped forward to be engulfed in the arms of her mother's friend.

Ti sank lower in the tub, letting the water rise to her chin as she continued to think of the day she'd spent with her grandfather. After she'd finished shopping, she'd met Samuel at the bank, and was introduced to the bank's president. Then as they'd strolled along the street, Samuel had continued to point out the various sights that were a part of Napa.

By the time they were finished it was late afternoon. As they'd driven back to the winery, Ti had turned to Sam.

"You sent me into Melissa's store purposely, didn't you?"

"Yes. Your mother and Melissa grew up together. I thought you would like to meet her," Sam explained.

"You could have at least come in and introduced me."

"Melissa hasn't spoken to me since your mother left the Valley," Sam stated bluntly.

Ti was taken aback by this. Melissa hadn't uttered one derogatory word about her grandfather, and in fact, had seemed warm toward him.

"I don't understand. . . ."

"Feelings run strong and deep in this valley. Good friendships last a long time, and anything that hurts someone isn't lightly forgiven."

"I think you're wrong about Melissa, she didn't seem angry at you at all," Ti had observed. Her grandfather had gazed at her for a few moments and then shrugged.

"Time changes people," he'd said.

Ti finished washing herself as she thought about her grandfather's words. Then she pulled the drain plug and stood, letting the water cascade from her skin. When the tub was empty, she drew the shower curtain, turned on the continental shower and wet her hair. As she lathered her hair, she thought about the people she'd met at the winery. Something was bothering Ti. . . .

Every employee they'd met today had been warm and friendly to them. She had seen immediately that it had not been an act for her benefit. The workers inside the winery itself all seemed genuinely glad that Sam was there. They spoke freely in his presence, and one had even argued with her grandfather about the temperature inside one of the vats.

But even as they argued, Ti had seen her grandfather nod several times at certain points the other man had brought up. When the discussion was over, they had both smiled at each other.

Everywhere they went, the people smiled and said hello. That, and their apparent warmth and liking for

her grandfather, bothered Ti. She remembered her
mother's description of Samuel Barkley as an unfeeling
demigod who oversaw everything with iron rules and
harsh words.

That person, and the grandfather she'd met yesterday, were two vastly different people. *Is the real Sam
Barkley hiding behind this benevolent mask?* she
wondered.

Ti rinsed out the shampoo thoroughly and shut off
the shower. She stepped onto the soft carpeting of the
bathroom floor and wrapped a towel around her body,
and another around her hair. Then she went into the
bedroom to get dressed for dinner.

Jase stood across from Sam in the parlor. Each had a
glass in their hands. Sam was dressed similarly to the
way he had dressed the night before. He wore a pair of
dark slacks, a white shirt, and a tie the same color as his
pants. An expensive tweed jacket, superbly tailored,
finished the look.

Jase was dressed in gray slacks, a blue-and-white
pin-striped shirt, open at the collar, and a blue blazer.
He shifted on his feet as he took a sip.

"I think she's beginning to relax a little," Sam said as
he glanced at Jase.

"Did she enjoy the day?"

"I think so. She was very interested in the winery.
She surprised the hell out of me with some of her
questions."

"Good," Jase said with a smile.

"When will the last of the crushing be done?" Sam
asked.

Jase stared at him as if he were a stranger. Then he
shook his head. "Today. Sam, what's wrong?"

Sam laughed and placed a hand on Jase's shoulder.
"Nothing, my mind's been playing tricks on me lately.

I'm not getting senile yet! It's just that having Ti here takes my mind away from business."

"It's more than that," Jase guessed wisely.

"Yes. I'm worried about her. I didn't know what to expect when she got here . . . out-and-out hatred, I suppose," he mused as he turned and looked out the window at the dwindling light. "But it wasn't there. Yes, it's under the surface, but she's trying to control her emotions. I don't think she'll be able to handle the strain for too long, it's dangerous."

"She has to work it out for herself."

"I know, I just wish I could help her," Sam said.

"She wouldn't accept it."

"Yes, I know . . ." Before Sam could finish, footsteps echoed from the hallway. Both men turned as Ti stepped into the parlor.

Jase knew he was staring, but he couldn't stop himself. She looked beautiful. Her black hair was piled on her head in a sensuous style that accented her cheekbones and eyes. She had one of her business suits on, but the way she wore it made it seem more like an outfit designed for the evening. The beige linen skirt reached a little past her knees, and the collarless jacket was open, revealing an antique silk blouse that rose to cover her neck in soft ruffles. The upper part of the blouse was an intricately detailed section ending in a V across the top of her breasts, and the smooth silk blouse was tucked neatly into the skirt. A slim gold belt cinched her waist and completed the look perfectly. Ti Barkley Calssen looked every inch a part of the house.

"I stand in awe," Sam said in a voice heavily laced with emotion as he stepped toward Ti. "You are very lovely, and I am glad you are here."

Even as her grandfather walked toward her, Ti's eyes were locked on Jase. She forced a smile to her lips as she fought against the sudden heavy pounding of her heart. He looked extremely handsome, and when he smiled the two craggy lines that ran near his mouth creased deeply. *Damn him!* she cried to herself.

Ti forced her attention to Samuel, and away from Jason. Her grandfather's words finally penetrated the fog that had held her mind captive, and she willed herself to answer him.

"I accept the compliment," she said self-consciously, and realized with a start that she spoke the truth.

"A drink?" Sam asked.

"What are you having?"

"Scotch," he replied.

"Not wine?" she asked incredulously.

The look that was on her face made both men smile. "Contrary to popular opinion, because we're in wine country doesn't mean we can't indulge in something different," Sam informed her.

"Could I have a glass of wine?" she asked.

"Of course," Sam replied with a smile.

As Sam crossed the room to the bar, Ti looked up at Jase. "Are you joining us for dinner?" she asked.

"If you can survive my company," he answered in a low, tight voice.

"I've survived worse, but I can't remember exactly what it was," she replied coldly.

"Survived worse what?" Sam asked as he handed Ti a chilled glass of white wine.

"Jet lag," Ti said quickly, and lifted the glass to her lips to avoid saying anything else.

"Jet lag?" Sam questioned Jase. Jase kept his face blank as he shrugged his shoulders innocently.

"This is wonderful," Ti commented as she tasted the wine.

"Private stock," he explained. "Every year I take a certain amount of wine for my own cellar. What you're drinking is from a truly great crop we harvested four years ago."

"Chenin Blanc," Jase added. "It's similar to the wine we had in Philadelphia."

Sam turned to Jase and asked him about the wine they'd had. As they talked, Ti drifted about the room trying to organize her thoughts. She wanted to strike out and hurt Jason, but at the same time she didn't want to do it in front of her grandfather. Perhaps it was her own pride that prevented it, but she promised herself she would try not to lash out again tonight.

Ti glanced at the walls, and was suddenly aware of the many certificates that were on them. She read several and realized they were awards of merit. One in particular, written in French, caught her attention.

It was a certificate of merit from the Institut de La Chambaue, awarding Barkley Vineyards first prize for a Cabernet Sauvignon wine grown in California. The certificate was dated 1899.

"Would you like to try that wine one day?" Samuel asked Ti as he stood next to her.

"It's awfully old, isn't it?" she asked.

"I didn't mean that exact year, although we have seven bottles of that vintage in the vault."

"Vault?" Ti asked.

"In the cellar there is a vault that holds several bottles from each year. However, we only keep the wines that have won awards. The wine that won that year is now worth almost two thousand dollars a bottle."

"But it's over eighty years old!"

"And it may very well be vinegar, but we won't know until it's opened," Sam explained.

Just then, Angela came into the parlor and announced dinner. With Jason on one side and her grandfather on the other, they walked from the parlor into a large formal dining room. Ti caught her breath as she saw the two large multitiered candelabrum, the only source of light in the room.

The room itself was beautifully appointed, the large oval dining table covered with an embroidered eggshell tablecloth and surrounded by rosewood chairs. White china dishes were set at three places, and the silverware gleamed from reflected candlelight. The walls were paneled halfway up, and the rest of the walls, until they joined the wood-beamed ceiling, were done in an elegantly simple wallpaper.

On each wall hung a painting, and when Sam guided Ti to her chair, she realized she was totally awestruck by the room. As she sat, she glanced first at Sam and then at Jason. Again she vowed to be polite to both of them throughout the meal.

Chapter 8

FOR THE MOST PART, DINNER WAS PLEASANT. THE FOOD was excellent, and the main course—a veal roast—had been prepared to perfection. As Angela cleared the empty plates from the table, Jase turned to Ti and smiled.

"Did you like the winery?" he asked. He had been aware of the many instances of silence that had hung between them all, and was trying for Sam and Ti's sakes to keep the mood friendly.

"I thought it was fascinating. I learned a great deal today," she admitted. "But I noticed you weren't around at all."

"No," Jase acknowledged with a nod of his head. "I was in the office catching up on my paperwork."

You mean you read and write, also? Ti almost spat out, but stopped herself in time and said, "From everything you've told me, I would have thought that would be the last place you'd be."

Jase nodded at her, and gazed into the swirling depths of her eyes as he spoke. "It is, but it's also part of my job."

"Like I was?" she hissed. Then she flushed, angry with herself for breaking her promise.

Jase stared at her silently, his face expressionless and his eyes apparently vacant. Ti noticed a vein throbbing boldly in his neck.

"I think I missed something again," Sam said in a low voice.

"Nothing important," Jase replied as he turned from Ti to look at his boss. "Just a disagreement we had on the flight here."

Angela's timely return saved all three from further explanations. She poured coffee for everyone, and asked if they were ready for dessert.

"I can't eat another bite," Ti pleaded. Both Sam and Jase echoed her words and Angela left the room.

Ti stared at the coffee cup, forcing her tense nerves to unwind. She looked up, and gazed at a small landscape painting on the wall. It looked familiar, yet different. She turned to Sam and asked about it.

Sam smiled as he glanced at the painting. "Your great-grandfather, my father, painted that when he was a boy. It's the Napa Valley at the turn of the century."

"You can see his love for the land in it," she observed.

"It was your mother's favorite painting," he said in a sad voice. Then he looked back at Ti and stared at her for a moment. "Ever since your mother left, this house has been lone—"

"Don't you use that pious tone!" Ti cried suddenly. The tension of the evening, combined with the barely contained anger of a lifetime, erupted as she cut off her grandfather's words. "My mother didn't leave by her own volition. It was your fault!" Logic and reason fled, and the old festering wounds and hurts could no longer be held back, nor did she want them to be.

She glared at Samuel, Jason forgotten for the moment, and continued her tirade. "It was you and your stupid rules! You cast my mother out into the world without any regard for her needs, and now you want me to love you? How could you even consider it?" she cried. Her eyes locked with her grandfather's and bored unmercifully into him. Slowly, forcing her heaving chest to still, Ti stood, threw her napkin on the table and walked out of the room.

Sam and Jase sat silently for several minutes after Ti had gone. Then Sam stood, a look of determination covering his face as he began to walk.

Jase rose quickly and placed a restraining hand on his shoulder. "No, Sam, let her go. Give her time alone. Her life is different from yours. Her feelings and emotions are foreign to you. You must give her enough time to get used to you, and your home."

Sam's shoulders sagged briefly under Jase's hand, but the older man straightened them again as he turned and nodded to Jase.

"You're right," he agreed. He'd lived many years, and in those years he'd learned a lot. He'd made many mistakes, and his worst mistake was still haunting him. He felt powerless to do anything about it, and for Samuel Barkley that was worse than anything else imaginable.

"Talk to her for me," Sam requested, his eyes meeting Jase's as he did.

"I don't think I should," Jase protested.

"She'll listen to you, she has already. Please, Jase. Someone has to talk with her and she won't let me."

Jase wanted to refuse, but if he did he'd have to

explain the reason to Sam. He couldn't do that. Sadly, Jase realized once again he had no choice. Slowly, he nodded his head and walked from the room.

After leaving the dining room, Ti had walked aimlessly around the grounds, until she found herself standing on a small hill overlooking the vineyards. In the cloudless, star-filled sky, the silvery half-moon lit the ground with soft light. The beauty that surrounded her helped to ease her troubled mind, and a gentle feeling of peace edged into her thoughts.

For the first time since her arrival here, Ti really looked around her. She breathed deeply, and smelled the scent of the land and the lushness of its foliage. The tranquility of the earth she stood on, and the quiet of the night, brought out a new feeling in her.

Ti sighed in confusion. Her outburst had been unwarranted, but she hadn't been able to stop herself. She had wanted to hurt her grandfather and shame him into admitting that he'd been wrong twenty-five years ago. She'd also wanted to punish Jase for his betrayal.

Her thoughts were too much for her right now, her mind too troubled. Ti bent and scooped up a small handful of dirt. She looked at it, feeling its moist grittiness against her skin.

She felt a sudden affinity with it, and all the land around her; it was a new and strange sensation. In all her years growing up in the city, she'd never known such a feeling of closeness with the land she stood upon.

Turning to look at the darkened hills, Ti thought she heard a sound nearby. She sensed another's presence and her eyes strained to pierce the darkness. Suddenly a form appeared a few yards away. Ti drew in her breath sharply as she recognized Jason.

"Stay away from me!" she commanded. The anger of moments ago returned with its full fury.

"We have to talk."

"We already did all the talking that's necessary. Or did my *grandfather* send you once again?" she goaded in open challenge.

"Yes, he did," Jase said truthfully as he pulled himself to his full height, barely a foot away from Ti. "But I would have been here anyway. Ti, you made me a promise—"

"I don't think any promise I made to you is worth keeping," she snapped at him. Even in the pale light of the moon, she saw the telltale vein on his neck throb in angry response to her words.

"You promised you would give your grandfather a chance. I don't give a damn about what you think of me, but I care deeply about Sam. Keep your word!" His voice cut at her sharply as he spoke. Then he spun on his heels and began to walk away.

Ti stared at his retreating back, her mind stinging with the ferocity of his words until she could hold back no longer.

"Don't you dare walk away from me!" she screamed. "I'm not finished with you yet!" But Jase ignored her and continued walking down the hill.

Ti lost all control at Jase's refusal to acknowledge her and began to pummel his back with tightly balled fists, but he kept ignoring her. Ti stopped and froze as she watched him continue to walk away.

"You *bastard!*" she screamed loudly.

Jase stopped suddenly, his shoulders stiffening at the word. He turned and looked back at Ti. Her hand was covering her mouth, and her eyes were wide as they stared at him.

Ti stared helplessly at Jase and saw the sadness

etched on his features. Her hand trembled as it covered her mouth, and she realized the intensity of her bitterness in that one angry word. Of all the people she knew, she was truly the only one who could be called a bastard. She had been born one.

As she gazed into his face, Ti's legs weakened and she fell to the ground. Deep sobs were suddenly wrenched from her throat, and she felt as if her soul were dying. She covered her face, unable to look at him any longer, unwilling to have him see her like this.

Jase stood frozen, staring at Ti. As she sank to the ground and his ears were filled with the sound of her racking sobs, he moved slowly toward her. He was torn between love and pity for her. When he was next to her, his heart finally overruled his mind and he, too, sank to the ground.

Silently, his arms went around her and he drew her close. He held her trembling body tightly, and let her give vent to the emotions that were tearing her apart. He let her cry and hold on to him until there were no more tears.

When her body finally calmed, Ti moved to free herself from his arms. She sat up and looked at him through large, wet eyes, and Jase saw the paths of her tears glint in the moonlight.

"I'm sorry," she whispered. "I didn't mean that."

"I know," Jase replied. Then he stood, and drew her to her feet. "Ti, you have to learn something right now. Something very important." He was aware of her eyes as she stared at him, waiting for him to continue.

"All of this will one day be yours," he said as he swept his arm in a wide arc. "There are a hundred people here in the Valley who depend on Barkley Vineyards for their very existence. There are another hundred on the outside, who need the vineyards to earn their living. That's why your grandfather wants you here. Ti, this is *your* land, your inheritance, your future." Jase paused as he tried to gather his thoughts coherently.

"That's why you and I are so unimportant. Any individual is unimportant unless they're part of the whole. That was what Sam was trying to tell your mother, but she couldn't understand it."

"Perhaps she didn't want to. Perhaps she didn't want the responsibility," Ti whispered as the enormity of Jase's words filtered into her mind.

"We don't have that choice. Someone once said to me that I wasn't the only person to be hurt by something I had no control over, and that I wouldn't be the last. But, he also said that the most important thing is to keep moving forward. Ti, you can't live in the past, especially in someone else's memory of the past. You can't live a life based on another person's, even if that person was your mother. You have to move forward and lead your own life."

Ti gazed into Jason's intensely drawn features for a long moment before she spoke. "And your long life has been so terrible that it gives you the right to talk to me like this?" she asked, knowing that she was again hurting him with her sarcasm but unable to stop.

"Yes," he answered in a low voice as his eyes searched her face. "You made a promise to me, at least try to keep that promise, if nothing else." Then he turned and walked away.

Ti watched until he was swallowed by the darkness. She drew herself to her full height, and slowly shook her head as she returned to the top of the hill. She wasn't ready to return to the house yet. She needed to calm the bedlam his words had caused.

At the top of the hill, with the stars blinking down on her in their purity, Jason's words echoed hauntingly in her ears.

She knew he had spoken honestly, and she realized that what he'd said had been the truth. But she'd been raised to fend for herself and to seek out opportunities and work hard to achieve success. Now, as she surveyed her grandfather's vineyards sleeping peacefully under the velvet blanket of the night, she had a frightening insight into one of the reasons Sam Barkley wanted her here. He wanted her to see what had always been hers. He wanted her to one day take her place as the head of Barkley Vineyards.

This sudden knowledge was as strong as a physical blow, and Ti staggered under its force. Everything she had believed in as she grew up was being threatened. Everything her mother had told her seemed somehow different.

Then she thought about Jason, and how his face had looked when he'd spoken to her. She had seen the fleeting sadness and hurt before he'd been able to hide them, when she had sarcastically spoken to him of his past.

At the same moment, she remembered another time, at dinner in Philadelphia, when Jason had begun to speak of his past, and had stopped suddenly. "My life began eight years ago," he'd said. She realized that that was when he had started to work for her grandfather.

What could have happened to Jason that was so terrible? Suddenly, Ti reached a decision. She would keep her promise and try to maintain an open mind and not make snap judgments about her grandfather. And, at the same time, she would try to find out exactly what Samuel Barkley really wanted from her.

With her mind made up, Ti descended the hill and returned to the house. Inside, everything was quiet. She wondered if her grandfather was still up, and walked toward the library. In the hallway, she saw a ray of light from the bottom of the door, and went to it.

She knocked lightly and waited. "Yes?"

Ti opened the door and stepped inside. Again she smelled the combined scents of leather and books, but this time the scent of tobacco was stronger. She glanced at her grandfather and saw that he was smoking a pipe.

"I . . . I came to apologize for my behavior," she began.

"There is no apology needed, just time to adjust," Sam replied in a gentle voice.

"I . . ." Ti faltered again and stopped. Something she'd never thought about rose in her mind. Ti laughed nervously, and shrugged. "I don't know what to call you," she admitted.

"I guess if we'd known each other all our lives, Grampa would be correct, but since we've just met, I think Sam would suit me fine."

Ti nodded her head slowly. "Thank you . . . Sam," she said.

"Your welcome, Ti."

Jase walked between the lines of full vats. In one hand he held a clipboard with several sheets of paper, in the other a pencil. His constantly moving eyes checked the seals on each of them, and at several vats he stopped and made notes. When he walked by the last one, he turned to the three men who followed and nodded his head.

"That does it for this batch," he said as he added another notation on the top sheet of the clipboard. As the men walked in one direction, Jase walked toward his office.

Just as he was about to open the door, he heard voices on the other side. The door swung open, and Sam and Ti walked in.

"Afternoon, Jase," Sam said. "Vats taken care of?"

"All done," Jase replied. Then his eyes shifted to Ti.

She stood behind her grandfather, dressed in jeans and a plain, western-style shirt. Her hair was pulled back from her face, and a week's tan glowed on her skin.

"Ti," he said in greeting as he looked at her.

"Good afternoon, Jason," she replied. Jase noted the absence of a smile on her lips as she looked at him. Not once since the night on the hill had she as much as smiled at him.

"We'll be in town for the rest of the day," Sam informed him.

"Problems?" Jase asked.

"Ti's found something in the accounts she's not happy with, and we want to straighten it out. You still going to Sacramento tonight?" he asked suddenly.

Jase nodded. "I'll be back the day after tomorrow. Everything is running smoothly here," he assured Sam as he started into the office. He stopped and turned back. "Juan will be finished with the number twelve barrel tomorrow, but if you get a chance, I'd feel better if someone oversaw the filling."

"I thought it would be another week?" Sam said.

"Santi's had an old barrel they were replacing. There were several planks in good condition. I bought two planks."

"Expensive?"

"Average," Jase commented. He nodded once more at Ti and Sam and then walked past them into the offices of the winery.

The offices were on the side of the main winery building. The office staff consisted of four people: the bookkeeper, an assistant bookkeeper/receptionist, Jase and Sam. As he walked through the office, Jase smiled to the bookkeeper, Sylvia, and went into his private office. There, he sat behind his desk and shook his head sadly at the pile of papers.

Jase had to go through them that day so he would be

caught up enough to cover his absence. In Sacramento, he had to appear before a House subcommittee investigating improper bottling and fermenting procedures. Jase had also made arrangements to meet with the Barkley distributor and go over the projected figures for next year's production.

But even as he looked at the papers, his mind wandered to Ti. She had been here for almost ten days, and for the last eight she had barely spoken to him.

He was fully aware of how deeply he'd hurt her, yet he knew he'd had no choice. *At least,* he thought, *she's living up to her word.* She was giving Sam a chance. And she seemed to be enjoying life here.

Jase had seen the change the very morning after she'd screamed at Sam and fled the dining room. Starting that morning, she'd begun to spend all her time with Sam. She listened and studied everything that Sam did, and every afternoon she would be in the offices going over the books with him.

While she had studiously and thoroughly thrown herself into learning about the winery and her grandfather, she had just as laboriously avoided any contact with Jase. When it was unavoidable and the three had to be together, Ti had only spoken to Jase when necessary, and only about business. Jase did his part, and had seen to it that he was always too busy to join them for a meal.

Jase knew what Ti was doing was for the best, but he couldn't suppress a desire for her which grew more powerful and more painful every day. When he saw her walking in the fields, watching the work being done on the harvested vines, his mind filled with the memories of the love they had shared so briefly, and he was hard-pressed to push back the need that arose.

But he had been the one who had informed her of the rules, and he could not break them. He would not plunge Sam and Ti into a disastrous situation that could otherwise be avoided. He could not do that to the man he respected and loved, no matter what he felt inside.

Jase was deeply troubled and had been ever since he'd met Ti. The haunting nightmares of nine years ago had returned, and with them had come long and sleepless nights. He knew his face reflected the lack of sleep, but he could do nothing about it. He had his own devils to exorcise, and he must do it soon, before they consumed him as they almost had once before.

He knew the trip to Sacramento would help him. It would take him away from the constant nearness to the woman he loved. But, because he was who he was, she was the woman he could not have.

With a determined effort, Jase wrenched his mind back to reality and the paperwork that had to be finished before he left that afternoon.

Ti lifted the bone china cup and sipped her coffee as she glanced at her grandfather. They had just finished a pleasant dinner of broiled chicken and fresh vegetables prepared by María. She felt tired, but good.

Ever since she'd decided to give Sam a chance, things had gone smoothly. The underlying currents of tension and hatred had diminished, and, as each day had drawn to an end, she'd found herself liking her grandfather more and more.

"That was some performance you gave today," Sam said as he gave her an approving nod.

"Thank you," Ti replied, enjoying the praise.

"I don't think I've ever seen Arnold so defensive."

Arnold was Arnold Mason, the president of the Napa Bank. Earlier in the afternoon Ti, Sam and Arnold had met at Ti's insistence when she'd discovered items in the accounts that pointed to several deposits in low-interest accounts.

"He had every reason to be," Ti declared. "After all, he'd had free reign over your money for years. The bank was making a nice profit on it, and you were seeing very little. In the next year, you're going to be amazed at the returns you'll get."

"I don't doubt that for a minute. Ti, you're a smart businessman, or should I say businesswoman?"

"Whatever," she responded with a smile. She knew he was trying, and appreciated his efforts. "I also think you should stop selling the pressings and produce a less expensive wine. There's a good profit margin in it."

Sam shook his head slowly as he gazed at Ti. She had a good business head, but she still had to learn more about the wine business. "Yes, it could be done, but there is something else to be taken into consideration. Tradition."

"Sam, I'm not talking about lowering the standards of the winery, nor am I saying to go into competition with the big wineries. Only that a less expensive but quality wine could help support the improvements of the standard wines."

"I understand that, but we have a tradition that goes back over a century. That tradition is also an obligation to the people who drink our wines," Sam explained patiently. "And by keeping our wines pure, we can fulfill our obligations without compromising ourselves."

"But we would be reaching a different consumer."

"Yes, but our name would be on the bottle. To use pressed grapes, and then follow all of our regular methods, would produce an inferior wine requiring the use of additives to remove the solids and stabilize the wine. I can't do that," he finished.

Ti nodded her head slowly as she tried to grasp what he was saying. One part of her mind analyzed the financial gains from doing what she suggested, while another part understood the depth of feeling that her grandfather's words had revealed.

"I don't really agree, but I haven't been here long enough to understand it all," Ti acknowledged as she took another sip of coffee.

Sam kept his face expressionless as he looked at Ti. Her last words firmly implanted themselves in his mind, and for the first time since her arrival, he allowed himself to hope that she was becoming a real part of his family. If she was already thinking in terms of staying longer to learn more, half his dream was becoming a reality.

"I think I'll take a walk. Would you like to join me?" Ti asked.

"I would like nothing better, and if I were ten years younger I'd go with you, but I'm a bit tired tonight," he said with a smile.

Ti nodded and stood. "I'll see you at breakfast?" she asked.

"Of course," he replied.

Ti left the dining room and went out to the garden, and into another crystal-clear California night. While she gazed at the myriad stars, she thought about her grandfather. With each passing day, she'd felt a lessening of her fears and hostilities, and a slowly growing warmth toward him.

The days had sped by quickly, filled with talk, activity and the work she had plunged into. The work itself was a release for Ti. She hated to do nothing, and going over her grandfather's accounts and investments had been fun, allowing her to use the skills she'd been trained to acquire.

By her third day in the Valley she had fallen into a daily routine. Each morning she would rise early and join her grandfather for breakfast. Then they would walk among the workers and see what was being done. After lunch they would go over the books, and when the sun set they would enjoy a quiet dinner.

It was at breakfast and dinner that Ti learned about her family. Each day, Sam would tell her another story about one of her ancestors. She also realized he refrained from speaking about himself, his wife and her mother, and Ti had not pressed him.

Ti went through the garden, and soon left it behind her as she walked along one of the many paths that criss-crossed the vineyards. She was aware that with each passing day she was falling more and more in love with the subtle beauty of the valley.

Walking in the cool evening air of the moonlit vineyards, Ti realized that the warmth which had been surrounding her and her grandfather had lingered. Then she stopped suddenly as a new thought struck her. Somehow, in the last few days, she'd lost the picture of Samuel Barkley as the terrible monster her mother had always made him out to be.

Her thoughts were suddenly flooded with visions of her mother, and guilt assaulted her relentlessly. Ti staggered under the impact, and fought with herself to hold back the flood of emotions that swept through her. She used logic as her weapon, struggling through the muddled paths, pushing onward through memories and feelings until she finally began to understand her heritage.

She saw her mother's life plainly, and saw also what had driven her to do what she did and be what she was. The hatred that had fueled her existence had been a part of what kept Jenna Barkley going. And even now, as Ti thought about her mother, she could recall only that one time when she'd told Ti the story of her birth, and what had preceded it.

But that story had made an indelible impression in her young mind, growing and festering until she could only see her grandfather as an evil ogre who cruelly dominated the lives of those around him.

Gazing at the moonlit hills, she felt an all-pervasive beauty and peace emanate from them, and, as she opened herself to it and basked in its glorious power, Ti realized that she had to reevaluate her thinking and redefine the goals she had chosen for her life.

Then she thought of Jason, of the way he had described the Valley to her in Philadelphia, and the way he had looked at her when he'd forced her to renew her promise to him.

Suddenly her heart was heavy and her eyes misted. There had not been one day since then when she had not thought of him. His handsome face haunted her in her dreams; his strong hands and powerful arms held and caressed her as she slept. No matter how she tried to rid herself of him, he stayed with her. She tried to deny her love for him, and refused to speak to him when he was around. But above it all, she knew she loved him deeply, and that saddened her because she knew her love would never again be consummated.

Shrugging her shoulders in resignation, Ti turned and went back to the house. As she entered, she heard the doorbell ring, but ignored it as she walked toward the stairs.

Before she reached the stairs, Angela appeared. Her face was fairly beaming as Ti looked at her. "There is someone here to see you," she informed Ti.

"See me?" she asked, puzzled by this unexpected event. She didn't know anyone in the Valley.

"Yes, Mrs. Daniels is here to see you."

Still puzzled, Ti followed Angela to the front hallway and saw Melissa standing there patiently.

"I hope you don't mind that I dropped in, but I was in the area and I thought I'd pay you a visit."

"Of course not," she said politely as Angela withdrew from the hall.

"I've been so busy since I saw you I didn't have a chance to call and set a date," she explained.

"It's quite all right," Ti said reassuringly. "Why don't we go inside?" Without waiting for a reply, she led the older woman into the parlor. "Drink?"

"Wine?"

Ti nodded, went to the bar, and poured two glasses of white wine. Then, after handing Melissa one, she led the woman to a chair, and sat across from her. Ti noticed how nervous she was, and knew Melissa must have seen the look for she smiled quickly and shook her head.

"I feel awkward right now, it's been so long since I've been here," she explained, and looked around the room. "It hasn't changed a bit." Melissa's brown eyes bored deeply into Ti's and then Melissa lifted her glass and took a long drink.

"I lied to you," she said.

"About being here?" Ti asked, shocked by the swiftness of the statement.

"No, about being too busy to call," she clarified. Melissa smiled nervously and took another quick sip from the glass she held in a tight grip. "After you left my shop, I started thinking about your mother and what she went through. Then I realized you might not even know what had *really* happened." Melissa paused for a moment and studied Ti.

"In one of the letters she sent me, she wrote that she wasn't sure if she would ever tell you the truth."

"She did," Ti stated.

"After I thought about what we'd said the other day,

I realized she must have, but I still wasn't sure if it was my place to say anything else. I decided to wait and see if you were going to be here for a while longer."

"I'm still here. Will you tell me about it now?" Ti asked in a low voice. She watched Melissa as the older woman stared at her, and finally, after several moments of silence, Melissa spoke.

"Tell me how you feel about Sam."

Ti shrugged. "I came here prepared to hate him, but I don't. I honestly don't know how I feel."

"That's good enough for me," Melissa said. Then Ti saw her take a deep breath. "Your mother and I grew up together. We had a close friendship, in fact we were more like sisters than friends. We did everything together, and we had no secrets from each other. I knew about your father from the beginning. But, even though I loved your mother, I fought with her. I told her she shouldn't marry Jamie. He wasn't good enough for her. He would only hurt and drag her down. I told her it wouldn't work.

"Those words almost destroyed the trust and love we'd always shared, but I wouldn't let it. After a while, things between your mother and myself were better, and I learned not to discuss Jamie. But no matter how I tried to hope things would work out, I knew they couldn't."

"Why?" Ti asked, interrupting Melissa's story.

"Because the Valley has its own rules. Because Jenna was a Barkley, and Jamie worked for her father. This Valley, and the people who live in it, are bound by traditions that have always been a part of it. When you come into the Valley, you come into a different world. And we keep it that way because it works. The Barkleys are among the oldest families in the area, and as such are treated like royalty. The wineries, and the families who own them, are the lifeblood of the Valley. They are the dynasties who keep the land alive, and the people who live on it understand this."

"You sound like someone who's living in the past."

"No," Melissa responded with a quick shake of her head. "You grew up in a different place, in an environment your mother chose for you. If you had grown up here, you would feel the same as I."

"I don't think so," Ti said matter-of-factly. "My mother didn't feel that way, either."

"But she did," Melissa countered softly. "Surely you can see that if she didn't feel that way, she would have faced your father with Jamie, and told him what they were doing. She wouldn't have tried to run away secretly, and your father would be alive today."

The shock waves of Melissa's words radiated through her body. Melissa had verbalized something she had not wanted to think about. As she had grown up, and thought about her mother's story, she had wondered about her father's death. But each time she did, she forced the unwanted thought away.

"I'm sorry if I've hurt you, but I had to tell you," Melissa said in a hoarse voice as the tears that had been welling up in her eyes spilled over onto her cheeks.

"It's all right," Ti replied in a whisper. "Please go on."

Melissa nodded, wiped the tears from her cheeks, and as Ti gazed into her eyes, she saw the true and unrestricted depth of feeling the woman had for her mother.

"When your mother left, everyone said your grandfather went insane. First he'd lost his wife, then his daughter. No one believed that he chased her away, or had threatened to send the child, you, off to be adopted by strangers. But Jenna had confided in me, and I knew it was the truth.

"For a year after your mother left, no one saw Sam

Barkley. Then he began to come into town again. The ravages of what had happened were written clearly on his face, and the change in him was seen by everyone.

"As the years passed, most of what happened was forgotten, or at least not mentioned. But Sam was never the same. Even today he rarely socializes, and when he does it's usually for business, a wedding or a friend's funeral." Melissa paused again and took another sip of the wine.

"I guess what I'm trying to say is that with all the pain and suffering your mother had to live with, your grandfather had his share to carry, also."

"If you were my mother's friend, why are you defending my grandfather?" Ti challenged.

"I'm not. I'm just trying to explain everything, but I gather I'm doing a bad job."

"No you're not. I'm sorry," Ti said, regretting her tone. "I'm very confused about it all."

"It's not easy. Both your mother and Sam are stubborn people."

"Why haven't you ever come to visit him?"

"I couldn't. When your mother left, I hated Sam as much as she did. I hated him for making her run away, I hated him because he forced me to help your mother leave and I hated him because I'd lost my closest friend," Melissa answered truthfully. "It took many years before I lost my bitterness toward him. But by then I was married and had my own business. My life had changed, and I didn't want to open new wounds."

"But you came here tonight?"

"Your mother was my friend. I owe it to Jenna to speak to you. Sam is your grandfather, and although he probably wouldn't say so, I think he needs you." With that, Melissa rose. "It's late, I think I should get home."

"Thank you," Ti said as she rose too, and walked Melissa to the front door.

She stood outside and watched until the taillights of Melissa's car faded from view before she turned and went inside the house and upstairs to her room, to think about the things she had learned.

Chapter 9

TI STIRRED RESTLESSLY ON THE BED AND OPENED HER EYES
to see the first gray streaks of dawn in the sky. Then she
closed her eyes and tried to go back to sleep, but two
minutes later she gave up.

She sat up in the bed and rubbed her eyes. What had
woken her? she wondered. Then she remembered. She
had been dreaming, and in the dream she had relived
her mother's story. She had seen her mother crying at
the news of Jamie Caissen's death, and had watched as
her mother, in the middle of the night, left the home
she had been born in.

Ti took a deep breath in an effort to calm her mind.
The dream had left her shaken, and recalled all the
memories of her life with her mother.

She thought about Melissa Daniels, and the story the
woman had told her three nights ago. She remembered
the compassion in her eyes when she spoke of the pain
that both Sam and her mother had lived with for so
long.

The hatred she had brought with her from Philadelphia had disappeared, and a warmth, and even a love, were beginning to blossom in her heart for the dignified man who was her grandfather. It was strange, she thought, that in her dream, she had not once glimpsed her grandfather. She had only seen her mother, and her mother's agony.

Finally, as the sun rose, and the sky lightened in multistriped fingers of blue, Ti left the bed to prepare for her day.

"What do you think?" Sam asked as he pointed toward a rolling section of land.

"Why now?" was Jase's reply to the question.

"Because she made me think about it for the first time in my life. Jase, in three years we can have the first crop bottled and in the stores."

"Under the Barkley label?" Jase asked incredulously.

"No, under a new one."

"Again, why?"

"Jase, I've worked my entire life under one principle. Then Ti came home, and she made me think. Why can't we make a less expensive wine, yet maintain the quality and integrity of what we believe in? Why can't people who cannot afford the cost of a really good wine have a wine available that is good, and can allow them to learn the difference between pure wine, and mass-produced domestics?"

"It's been tried before and found unprofitable," Jase reminded him.

"Because they tried to do it in too big a way. Ti gave me an idea and I think it will work."

"So you're going to buy this land?"

"No," Sam said with a smile, "I already bought it."

"Then why this meeting?"

"Because I wanted to thank you again for bringing Ti home," he explained as his voice turned serious and he gazed deeply into Jase's eyes.

Again, Jase felt the agony of guilt and he couldn't hold Sam's stare. Instead, he looked at the land around him. "Sam, she's only been here for a little while. I hope—"

"What?" Sam asked, cutting Jase off before he could finish. "You hope I'm not building castles in the sky? Jase, I'm sixty-four years old. Ti is my only blood relative. I have to build those castles while I can."

"I know," Jase said in a low voice.

"There's something else," Sam continued. The tone of his voice made Jase face him. "The new winery operation will be set up as a stockholder corporation. Barkley Vineyards will hold a large block of stock, and another large block will be purchased under the name of Jason Patten."

Jase stared at Sam for a long moment before he was able to speak. "Sam—" he began, but was cut off again.

"Jase, you've been as close to me as any son could have been. We've been through a lot together, and this is my way of thanking you."

"But—"

"No buts," Sam interrupted as he placed his hand on Jase's shoulder. "A simple 'thank you' will suffice."

Jase nodded his head, and then gazed at the land again. "Thank you," he said as he swallowed forcefully.

"It's not that easy!" Jase challenged in a louder voice than he intended. Ti glared at him from across the table, and he was aware of the way the candlelight reflected in her eyes.

"Yes it is!" Ti stated in a defiant voice. "I've already

charted everything. In five years the new winery will be showing a profit!" she concluded emphatically.

"If everything goes according to your plans. What if there's a frost? What if there's a hailstorm? Or what happens if the crop just isn't any good?"

"It will be," Ti said as she stared at him in open challenge.

Jase sighed as he shook his head. "Ti, I'm not trying to fight with you, all I'm doing is telling you what can go wrong."

"You seem to dissemble the facts to suit yourself, and you do that quite well, but I'll be damned if I'll listen to your pessimistic dogma. Don't you realize that all you ever speak of is the negative aspect of things? Damn it, Jason, there's more to life than the bad times!" Ti snapped.

"And you're the optimist?" he retorted through clenched teeth. He stared at her, his nerves turning to ice in response to the barrage of heated words she'd shot at him. Then he saw her glance quickly at Sam, and realized they'd both forgotten his presence as they argued.

Sam was looking at Ti strangely before he moved his eyes to Jase. Finally, he shook his head. "We've been sitting here for an hour, and all I've heard are the two of you arguing. You sound like an old married couple," he said in jest.

Ti flushed at his words and at the same time saw Jason's eyes flick to her for a moment before returning to Sam.

"Sorry," Jase said in a subdued voice.

"No apologies needed. I'd just like to finish this meal on a quieter level."

"I only have one more question," Jase said. Both Ti and Sam looked at him expectantly. "Has a name been decided for the new winery?"

Sam smiled and nodded to Ti. "Gentle Winds," she answered. "The Gentle Winds Vineyard."

Then in silent, mutual agreement, there was no further discussion about the new winery. They finished the meal in a strained yet peaceful silence. When Angela served the coffee, Ti excused herself from the table and went outside.

Her mind worked frantically, and she tried to settle it by strolling along the vineyard paths. She'd become upset when she'd found both Jason and Sam waiting for her in the parlor before dinner. As soon as she'd seen Jason, she knew he'd be joining them.

Jason had returned yesterday, but had not spoken a word to her except for hello. She too had avoided any contact with him, but at the same time had wondered how long this situation could go on.

"Forever," she told the moon. Jason's principles seemed firmly and unshakably rooted in him, and she sensed he would not allow himself to bend. *It isn't fair,* she thought, *it just isn't fair.*

While she sat across from him tonight, her heart had beat crazily as she gazed at his handsome face, and her desire for him had grown so strong she'd wanted to cry out.

In defense, she'd argued and fought with him, challenging everything he'd said and throwing it back at him. She would not let him see how much she wanted him, how much she loved him, how much she ached for him.

He set the rules, she reminded herself. But it wasn't fair that she had to play by them. Ti sighed softly in the night as she continued to walk. She looked around, searching out all the hidden spots of beauty that the moonlit landscape offered in another effort to ease her troubled mind and body.

A few minutes later, Ti reached a lone, grassy knoll and sat on the grass.

Shortly after Ti left, Jase said good night to Sam. But even as he walked from the room, he felt Sam's eyes on his back. He knew Sam was wondering what had happened between him and Ti to bring about the arguments they had every time they were together. Jase only hoped he wouldn't guess the real reason.

As he walked toward his small house, he was conscious of the restlessness that rippled through him, and knew he would not be able to settle his mind for a while. He also knew that what he needed was to talk to Ti. But he had no idea where she was. He decided to take a walk and see if the exercise would help him to relax.

He looked around and smiled as he thought about his destination—it had been a long time since he'd felt the need to go there. It was a private place he always went to when he needed to be alone. He'd discovered it when he first started at the vineyards, and had gone there often. It was a unique spot, a low hill in just the right location—it not only overlooked the old and stately main house, but, in the daytime, he could clearly see the lush and vibrant beauty of the Valley.

He walked toward the hill, and when he reached it and stepped onto the level grass top, he froze. Ti was sitting no more than ten feet from him with her back to him.

He stood there silently, watching her, and felt the loneliness of the last nine years well up in him. Mixed with that loneliness were the surging desires that had been torturing him since he'd first met the dark-haired woman. Slowly, Jase began to walk toward her.

Although her thoughts were thousands of miles away, and many years in the past, Ti was suddenly aware of someone near her. She opened her eyes and turned. Her breath caught loudly when she saw Jason standing a yard away. Recovering quickly, she rose to her feet and stared at him.

"I have to speak with you," Jase said in a husky voice. "I . . ." He stopped. Words were no longer possible. His emotions overcame him and he stepped close to her. His arms went around her and he drew her hard against him.

Ti's voice failed her completely when Jason spoke. Her heart hammered furiously in her chest as she tried to breathe. Then his arms were around her and she was being pressed to his chest. His lips covered hers, pressing hotly in demand, and lances of fire tore ruthlessly through her body. Her tense, stiff muscles loosened, and she melted against him.

Her mind was rocked by her body's reaction, and she knew she was again a prisoner of her own desires. Then nothing else mattered as she returned Jason's passionate kiss. Her body pressed against his, and her arms flew around his back.

His tongue burned an entrance into her mouth, and a low moan tore from the back of her throat. Slowly, with their arms entwined around each other, they sank to the earth's soft carpet of grass.

In a haze of floating stars, Ti let herself free to Jason's hands and lips as he began to undress her. As his hand slipped under her bra, she gasped. When her blouse was open and his lips traced a fiery path along her stomach, her back arched, and her hands gripped his hair tightly.

Suddenly she was sitting up, kissing him as passionately as he kissed her. Her hands roamed across his back as her breasts were flattened to his chest. Heat, desire and need filled her to the breaking point. She knew she should stop herself, but could not summon the willpower to do so. His hands were burning embers racing across her skin. His mouth called to her silently, as it caressed her skin. Then she was undressing him, even as he undressed her. A moment later they were both naked and gazing into each other's eyes. As one, their hands rose and they embraced each other tenderly. Slowly, almost hesitantly, their lips met.

It was a light kiss, a tasting, until neither could control the hunger that consumed them, and they fell to the ground.

Ti was conscious of the soft, prickly blades of grass beneath her, but that sensation was driven from her mind as Jason's body covered hers. Hungrily their mouths met, and as Ti's hands caressed Jason's back, his hands stroked her sides lovingly.

Their kiss lasted for an eternity. Ti's blood turned to molten fire, her body the center of a volcano. She could feel Jason's every sinew and muscle. Then he drew his mouth from hers, and Ti cried out in protest. She opened her eyes to look at him. His face was framed by a thousand stars, but even in the dark she could see his eyes caressing her face. Then he moved, and his mouth returned to hers for a brief moment before sliding away again. She luxuriated in the sensations his lips created upon her as they trailed across her neck on their quest for more.

"Ohhh," she moaned as his mouth caught her already erect nipple and lavished it with attention. Tiny pinpricks of pleasure radiated inward from her breast. Then his mouth journeyed to the other breast and gave it the same attention. The stars swam dizzily in her eyes, and Ti was forced to close them.

Jase kissed one breast as he caressed the other. The taste and texture of Ti's skin was maddening. His desire surged in waves through him, and even as he kissed and touched her, he glanced at her moonlit face. Ti's eyes were closed and her lips were curved in the faintest of smiles. Jason smiled also.

Then the smile disappeared as he returned to her mouth. He felt her hands go around his back, and felt her nails as they dug into his shoulders urgently.

Ti cried out again as Jason's mouth left her breast. Then her body arched and she opened her eyes again as Jason's body fitted over hers. Their eyes met in a blaze of desire and agreement.

There were no further explorations, no slow caresses, for the passion controlling them both would not permit it.

Their mouths joined, and Ti's breath escaped in a rush as the heated tip of his manhood pressed against her thigh. Her hand moved of its own volition, and even as she adjusted herself for him, she captured and guided his pulsating hardness into her.

Jason penetrated her deeply and Ti cried out as he filled her. Her fingers dug into the muscles of his back and her teeth bit into his shoulder. In response, Jason stopped and held her tightly.

Then, as the powerful tension that held her in thrall eased, and the throbbing that filled her very core changed into a rocking, waving desire, Ti freed his shoulder and began to kiss him passionately. They moved together slowly, their bodies adjusting together beneath the dark, velvet sky.

Then all thought fled and the volcano erupted within Ti as Jason thrust deeper. She wrapped her legs around his, and met each powerful thrust with one of her own. There was nothing in creation except themselves, and together they drew from each other and rode the undulating waves of their love until they finally crested in a cascading rhythm of love and fulfillment that left them both weak and shaken.

They were locked together for endless minutes until their breathing gentled. The low hum of a plane washed over them, but they heard nothing except the beating of their hearts.

Ti's hands loosened on Jason's shoulders, but instead of leaving them she caressed his back in slow circles while his lips wandered along the contours of her face and neck.

Ti unlocked her legs and freed her lover. He moved slowly, holding back their separation for as long as possible, until finally he was no longer inside of her. Then he lay down next to her, with one of her arms still under him, and pulled her tightly into his side.

Her free hand reached up and stroked his cheek as she gazed into his face. She was afraid to speak, and sensed he felt the same. She lifted her head and kissed the corner of his mouth.

"I missed you," she whispered into his ear as she buried her face against his neck. His hand rubbed her back reassuringly, and his chest rose as he took a deep breath.

"We've been punishing ourselves for nothing, haven't we?" she murmured after the silence had become unbearable.

"No," he replied, "you know that."

Ti held her breath until she realized that the anger she'd thought was there, had gone. In its place was a new knowledge; Jase was right.

"Yes," she said, "I think I understand a little. But it's all so new, so strange," she admitted as she pulled her arm free from under him and sat up. She smiled gently at him as he, too, rose until he was gazing into her eyes.

"I was hurt when you rejected me on the plane," she began and as Jason began to reply, she placed two fingers over his lips to silence him. "Wait. I felt betrayed by you. I thought you lied to me in order to get me to come here. After two weeks I see how wrong I was. You didn't betray me, you thought you were helping me."

"I was trying to."

"I know," Ti comforted as she grasped his hand and lifted it to her cheek, where she pressed it to her skin. "I've learned a lot about the Valley, and about the way the people here think and act. That night, when you told me about the vineyards, and about Sam's responsibilities to the people, and what you think he's planning for me, I began to realize what you meant, and also understood you a little better.

"At first I didn't want to, I was afraid. I had so much hate and distrust within me, but I'm learning," she said and then moved Jason's hand to her mouth and kissed its back lingeringly.

"Then you can understand how I can love you, but can never have you for my own."

"I can accept it for now, but I can never believe in it. The concepts you adhere to are not mine, but until something happens to make it the way it should be I won't fight you. I will do what I must, but I shall not give you up!" she vowed fiercely as she stared unflinchingly into his eyes.

"I love you, Ti," Jason whispered in the night. "I don't want to hurt you."

"You can hurt me more by not loving me," she told him as she leaned forward and let her breasts brush lightly across his chest. "You can hurt me by denying us each other," she said in a louder voice.

"Ti," he crooned as he raised his hands and cupped her face between his palms.

"Love me in the dark, love me behind closed doors if you have to. I don't care anymore, so long as you love me," she whispered, knowing the truth of her words, and realizing she could not return to the empty, lonely feeling she'd had when she'd denied her love.

Ti awoke with a start. The sun was a powerful ball that filled her window. Shaking her head, she looked at the clock and saw it was nine-thirty. Then she lay back. As her head nestled on the pillows, her mind ran free.

She had good reason to sleep late, she thought, as the memories of the past week ran through her mind. Ever since she and Jason had made love on the hill, things had once again changed, although to those around her, especially her grandfather, everything remained the same. Ti and Jason's daytime meetings were marked by formal cordiality; however, the terseness that had been a thick wall was gone.

By mutual agreement, she and Jason stayed apart from each other as much as possible during the day. She knew what she wanted for the future, and was determined to have it. She also knew that it would take a while to prove to Jason the foolishness of his *rules,* but in that, too, she was determined. It was only a matter of time, she thought, before she could wear away his stubborn veneer. And she knew it would soon be time to do the same with her grandfather. If he wanted her acceptance, then he must be willing to accept not only her, but the man she loved.

Ti's days were filled with learning, and she enjoyed the time she spent with her grandfather. But at night her life changed. At night she came alive. At night, after everyone was inside, she and Jason would walk in the fields. They would talk of a hundred different things. They would hold hands and be reassured by the warmth of their touch. Later, they would lie in his bed and make love.

But always she would leave him to return to the main house, and her bed.

Ti yawned and stretched languidly. A smile formed on her lips as she thought about what had happened last night.

Ti had left her grandfather's library after spending an informative half hour with him, learning more about the woman she had been named after. Her head was filled with her grandfather's words, and she felt, for the first time, a kinship with her ancestor. Ticonderoga Bennett Barkley had been a strong and willful woman who had loved her husband fiercely, and had stood by his side throughout many hard, adventurous and exciting years.

As she crossed the living room, Ti wondered if she'd be able to have the same chance with Jason. When she reached the front door, Angela appeared with a napkin-covered tray. The housekeeper smiled at Ti in greeting.

"More stories?" Angela asked. Ti laughed and nodded her head. "Your grandfather likes to tell them to you. He wants you to know about where you came from."

"I know," Ti agreed. "Is that for Sam?" she asked as she glanced at the tray.

"No, for Jase. He is still working and asked for some dinner."

"I was just going to the office, why don't I take it?" Ti asked, hoping her voice was not betraying her.

"Thank you," Angela said with a smile and an unreadable expression. "Tell him not to work too late," she added.

"Do you worry about everyone?" Ti jested.

"I'm a mother, I've been trained to worry," Angela replied only half in jest, as she handed Ti the tray.

"You're a love, also," Ti said suddenly as a wave of

emotion washed over her. She knew she was blushing, but could not stop herself.

"Thank you," Angela said. "I am glad you've stayed." She turned and walked away.

Ti shook her head slowly and left the house. She walked quickly to the offices, and entered. "Delivery!" she shouted. A moment later she met Jason halfway. "Hungry?" she asked as she held out the tray.

"Not for food," he answered as he ignored the tray in Ti's hands and leaned over it to kiss her.

Ti's lips exploded as he touched them. "Don't do that!" she ordered as she pushed the tray into his stomach.

"I can't help it," he replied with a smile and a wicked gleam in his eyes.

"Eat!" she ordered again. The smile stayed in place and the gleam grew bolder. "Jason!" she cautioned.

"Yes ma'am," he replied as he finally took the tray and led her into his office. Jase put the tray on top of the papers on his desk and took off the napkin. Then, as Ti sat on the couch across from him, he began to eat. She watched him and suffered through the endless minutes until he was finished.

"You're beautiful," he marveled as he sipped his coffee.

"So are you," she responded.

"I thought we agreed that I was handsome, and you were beautiful," he teased.

"No," she replied, her voice serious but her words light as she studied his face. "The handsomeness is the overall picture; but your beauty is in your face and eyes and hair and mustache and body and hands and fingers and toes and legs and arms and back and . . ." Ti stopped, unable to say aloud what she'd just thought, but the color that suffused her face must have told him.

"And?" Jase asked, holding back a laugh at the way she went on.

Ti felt the heat from her blush spread from her face all the way down to her toes. Suddenly her mouth was dry and she tried to moisten her lips with her tongue.

"And," Jason prompted again, but Ti shook her head. "I love you," he said in a low, strong voice.

"I know," Ti whispered as she tried to smile.

"What's wrong?" Jason asked.

"Nothing," Ti lied, not wanting to bring up the touchy subject of Valley principles. "Are you finished here?"

"I can be."

"Let's walk off your dinner."

"I have a better idea," Jason said as he gazed at her meaningfully.

"Really?" she asked as she stood and challenged him.

"Really." He smiled.

Again Ti's mouth was dry, and her heart raced. Nothing had changed since the first time she and Jason had made love. When he looked at her as he did now, everything stopped and all she wanted was him.

"Jason, someone will see us," she cautioned.

"No they won't," he replied.

"Jas—" His name was cut off as his mouth covered hers. Ti's hands went to his back as she pressed herself to him. Whatever protest she'd had in her mind disappeared as his lips devoured hers. Her nipples stiffened against his chest, and her breathing became labored. She tore her lips from his and buried her face on his chest.

"I love you," she whispered as her fingers massaged his back slowly.

Jason stepped away from her and turned off the light in the office. The low light from the other room filtered in softly, and Ti watched Jason come back to her. She stayed still as his fingers unbuttoned her shirt.

When her shirt was open, he slipped it from her shoulders and unsnapped her bra. When that, too, was gone, she heard his sharp intake of breath and saw his eyes move to gaze at her breasts.

"Those," Jason said in a husky voice, "are what you call beautiful." Then he bent and cupped her right breast in his hand. "And this, also," he whispered as his lips surrounded her nipple.

A lightning bolt exploded within her right breast and shot through her body. Then he stood straight.

Ti stared at him as she forced her hands and arms to move. Slowly, her fingers went to the buttons of his shirt and opened them one at a time. When the shirt was opened and pulled free of his pants, she took it from his shoulders.

"And this," she said after she found her voice, and had traced a light path across his chest with her fingernails, "is what *I* call beautiful." Bending, she took his nipple in her mouth and teased it gently between her teeth. The tip rose firmly against her tongue, and another chill tremored through her body.

Then, as if she were in a trance, she sank slowly along his length. Her mouth explored the fine hair of his chest, and moved downward over his finely muscled abdomen.

Her mouth and hands stopped at his belt. Slowly, she unfastened the belt and opened his jeans. Her head lifted, and she gazed up into his eyes as she drew his pants down. Then her hands skimmed lightly along the back of his thighs, and she felt a tremor pass through his muscles. She could scent his heady male fragrance as her lips roamed across the front of his thighs.

Then his hands were in her hair and she was being lifted up. Their lips met, and their tongues began to dance. Electricity raced along the length of their bodies. Suddenly Jason stepped back, and his feet became tangled in his jeans and he fell on the floor.

Ti stood paralyzed, until she could no longer hold back the laughter that rumbled in her chest. Jason scowled up at her for a long, dark moment, but still she couldn't stop herself.

With his eyes squinting almost closed, and his chin jutting forward stubbornly, he spoke. "And I suppose you call this beautiful, too?"

Ti almost fell on top of him in her effort to stop laughing. She offered him her hand to help him up, but instead, he grabbed her and pulled her down on him, completing the ungainly heap they had become.

"You! You . . ." Ti yelled as she tried to free herself. But suddenly she stopped fighting and looked at him. Her breath flew from her. She bent and covered his mouth with hers.

They kissed deeply for a long, endless minute, until Ti drew away slowly. Her breasts rose and fell in a powerful rhythm as she stroked his cheek gently.

"I want you," she murmured. Then she moved, and turned. She took one of his feet in her hands and pulled his boot free. When the other boot was freed, she stood and gazed at him. She wanted to smile, but couldn't. Instead, she kicked her shoes off and slipped her skirt and panties from her hips. Then she returned to the floor and to Jason.

As he began to take his underwear off, she stopped him. Her lips sought his, and her tongue darted excitedly into his mouth. When he returned her kiss, she suddenly pulled away and looked into his eyes. Then her mouth traveled to his neck, and she tasted its slight saltiness. Tantalizingly, Ti flowed along his body. Her hands were everywhere, caressing, massaging, teasing and stroking.

She was lost in the quest of exploring Jason's body. Each time she had she'd discovered new secrets, and each new secret revealed more about the man she loved.

His hand was on her back, moving in languid circles, but she refused to be distracted as she lavished him with moist kisses and warm caresses.

She bit and teased each of his nipples in turn, and then wove her tongue along the arrow of hair toward his stomach. His muscles tensed beneath her lips, and the same tension filled her and made her moist and ready for him. But she held herself in check, and didn't respond to the deep, masculine moans floating above her.

Suddenly her fingers touched the elastic of his briefs, and she rolled them down. As she guided the material slowly along his thighs, her mouth caressed his skin. She removed the last vestige of clothing, and turned to gaze up along his length.

His eyes were fastened on her, and his chest rose and fell powerfully. Not rushing, Ti moved up along his length. Her fingers teased the inside of his thighs as her mouth kissed every inch of skin she passed over. Soon her hand was filled with the pulsing rhythm of his rising manhood, and her lips again followed her hand's path.

"Ti," Jason moaned in a husky voice.

She ignored his call as her lips followed their own dictates. The heated satin skin vibrated within her hand and against her lips. His low moan echoed, even as his hands wound through the long waves of her hair. Then her eyes closed and her lips continued their new exploration, until finally, she could no longer think.

Her hands moved upward, and her nails raked lightly across his abdomen. Jason's back arched, and he moaned again. Slowly, Ti's mouth resumed its journey upward. She moved like liquid, sliding along his stomach until finally her lips were on his. Suddenly, she lifted herself, only to return and engulf him.

She stayed like that, frozen in time, as he erupted within her depths. Then, after a century of stillness, Ti began to move. She took Jason slowly, never hurrying, never varying her pace as he joined with her in movement.

As she made love to Jason, she watched him, drinking in the masculine beauty she had spoken of. She watched his face, his eyes and his chest, luxuriating in the smoothness of his rippling muscles. The strength of his hands as they held her hips brought out even more of this feeling.

Ti knew she was living a moment frozen in time, and didn't care. She felt his love, and she knew he must feel hers. Then he moved, and his hands cupped her breasts. Tingling waves of pleasure spread through them and joined the other sensations that were steadily rising from her very center.

She closed her eyes, unable to watch him any longer as her pleasure grew stronger, and her need for him climbed to insurmountable heights. She felt herself grow tense, and urged him to join her. A low moan issued from deep within her throat, but was suddenly replaced with a cry of protest as Jason's hands left her breasts and returned to her hips. He gripped her small waist and stopped her from moving. Her eyes snapped open as she gazed at him.

Jason sat up without breaking their bond. With a fluid movement, Ti unbent her legs and wrapped them around his waist. Jason's arms went around her, pulling her even tighter to him as their mouths joined.

Together, with new and powerful sensations, they blended their bodies. With their eyes open and fixed upon each other, they took their love upward, until they were flying above the earth.

The universe shattered with bright, swirling colors inside Ti's mind; and then she too exploded with wave after wave of undulating release as Jason grew stronger and stronger within her, until his cry joined hers and he filled her with his searing essence.

With a great effort, Ti pushed away the memory of the previous night, tossed the covers from her and stood.

Jason had been beautiful, and she only wished she could wake up with him in the mornings. *Stop!* she commanded herself as she walked toward the bathroom. She paused at the door, as a knock sounded.

"Yes?" she called.

The door opened and Angela entered. "Good morning. I'm glad I didn't wake you."

"I woke a few minutes ago," she said.

"*Sí.* . . . Your grandfather asked me to tell you that he would like you to meet him in the storage cellars."

"When?"

"When you are dressed," Angela said with a smile. "I have biscuits and coffee ready for you when you come down."

"Thank you. I'll be down as soon as I shower and dress."

"*Bueno.*"

Ti watched her leave and then turned to the bathroom. Would Jason be with Sam? she wondered. She hoped so.

Sam Barkley was alone when Ti found him in the storage cellar. Only a few lights burned in the cavernous room, but even with the low light Ti could clearly see the endless rows of barrels waiting for the right moment to be drained.

She saw her grandfather walking between the rows of

barrels, his white hair and beard glowing against the darker background of the wooden walls. He wore a light Windbreaker, the same type as the one she had put on outside the storage room's door. The temperature in the room was chilly enough to warrant the jacket's use.

Sam Barkley turned and saw Ti. He smiled and walked toward her. "I take it you slept well?"

"Very. Sorry I missed you at breakfast."

"That's quite all right," he said with a smile. "How is your palate this morning?" he asked.

"I can still taste María's biscuits," she replied.

"That shouldn't make any difference."

"What shouldn't?"

"I've opened a barrel and I want your opinion," Sam informed her as he gazed into her eyes.

"You're kidding," Ti protested.

"I'm very serious. You have to start learning about this part of the wine business, too. You're very good with books, now it's time to develop your taste."

"Oh? I thought I was born with good taste. After all, I am a—" Ti cut off the last word before she spoke, and turned from Sam for a moment to regain her equilibrium.

"Say it," Sam ordered in a low voice.

"Sam, please," Ti pleaded, her nerves suddenly taut.

"No. You've been here almost three weeks. There's been nothing to keep you here except yourself. Ti, you have to say it."

Slowly, with tears welling in her eyes, Ti nodded her head.

"I'm a Barkley," she said in a hoarse whisper.

"Yes. Now, if we can get on with our purpose for being here," Sam continued as he tried to hide the emotions that filled his voice.

Ti nodded hesitantly. He had gotten her to admit she

was part of his family. She was grateful he hadn't pushed it further.

"This lot is from nineteen fifty-eight. It was a good year, not outstanding, but good. I think it's time to taste it and decide if we want to bottle it this year, or wait."

"What is it?" Ti asked.

"A Pinot Noir. We have enough stored to make two thousand cases, which is a quarter-million bottles."

"Quarter of a million," Ti echoed. For the first time, the enormity of the winery struck her. Up to this point, all the facts and figures had been on paper. Now, her grandfather was asking her to share in a decision that could bring in millions of dollars to the Barkley winery.

She watched Sam's smiling face as he went to the second barrel in the first row. She noticed that the plug had already been pulled, and two wineglasses sat next to it.

She stared in fascination as Sam dipped a ladle into the keg and filled both glasses. Then he picked them up and held one out for Ti.

She took the glass and sniffed the fragrance of the red wine. Then she looked at her grandfather. "I've watched those TV commercials that show wine tasters. Am I supposed to swirl it first, or smell it?"

"Swirling wine is theatrical. Smell it, enjoy the bouquet, and then sip it. Let it flow across your tongue. This wine, if it is ready, will be very dry. It should tingle when it meets your tongue." He lifted the glass to his lips.

Ti did the same. Then she took her first sip. Even as she tried to analyze its taste, she realized she couldn't. It was very smooth, yet full and more fruity than acidic. Her tongue came alive and, as Sam had forecasted, it tingled as the wine flowed across it.

Ti realized instantly that this was the finest wine

she'd ever tasted, and that if it wasn't ready, she would never know it.

"Well?" Samuel Barkley asked. He hadn't missed the spark of excitement that had flashed in her eyes when she'd taken her first sip. Even as the wine had rolled through his mouth, he knew she knew.

"It's incredible."

"I know, but is it ready?" Sam asked.

"I don't know, but if it isn't, then someone is missing out on something."

Sam laughed and suddenly he leaned over and kissed Ti on the cheek. "It is ready," he declared.

Ti flushed with pleasure as she watched her grandfather. That was the first time he'd kissed her. She didn't know which made her happier. The fact that she had been right about the wine, or his kiss.

"Come," Sam said, interrupting her thoughts. "Let's get outside, I'm starting to feel the cold in my bones."

Ten minutes later they were in the garden behind the main house, walking along the center path and basking in the sunshine. Halfway through the garden, Sam stopped and looked at Ti. Then he glanced at the sun. "Winter will be here soon," he commented.

Ti gazed at him for a moment, then cocked her head as she watched a bird fly from one tree to another. "Do the birds stay year round?" she asked.

"Some do," he answered in a faraway voice. Then he glanced from Ti to the hills surrounding the vineyards. "Do you like it here, Ti?"

Ti didn't answer the question immediately. She thought about it for a moment. She knew it hadn't been asked lightly. "Yes," she said simply.

"The Valley is very different from what you know," he began. Ti nodded in agreement. "The people are different, also. They have their own ways, their own sense of right and wrong."

"So I've been learning," Ti said.

"Everyone, the owners of the wineries, the people who work them, the bankers, the businessmen, everyone and everything interact together. Without those types of interrelations, it wouldn't be the same."

"That fact has been driven home very pointedly," Ti stated as she looked at her grandfather. Just then, a small bluebird cried out from the tree above them. Ti's eyes flicked upward for a moment and then returned to rest on her grandfather again. "I heard it from Jason, even before we landed. Then Melissa told me. I can understand some of the things about the Valley, but not all of them."

"Nothing happens in the Valley that doesn't affect something else."

"This isn't an insect colony," Ti countered tersely. Then, with a shrug she went on. "A closed environment stagnates. Values don't change with the times. That isn't good."

"Sometimes it is. Sometimes it's for the best," Sam said in a gentle voice as his eyes searched Ti's face.

Ti waited before she spoke as a warning sounded in her mind. She wasn't sure what it was, but she listened to her intuition.

"Things have a way of happening here," Sam explained as his arm swung out. Ti followed his pointing finger and watched it glide across everything around them. "Cause and effect are part of the environment. When something happens that's different, people's reactions are not always good. A lot of harm and bad feelings can develop."

"You're talking about my mother and father."

"No, Ti, I'm not," he told her. Ti thought she heard a note of sadness in his voice and gazed at him for a long moment until, with a sinking sensation, she realized he knew about her and Jason.

"I'm sorry you had to find out before we could tell you," she whispered. Her head and shoulders were held straight, and her eyes challenged him defiantly.

"Would you have told me?" he asked in a level voice.

"Yes."

"It's not the way of the Valley," Sam said.

A blast of anger burned through Ti as she stared at her grandfather. Everything she'd felt for him earlier was consumed within the fire, and the loathing for him with which she had been raised emerged fresh and unchanged.

"But it's my way! I'm not from here. I'm not part of what you believe in! I am my own person. I will not have the restrictions of your antiquated codes forced upon me!"

Sam stood still against Ti's withering blast, his heart heavy with her words and the knowledge that he was about to lose her. Slowly, holding his emotions in check, he spoke. "And Jase? He agrees with you?"

"Damn you!" Ti cried as her fists clenched and unclenched ineffectually at her sides. Her chest was tightly constricted as she stared at Samuel Barkley's stoic face. "He's just like you! He loves me as I love him. But he's just like you," Ti repeated, unaware of the tears spilling onto her cheeks. "He won't allow us . . . He won't accept that our love can surmount the prejudices of this place. And his misguided loyalty to you is our biggest block," she cried.

"It's more than that, Ti. Try to see it through his eyes," Sam pleaded as he lifted her balled hands and held them within his.

Ti stared at him as if she'd never seen him before. Then she yanked her hands free and crossed them over her breasts, hugging herself as she watched her grandfather.

"He grew up on a vineyard. His parents worked the winery all their lives, and as Jason grew, he, too, worked within the system. He is as much a part of the Valley as I am. The things that govern his way of life are a part of everyone here. Jase knows what he has to do, and he does it."

"You sound like every bad movie I've ever seen," Ti snapped. Then her voice lowered and her eyes narrowed. "A man has to do what a man has to do," she drawled in a perfect imitation of a macho movie star.

"Sometimes a cliché is the only way to say something," Sam told her.

"I won't live my life by someone else's standards."

"Have you ever heard of compromise?"

"I'm a Barkley, remember? You said so yourself. The Barkleys are stubborn, they don't compromise!" Ti stated with finality. "What you and the others here won't understand is that the morality you force on everyone is wrong!"

"Ti, no one is forc—"

"It was wrong twenty-five years ago when you forced my mother to run away, and it's just as wrong today!"

"You don't know the way of the Valley," Sam protested.

"I don't have to know something intimately to know when it's wrong!"

"Right or wrong, it's still the way of the Valley," Sam insisted.

"Then, *to hell* with the Valley!" Ti screamed.

Whirling suddenly, Ti ended this fruitless battle and walked away. She held herself rigid, refusing to turn and so much as glance at her grandfather. She was still fuming at Samuel Barkley's inability to understand her. She was also hurt, and slowly, as she left the garden, her heart began to break again. She knew she must face Jason soon, and knew also that she would force him to make a decision between his work and her.

"It isn't fair," she whispered as she entered the house. She didn't see Angela as she walked past the housekeeper, nor was she aware of the steady stream of tears that fell from her eyes. All she knew was that she was once again on the verge of losing something important. She might lose Jason forever.

Once Ti was within the privacy of her room, she threw herself face up on the large four-poster bed. Staring at the beige linen canopy, her eyes became unfocused.

Her mind was a jumbled, confused maze of conflicting emotions. Logically, she knew she should pack and run away as quickly as possible. But emotionally, she couldn't bring herself to do it.

It was only this morning that she had begun to realize she was coming to love her grandfather in spite of what had happened to her as a child. In three weeks she'd learned a lot, and had thought she'd penetrated Sam's heart. Now she knew she had been wrong.

And to top everything else off, the man she loved, the man she had given her heart, soul and love to, was nothing more than a younger duplicate of Samuel Barkley.

Jason had the same ideals, the same goals and the same inhibitions and prejudices that her grandfather had.

"They're both fools!" she cried aloud in a sad voice.

Sam Barkley watched Ti walk away from him. He wanted to stop her, but was unable to. She had to learn things for herself. She had to learn that to do what she wanted would make her an outcast. It could hurt her and Jason, and possibly ruin whatever chance they had together.

But he could not tell her that. She wouldn't accept it from him. No one who had not grown up in this valley would be able to fully comprehend the magnitude of what she wanted. *But then,* Sam thought as he shook his head and smiled, *she said it herself. She's a stubborn Barkley.*

Chapter 10

TI GAZED INTO THE MIRROR AND APPLIED THE FINAL BRUSH
stroke to her makeup. She had spent a restless,
thought-filled afternoon in her room, and by the time
darkness had fallen, she knew what had to be done. It
had been a difficult decision, but after looking at her
options she realized it was the only one she had.

She could not remain in the Napa Valley as things
were. She could not lead a life of loving behind closed
doors. And she would not be ruled by the unspoken
laws both Jason and her grandfather adhered to. She
was her own woman, and would accept nothing less
than the life she chose for herself.

With a sigh, Ti flicked back a strand of hair. At first
she had thought to pack and leave, but as the day ended
and evening came, she'd decided against that impulse.
If nothing else, she would not leave here as her mother
had, disappearing into the night. She would face her
grandfather and tell him she was going, along with her
reasons why.

Standing, Ti smoothed out her skirt and adjusted the blouse before putting on her jacket. She had decided she would have a final meal with her grandfather.

In the dining room, Sam sat at the head of the table, holding up a carafe of wine and looking at it in the reflection of candlelight. He had been pleased when Angela told him Ti was joining him for dinner, and had decided to use some of the wine they tasted this morning to have with dinner.

"It has a lovely color," Ti observed as she entered the dining room. She smiled as Sam stood, but waved him back to his chair as she seated herself.

"It does. I think you'll like it," Sam replied with a smile as he poured the wine into her glass.

Ti was tense, but did her best to hide it as she lifted the glass and sipped. She recognized the taste instantly, and her smile was no longer forced. "It's even better. The woody taste is still there," she added in surprise.

"Certainly. That's why we age the wine in wood. If we used steel vats we would lose most of the richness and fruitiness."

Ti nodded her head in understanding as she watched her grandfather's face proudly display the emotions of his words. Then she saw his eyes flicker and his face change. Intuitively, she knew what he was about to say. She wanted to scream to keep him from saying the forthcoming words, but nothing came out. Instead, she watched as Sam took a deep breath.

"Ti, what happened in the garden today . . . I'm sorry we had to argue."

"I'm not," she said suddenly. Sam started to speak again, but she wouldn't let him. "It had to come out sooner or later. I'm returning to Philadelphia tomorrow. I can't live under your senseless rules. I'm sorry, Sam, I can't live the life you want me to." By the time she uttered the last word, her voice was barely audible.

Ti's throat tightened as she watched her grandfather's face go through a range of expressions. She knew she'd hurt him deeply, and again the conflicting emotions that turned her mind into quicksand emerged. Willfully, she swallowed and forced herself to remain calm.

"No!" Sam yelled. The quiet of the house was shattered as he rose and slammed his hand on the table. China jumped and silver clattered. Sam's wineglass fell over and Ti watched the burgundy liquid spread across the white tablecloth.

"No!" Sam repeated angrily. "You will not do this to me! I've waited twenty-five years to have a family again. I will let nothing interfere!" he said in a loud, flint-edged voice.

For the first time since she arrived at the vineyards, Ti saw rage in her grandfather's face, and fearfully remembered her mother's words about his temper. She stared wide-eyed as he walked ominously toward her.

Without warning, Sam grabbed Ti's wrist and dragged her from the table. She tried to fight him, but she was no match for his strength and determination. Silently, Ti went along with him, her wrist tightly imprisoned in his viselike grip.

Sam pulled her to the stairs and forced her to walk up them. He did not say a word. His anger at being so close to losing her stopped him. Instead, his reaction had been swift and certain. *It is time for her to know!* he screamed inside.

Ti almost had to run to keep pace with her grandfather as he walked swiftly down the hall, stopping finally at the end of the foyer. Once again, Ti tried vainly to free her wrist. Then, as Sam reached for the doorknob, he opened his hand, released her wrist, and spoke without glancing back at Ti.

"This was your mother's room," he said. Then he pushed the door open and stepped aside for Ti.

His words sent a chill coursing along her spine. Ti's first thought, as he released her arm, was to run from the madman he seemed to have become. His words stopped her even before she'd lifted one foot. She stood rooted to the spot as she watched the door swing open. For the three weeks she'd been here, she'd never ventured into any of the rooms on the upper floor. She had wanted to see her mother's room, but had been afraid to bring the subject up.

The room was dark, but she tried to see inside anyway. Sam stepped aside, and Ti hesitantly moved into the doorway. As she did, Sam spoke in a voice heavily laden with emotion.

"When your grandmother died, I thought my life had ended. Everything turned dark for me. Not even Jenna had been able to break through my depression. I had fallen in love with Katherine the moment I met her. I was seventeen at the time. We were married soon after that. A few years later your mother was born. Every day was beautiful, filled with life and love. Then your grandmother became ill. It was as devastating a disease as it was swift. Within two months Katherine died, and part of me died with her.

"I know I took a lot of it out on Jenna, but I didn't realize it at the time. I was destroyed, I had lost the most important thing in my life." Sam paused for a moment, his eyes vacant and unseeing. "I know that sounds terrible, because I still had Jenna. I don't mean I didn't love your mother, I did, but the love I shared with your grandmother was special, it was strong and it was good. In my grief, I forgot that Jenna had also lost the mother she loved. Instead of sharing our grief to lessen it, I did just the opposite and withdrew into myself.

"I became a dictator, and worse, I didn't see what I was doing to my daughter. I loved her, but I could no longer express it. Instead, I gave orders and ultimatums. I was wrong.

"After your mother left, I realized just how wrong I had been. It wasn't something that happened overnight. It took a long period of adjustment and understanding. Finally, I came to terms with myself, and was ready to face the world and make up for my mistakes."

Suddenly the room exploded in light, and Ti blinked away afterimages of orange and red. When her eyes cleared, and adjusted to the brightness, she gasped in disbelief.

Piled in sloppy disarray on the top of her mother's bed were hundreds of letters. "Those are all the letters I sent your mother. Two a week from the time I realized what I'd done to her, until she died. Look at them!" Sam commanded in a low, hard voice.

"Not one was ever opened. Every last one of them was returned unopened. Every time I called on the phone, Jenna hung up on me. Ti," Sam said and for the first time since he'd opened the door he turned to face her. His hands went to her shoulders and his eyes held hers. "For twenty years I poured out my heart to your mother. I begged her for forgiveness. Not once did she consider it. Not once did she even try to learn what I wanted—"

"She couldn't help it, Grandfather. She was hurt badly."

"So was I," Sam said as he left the room, closing the door behind him to let Ti have the room to herself. He blinked his eyes furiously to try and stop the moisture that filled them from spilling over. He wasn't sure what had brought it on, his own memories or the fact that for the first time, Ti had called him "Grandfather."

Sam stood in the hall, listening to Ti behind the closed door. He hadn't meant to be so brutal in showing her this room. He loved her, as he had always loved his daughter. He needed her here, to help him live his waning years in peace. He did not want to die as he had lived in the past—alone.

Sam took a deep breath and went to the stairs. At the bottom, Angela waited for him.

"You told her," she said.

"Yes. I had to," he admitted.

"You should have done so sooner," she stated.

"It wasn't time. Tonight was the time. I must speak with Jase," he said as he walked to the front door.

"It will be difficult," Angela whispered.

"I know," Sam replied wearily.

Inside her mother's room, Ti stood motionless. Her mind whirled with her grandfather's words as she looked about her. *Mother's room,* she thought. Her eyes roamed over everything greedily. The bed was a smaller version of the one she had been sleeping on for the last three weeks. A triple row of shelves decorated the center of one wall; on them were three neatly arranged rows of dolls.

Ti walked to them, and through her misted eyes, saw some of her mother's childhood passion in the dolls. Forcefully, she tore her eyes from them and turned again. She walked to the dresser and looked at its top. On it was a small silver brush and comb. Dust covered everything, and Ti realized that no one except her grandfather ever came into this room.

Slowly, she turned toward the bed. She reached it and pushed a pile of letters aside so she could sit. Ti picked a letter at random and opened it. She took a deep breath and began to read. When she finished the letter, she reached for another.

* * *

"I don't know what to say," Jase replied. He'd just finished a light supper when he'd heard a knocking on his door. He'd been surprised when he'd opened it and found Sam standing there. For fifteen minutes he'd listened to Sam talk, and heard the words he'd feared must one day come. Sam knew about Ti and himself, and he was fighting to keep his granddaughter. Jase understood completely, and knew what his obligations were.

What bothered Jase most was that he'd violated the trust Sam had placed in him. He'd looked upon Sam almost like a father, and their relationship had always had a father/son quality to it. Now, that relationship was shattered.

"Sam, I'm sorry for what happened, and I want you to know that I'll never allow you to be embarrassed by what I've done."

"Embarrassed?" Sam asked as his eyebrows arched.

"I'll be gone by morning," Jase stated.

Sam ignored Jase's words as he gazed at him. Eight years had created a strong bond between them, and although thirty years separated them by age, it had never been a significant factor in their relationship.

"How do you feel about Ti?"

"I wasn't playing with her, if that's what you're asking."

"It isn't."

"I'm in love with her," Jase replied truthfully. "And I'm afraid because of it."

"You've never been afraid of anything," Sam said as he searched Jase's face. "Or is it me you're afraid of?"

"No, it's me," Jase admitted suddenly. Then his face turned hard and Sam knew Jase would not speak further on the subject. "Thank you Sam, for everything you've done for me." Jase stood as he finished speaking.

Sam knew that nothing he could say would stop Jase from doing what he thought he had to. Instead, he looked at Jase for a long time before he turned and left.

Outside in the cool air, Sam paused. How had he managed to get what he wanted, yet at the same time lose it? *Nothing's lost yet!* he told himself determinedly.

Inside, Jase stood by a window and watched Sam walk away. Refusing to allow his mind to dwell on what could have been, Jase went into his bedroom. From the closet he took out a large suitcase.

His mind was filled with his words to Sam. Yes, his love for Ti had made him afraid—not of Sam, or of Ti, but of himself. Ever since he'd met Ti, the nightmares of his wife and daughter's deaths had returned to haunt him. And with it had come a new fear. A fear that if he were to marry Ti, something just as terrible would happen to her. He couldn't go through that again. Quietly, knowing that the best part of his life was ending, Jason continued to pack.

The gentle rays of the early morning sun caressed Ti as she sat in a chair near her window. Her eyes were closed, and her body was as relaxed as it had been all night.

The sounds of the vineyard coming to life reached into the room, but Ti didn't hear them. Her mind was too involved in trying to analyze the intricacies of last night's discoveries.

After Sam had left her in her mother's room, Ti had begun to read his letters. She read one after another after another, until finally, near dawn, she had finished the last one.

At the beginning, she'd felt numb. But as the hours

passed, and she absorbed more information, her mind had started functioning again. When she'd finished reading the last of the hundreds of letters, she'd let herself cry.

Then she'd returned to her room, exhausted but unable to sleep. Her mind had been churning at a frantic pace and Ti knew that nothing would settle it at this point. She had wanted to speak with Jason, but decided against waking him. She knew he would understand her absence last night, especially when she told him the reason for it. Instead of trying to sleep, she'd undressed and put on a robe, then settled herself into the chair just as the sun had risen.

With the realization of what had happened to her mother and Sam, a deep, pain-filled sadness washed through her mind. *How foolish*, she thought. *How pitiful.* For all those years, Jenna and Samuel Barkley had been separated by pride and the inability to communicate. It wasn't her mother's refusal to read Sam's heartrending letters, but the earlier unwillingness of either of them to speak and comfort each other during the time of their great loss.

Two lives had been wasted because of it, and Ti saw clearly just how it had happened. Taking a deep, shuddering breath, Ti mourned again the loss of her mother. Jenna would never know what could have been hers. Then another thought struck Ti. She no longer felt the penetrating anger and hate for her grandfather that had threatened to consume her last night.

The past twenty-five years of loneliness could have been avoided if only Sam and Jenna had been able to talk and listen to what each had to say. Then another chilling thought caused her to shiver uncontrollably. What had happened between her mother and grandfather was being repeated between her and Jason.

Jason's moralistic ideals concerning the Valley were

the same as Sam's. It was the wedge that was opening a chasm which might never close. Ti refused to think of that possibility. *No,* she declared to herself, *I will not accept that!*

Determined to speak to both Sam and Jason, Ti rose from the chair. Ten minutes later she was dressed in jeans and a checked shirt. Her long hair was pulled back from her face and clipped at the nape of her neck.

As she slipped on her Docksider loafers, there was a knock on her door. "Yes?" she called.

"There's a phone call for you," came Angela's voice.

Ti paused for a moment, wondering who it could be. "Did they say who it was?" Ti asked.

"*Sí.* Miss Daley from Philadelphia."

"I'm coming," Ti called as she strode quickly across the room. She was suddenly excited as the lawyer's name reverberated in her mind. As she walked toward the stairs, another thought struck her. When she had spoken to Ann Daley the day after she'd arrived in California, Ann had been certain it would take at least six months for her case to come to court. Why was Ann calling her now? Had Matheson and Company offered a settlement?

Ti reached the main floor and went into the parlor. She hesitated for a moment before picking it up, then suddenly grasped it and heard her lawyer's voice clearly.

"We've had a bit of luck," Ann said after they had greeted each other.

"Luck?"

"There were two court cancellations. We got one of them."

"You must be pretty influential to get us moved ahead of the others," Ti commented jovially.

"Don't they have TV in your part of the country?" Ann asked in a strange voice.

"Of course. . . . What are you talking about?" Ti demanded as a strange feeling swept over her.

"You don't know?"

"If I knew, I wouldn't be asking, would I?"

"I don't know you well enough to answer that, but you and I have become minor celebrities. That's why our case was given precedence over the others."

"Ann, no more double-talk," Ti pleaded.

"Remember that luncheon with Cybil Ashe?" Ann asked.

"Yes."

"She ran the story, and for some reason it was picked up on by the wire services. Several newspapers around the country printed it, and last week I was interviewed on network news. Ti, you're becoming famous. The hue and cry has been picked up by several women's organizations!"

Ti was silent for a moment as she digested these facts. "Ann, this is not what I'd intended. I just want my record cleared up, and my life straightened out."

"Strategy. Remember what I said. The more publicity we get, the better it is for us. Do you want to know our court date?" Ann asked, ignoring Ti's protest.

"Yes."

"Monday."

"But today's Friday."

"My goodness, do they keep track of those things in California?" Ann retorted good-naturedly. "Seriously, I think we have a hell of a chance, Ti. It's going to be a fight, but one we can win."

"I hope you're right, Ann," Ti murmured.

"I am. When will you get to Philadelphia?"

"I'll try to get a flight today. Can you do me a favor?" Ti asked.

"Of course, if I can."

"Could you have my phone and electricity turned on so I can stay at my place?"

"Sure," the lawyer replied, then took the necessary information from Ti.

"See you Monday morning in my office. Eight o'clock sharp!"

"Yes, ma'am," Ti said with a smile as she hung up the phone.

Ti picked up the phone again, and called the airlines. She made a reservation to Philadelphia, and then went to look for her grandfather.

She spoke briefly to Angela, who informed her that her grandfather was in the garden, waiting to speak with her. Ti was surprised; it was seven o'clock and by now her grandfather was usually at the winery.

As Ti walked toward the garden she realized that Sam had probably wanted to find out Ti's reaction to last night. Ti shook her head slowly. If nothing else, Samuel Barkley was a brave man. Ti wasn't sure she could do the same thing after baring her soul to another.

Ti saw him sitting at the glass-topped table, drinking a cup of coffee and watching the birds wander in the trees. She walked slowly toward him, her thoughts replaying last night's drama and her heart wanting to reach out and comfort him.

"Sam," she called tentatively. Sam turned and looked at Ti.

"Good morning," he said in a level voice. "Coffee?"

"Please," Ti replied as she sat across from him.

"I have to leave today," she said suddenly. She saw her grandfather's hand freeze in midair and felt his eyes bore into hers. "It's not because of last night," Ti continued, and explained about the lawsuit, concluding with Ann Daley's call this morning.

"Do you really want to go up against a large corporation?" Sam asked as he studied her carefully.

"Yes!" Ti answered defiantly. "I was good at my job. And I won't let some hot-to-trot man take it away from me because I didn't come through for him!"

"You can be hurt by this," Sam cautioned.

"Not any worse than I've already been. Sam, they're punishing me for being a woman who wants to do something with her life."

"You have me, and the winery."

Ti stared at her grandfather for a long, silent minute. Her throat constricted and her eyes filled with moisture. "I . . ." Ti tried to speak but couldn't. Then she smiled and nodded. "Thank you, Grandfather. But"—she took a deep breath—"I have to do this for myself. Even if I never work in Philly again, I have to do this."

"I realize that. I just wanted you to know."

Ti nodded again. Then, without touching her coffee she rose. "I have to tell Jason about this," she informed Sam. She watched her grandfather's face change, and saw a flash of sadness in his eyes. "I love him, and that won't change."

"Ti," Sam said as he looked into his granddaughter's face, "Jase is gone."

Ti stared at Sam as if he were a total stranger. When she finally spoke, her voice cracked with emotion. "What do you mean?"

"He's gone. He left late last night," he added. Although he tried, he couldn't keep the sadness from his voice.

But Ti did not hear Sam's tone, only the words he spoke. Anger whipped through her like a tornado. "How could you!" she hissed. Then she turned and walked out of the garden.

Sam watched her retreating back and forced himself to stay seated. He wanted to chase after her, to tell her that it had not been he, but Jase who had made the decision to leave. But he held himself back. He knew she needed time before he spoke to her again.

Ti looked at her watch. It was nine-thirty. Then she looked at the bed. On it was her packed suitcase, and on top of that was the airline ticket Jason had given her in Philadelphia as part of their arrangement. Then she glanced in the mirror. She was ready to leave. She wore a conservatively cut gray business suit, with a white cotton blouse buttoned up to the base of her throat.

Ti walked to the window and gazed out at the vineyards. The sun bathed them in a warm glow, and Ti realized she would miss them terribly. Even now, after the harvest was over, and the vines were dormant and turning brown, they still held a fascinating beauty.

But they were not for her; not after what had happened today. She wanted to blame her grandfather, but realized that he was a prisoner of his upbringing, just as Tom Hutchings had been a prisoner of his environment when he'd tried to seduce Ti. No, she didn't hate her grandfather, she felt sorry for him. He was a rich and successful man, but he was also a lonely and poor man who had lost the love and respect of his family.

Ti's door opened, and she turned to see who was there. Her breath caught in her throat as she faced Sam Barkley.

"Will you be coming back?" he asked simply.

"No."

"Ti, by now you must know I love you. I lost your mother because of my own stubbornness and stupidity, I don't want to lose you."

"You should have thought about that before you fired Jason," Ti answered hotly.

"Would you believe me if I said that wasn't true, that I didn't fire him?"

"I wouldn't believe anything you told me," Ti retorted, unrelenting in her belief.

Sam sighed audibly. "I'm sorry it had to come to this. The limousine is waiting downstairs. Good-bye," he whispered. His stiff features dissolved momentarily and his vulnerability showed in the moist depths of his eyes. Then, without another word, he turned and walked away.

Still feeling the anger and resentment within her, Ti picked up her suitcase. She left the room without a backward glance and walked along the hallway and down the stairs. Standing at the bottom was the chauffeur and Angela.

George, the chauffeur, took Ti's suitcase and left. Ti gazed at the housekeeper. "Thank you," she whispered.

Angela nodded silently. Then, just as Ti was about to leave, she spoke. "Do not turn away from him. He is a lonely man and he loves you."

Ti wanted to say something, but couldn't find the words. Instead, she nodded her head and walked outside and into the waiting limousine.

As the automobile pulled away, Ti fought against the desire to turn and look back. Too many things had happened here, and she didn't want to see the cause of her sadness.

Then, as they reached the highway, Ti could no longer control her raging emotions. She buried her head in her hands as her sobs echoed within the soundproofed confines of the limousine's back seat.

Ti's tears gradually stopped and she took a deep, shuddering breath. The last two days had been a constant assault on her emotions, and when she'd entered the limousine, she had no longer been able to maintain the barriers she'd built as a defense. But the tears had their own value, she realized as she wiped the moisture from her cheeks. They had provided a catharsis for her tortured mind, and now that they had stopped she was beginning to feel better.

She had learned a great deal in the three weeks she'd been in California. She'd learned about herself and the way she felt about others. She had found love, and lost it. She had found a family, and had given it up. *But I have myself, and I am stronger for it,* Ti reminded herself, and felt a renewed strength for life build within her.

Jason was wrong, he was wrong to have left without speaking to me. I may be a Barkley, but I am not from the Valley. We could have made a life together—a good life. But he suffers from the same disease as my grandfather: foolish pride and a stubborn, outmoded sense of responsibility to something that is wrong.

"But I still love you," Ti whispered aloud. The limousine slowed unexpectedly. Ti looked out the window and saw they were driving through a cemetery. A few puzzling seconds later, the limousine stopped.

Ti didn't know what to expect as she watched the driver leave the limousine and walk around the car to her door. He pulled it open and bent his head so he could speak to Ti.

"What are we doing here?" Ti asked.

"Mr. Barkley told me to bring you here and show you something," he said as he offered Ti his hand.

She sighed with resignation and let him help her out. Then, as she stood she looked around. It was a small, neatly laid out cemetery with even rows of gray headstones.

"This way," the chauffeur directed and Ti followed

him. George stopped at a gravestone about a hundred feet from the limousine, nodded his head to Ti and walked away.

Hesitantly, Ti stepped closer to the grave and read its inscription. Her breathing stopped, and she felt her heart slow. Forcing herself to take a breath, she reread the carved letters.

SUSAN CLARKE PATTEN
BELOVED WIFE AND MOTHER
CLAUDIA JANE PATTEN
DAUGHTER

Several minutes flew by as Ti struggled to understand the meaning of what she'd just read. Jason had never mentioned a wife and child, but as she looked at the dates engraved in the stone, she knew it must be so. With a sudden flash the words he'd spoken weeks ago returned—"My life started eight years ago . . ."

Turning, Ti walked back to the car. A strange mingling of hope and despair rippled through her mind.

"George, do you know if Mr. Patten comes here often?"

"All the time," the chauffeur replied.

"I think you'd best tell me the story." She gazed at George and waited. He spoke quickly and Ti was aware of his discomfort. When he finished, she was shaken to the core. She nodded her head, and in a voice choked with emotion she thanked the chauffeur.

"Is there any writing material in the car?" she asked.

"Yes, ma'am," George said, pointing to the back of the partitioned seat. "In the desk."

"Thank you. Please wait until I'm finished," she told him as she sat in the seat, lowered the desktop, and wrote a letter. After sealing the envelope she left the limousine, returned to the grave and placed the envelope on the base of the headstone. Then she put a small rock on it to keep it from blowing away. If Jason came here regularly, he would find the letter. Ti walked back to the limousine, sat and closed her eyes. She had a lot to think about, and a lot to understand.

An hour later, the limousine stopped in front of the air terminal. George took her suitcase from the trunk and walked with her to the ticket desk. After she checked in, and was assigned to her seat, she turned to the chauffeur and thanked him.

"I'm to stay with you until you board," he informed her.

"My grandfather's orders?"

George nodded.

"Very well." Ti sighed in resignation as she gazed at the chauffeur's face. "Then we might as well go to the gate." With that, Ti and George walked through the ultramodern San Francisco airport, through the security check, and down what seemed to be an endless corridor flanked by departure gates on all sides. Her gate was at the far end, and by the time they arrived the flight was being called.

Ti walked toward the boarding door. When she reached it, she turned to George. "You can tell Sam that I got off all right, and thank you, George, for telling me about Jason."

George smiled at her and nodded his head. Just as Ti turned, he spoke. "Miss Barkley?"

Ti stopped herself from getting angry and reminding him her name was Caissen. Instead, she turned and looked at him. "Mr. Barkley asked me to give you this," he said as he handed her an envelope. "Have a good trip," he added. Before she could reply, he turned and walked away.

Ti watched him for a moment before she, too, turned

and walked through the doorway to the plane. Inside, she fastened her seat belt, and opened the envelope.

"Dearest Ti," she read. "I know that you feel hurt and angry, and I therefore must set things right."

A sudden vibration passed through the plane, and Ti pulled her eyes from the letter. She glanced out the window and saw that the plane had begun to move. She realized she was on her way home. She looked back to the letter in her hands, and began to read again.

I did not fire Jason. It was his decision to leave, and there was nothing I could do to prevent it.

Ti, I am too old, and have lost too much in my life to even consider losing you, now that I've found you. I learned my lesson with your mother, and have come to terms with myself and my actions.

There is something else that must be said, and although I have written this letter before speaking with you, it was with the certainty that your hurt and anger would stop you from listening to me that I chose this method of communication.

It was not I who was against your love for Jason. As I wrote above, I have learned my lesson through much loss and pain, and would never make that mistake again. But I could not find a way to explain this to Jason. He is of the Valley, and has always lived within its bounds. You see, Jason must stand up for what he wants, and rid himself of the other demons that are within him.

Perhaps one day . . .

Ti tried to read the rest of the letter, but her eyes misted and she closed them. *Why?* she asked herself. *Why are they so foolish?*

The sun was setting when Sam Barkley's doorbell rang. When it rang a second time, he rose from the parlor chair and went to the door. He opened it and gazed into Jase Patten's chiseled features.

"Is she here?" Jase asked.

Sam stared at him. A warm feeling washed slowly through him, but he kept the smile he felt from showing on his face. "No," he said with a shake of his head. Then he stepped back and motioned Jase inside.

"What happened?"

"A couple of things. You know about the lawsuit?" Jase nodded. "Her lawyer called with the court date. It's Monday. She flew back today."

"She could have waited until tomorrow, or Sunday. You said a couple of things. What else?" Jase asked quickly as he looked into the face of his friend and mentor.

"You. You hurt her by leaving. You hurt her by not explaining things to her, and you turned her against me again. She thinks I fired you," Sam answered in a low voice.

"I tried to explain everything to her," Jase said.

"No, you explained well enough about the Valley, but not about yourself."

Jase gazed at Sam for a moment as the older man's words sank in. Then he nodded at the truth he'd just heard.

"I'm sorry, Sam. I thought I had wronged you and let you down. When I realized I was in love with Ti, I started to get this feeling that if I married her something terrible would happen . . . like with Susan. I didn't want Ti to be hurt by me."

"If you really feel that way, what are you doing here?" Sam challenged. He glared at Jase, his face suddenly hard and unrelenting.

"I was wrong about myself, and I don't give a damn about what the people in the Valley have to say! I realized that early today, and I came back to ask Ti to marry me."

"Really? And just where would you live? Philadelphia?" Sam asked sarcastically.

Jase looked at him, and Sam saw his eyes harden with determination. "It doesn't matter where we live, just that we do it together."

"Damn. . . . It's about time," Sam said. The rough edge in his voice disappeared, and the hard planes of his face softened. "You two children better grow up fast, I'm tired of waiting."

Jase stared slack-jawed at Sam. "You won't try to stop us?"

"Son, it was you, not me, who stopped you. I may be old, but I'm not stupid. I saw how much in love you both were when you first brought Ti home. But you never asked me, you just took it for granted I wouldn't approve. Hell, I wouldn't have given you stock in the new vineyard if I disapproved."

"Sam—"

"I just don't want you and Ti running off to get married. A marriage can't survive if it starts off like that. That's what was wrong with my daughter, that and my own foolish pride." Sam paused for a moment as his eyes flickered around the room. "Only, neither Jenna nor I realized what the problem was until it was too late. Damnit, Jase, I'm glad you learned before it happened to you, too. Now, what are you going to do about it?"

"I don't know yet," Jase replied as he smiled and pulled out a white envelope from his pocket. "After I made my decision, but before I came back, I stopped at the cemetery. I found this on the gravestone. That was your doing, wasn't it?"

"So?"

"So, thank you."

"You're welcome. And Jase . . ."

"Yes?"

"In the future, try to talk things out, *all things.*"

Chapter 11

TENSION SWIRLED THICKLY IN THE AIR, SATURATING EVERY inch of the courtroom. Ti held her head up and looked straight ahead at the empty desk and platform that would soon be occupied by the judge.

Voices whispered behind her and made her think of her entrance a few moments before. Even though Ann had warned her that there would be journalists and television reporters waiting for them, she had not really believed it.

When they'd stepped out of the taxi, she'd seen a human wave rush toward them. Questions had been thrown at her from every direction, but she had listened to Ann's advice and had shaken her head and politely refused to answer.

When they were almost at the door of the court-house, the reporters left them in another rush to converge on the Matheson people. Tom Hutchings answered several questions, as did the two attorneys who accompanied him.

"Theatrics," Ann had said.

A shadow crossed her eyes and Ti looked up. The two defense lawyers were standing before her and Ann.

"Could we have a word with you, in private?" one of them asked. Ti gazed at him and noted the immaculate cut of his suit. In fact, everything about him seemed to be perfect; she didn't like him at all.

Ti watched Ann walk a few feet away and speak to the men. A moment later, she saw anger written across Ann's features. Although she couldn't hear what was said, Ti knew it boded no good for her. Suddenly Ann walked away from them and returned to the table.

Ti's nerves were already stretched to the breaking point, and her lawyer's actions hadn't helped. She looked at Ann questioningly.

"Let me cool down first," Ann said. The lawyer stared across the courtroom at the Matheson lawyers and Tom Hutchings. Then she turned to face Ti. "We've got a problem. Your ex-boss is going to testify that it was you who made the advances to him, not the other way around. He's going to testify that he turned you down and fired you because of your moral conduct."

"He's lying!" Ti cried.

"But he's still going to testify to that. We can drop the suit."

"No we won't. I don't care if he does lie. I'm going to tell the truth! I will not have my life ruined because of him."

"Ti, it looks like it's going to get messier than I first thought," Ann warned as she studied Ti closely.

"You told me that the first time we met. Are you afraid of losing the case?"

Ann smiled. "No. I just want you to know what might happen. They also said they have another witness who will also testify that you made advances to him."

"Never! Damnit Ann, can you beat them?"

"We'll soon find out," Ann replied.

A hush swept the courtroom as a door on the far side opened. The noise was replaced by an electrical silence that crackled in Ti's ears. She saw a figure emerge, and stood with everyone else as the clerk called the court to attention.

Ti watched the judge, and was momentarily startled to see a tall, gray-haired woman clothed in black judiciary robes.

"She's wonderful," Ann whispered as the clerk spoke and announced the case.

Ti sat at the same time as Ann. "Who's wonderful?"

"The judge. I've known Alice Osborne for a long time. She's fair."

After several minutes, the formalities of the case were cleared and the judge asked Ann Daley to call her first witness.

"The plaintiff calls Tom Hutchings to the stand."

Ti watched closely as Hutchings rose and walked toward the witness chair. He was dressed somberly in a brown three-piece suit. His hair was combed neatly in place, and his face was cleanly shaven. As he passed Ti, he nodded.

After he was sworn in and seated, Ann walked up to him. "Mr. Hutchings, what is your position at Matheson and Company?"

"Vice-President and Director of Financial Planning."

"I see, rather a prestigious title. . . . Would you tell the court exactly what financial planning is?" Ann asked.

"Objection, Your Honor!" called the head defense attorney. "The question is immaterial."

"Your Honor," Ann cut in, "the question is material in establishing my client's qualifications for her job."

Judge Osborne looked at Ann and nodded her head. "The objection is overruled. Continue, Counselor."

"Thank you. Shall I repeat the question, Mr. Hutchings?"

"My department is in charge of the financial planning for our company's future. I look into market trends, make assessments, give advice and suggestions about investments and acquisitions based on corporate projections."

"A rather difficult job. Is a lot of training and education necessary to do this job well?"

"Yes," Hutchings stated.

"And when you hired Ms. Caissen, did you think her educational background was sufficient?"

"Yes."

"How many people are in your department?" Ann asked suddenly.

"Seven."

"And they all do the same thing?"

"No. Two are secretaries. Two are statisticians, and two are my assistants."

"I see," Ann said as she looked at him, and then at the pad in her hand. "Tell me, Mr. Hutchings, at the time Ms. Caissen was employed by your company, was the other assistant a man or a woman?"

"A—"

"Objection!" yelled out the defense lawyer. "That has no relevance."

"Your Honor," Ann said as she turned to face the other attorney. "If you will allow me to continue I will show the relevance of my question."

"Mr. Overton, I think your objection is out of line," the judge said as she looked at the attorney. Then she turned to Tom Hutchings. "You are directed to answer the question."

"A man," he said.

"I see. Tell me, Mr. Hutchings, did you think Ms. Caissen a competent employee?"

"Yes."

"More so than your other assistant, who was with you for"—Ann paused as she glanced down at her notes—"over a year?"

"No."

"Then why was Ms. Caissen required to work late on the night in question, rather than the male assistant?"

Tom Hutchings looked at his lawyer for advice, and the lawyer smiled and nodded his head. Ti heard Tom Hutching's voice change imperceptibly, and to her ears he sounded as if he were reading a prepared statement.

"Ms. Caissen had been assigned to this project, and as my assistant on it, *her* presence was required, not the other assistant's."

"That's a lie!" Ti shouted suddenly. Ann whirled and walked toward her with her hand outstretched in an order for Ti to be quiet.

"Miss Caissen," the judge said as she looked at Ti, "please refrain from calling out. It is up to the court to decide whether or not the witness' statements are true."

"Yes, Your Honor," Ti said in a low voice.

"Easy, you'll have your chance," Ann whispered.

"So, Mr. Hutchings, what you're saying is that it was because Ms. Caissen was assigned to this project that she had to work late with you?"

"That's correct."

"Well then, was it your idea to take her to dinner after you'd finished your work?"

"Matheson has a policy that if the executive employees work late, the company pays for their dinner," he explained.

"I see. It must be very nice to work for a company that treats its employees so well," Ann said with a smile as several titters broke out in the courtroom. "Your Honor," Ann said as she walked to the judge's bench, "I would like to offer for evidence this copy of the check from the restaurant where Mr. Hutchings and Ms. Caissen had dinner. Please note that the total bill is one hundred and ten dollars, and that nine drinks had been served."

"Objection!" came the weary voice of the defense attorney.

"What grounds, Mr. Overton?" asked the judge.

"Immaterial."

"I will reserve judgment until later. For the present I will accept this bill as evidence, but, Ms. Daley, I hope you will clarify what the evidence is."

"At the correct time, Your Honor."

"Very well, proceed."

"Thank you. Mr. Hutchings, after dinner you accompanied my client home, is that correct?"

"Yes."

"Is that also company policy?" More twitters came from the court observers, but Ann paid them no mind as she waited for Hutchings to answer. "Well?"

"Matheson and Company provides conveyance home for all their female employees if they work after-hours."

"And an escort to their apartment?" Ann snapped quickly.

"Objection!"

"Sustained. Counselor, please refrain from—"

"My apologies, Your Honor, I withdraw the question," Ann said before the judge had finished. She walked back to the table where Ti sat and placed a hand on Ti's shoulder. "Mr. Hutchings, why did you accompany Ms. Caissen to her apartment door?" As she finished her question her fingers pressed into Ti's shoulder in warning and restraint.

Hutchings looked directly at Ti as he spoke. "Why don't you ask her that?"

"Your Honor!" Ann called.

"The witness is directed to answer the question."

"I don't want to embarrass the lady," Hutchings said.

The judge stared at Hutchings for a moment before she spoke. Her voice was firm and authoritative. "Mr. Hutchings, I will not repeat myself a third time. You are directed to answer the question."

Hutchings's eyes bored into Ti's as he spoke. "Ms. Caissen asked me to accompany her. She said she'd had too much to drink and was unsteady and needed my *masculine* help."

Ti tensed as he spoke, and almost shouted, but Ann's warning fingers kept her at bay. "He's lying again," she whispered. Ann nodded and released Ti's shoulder. She walked slowly toward the witness stand.

"And?" she prompted.

"And I escorted her upstairs."

"Where you tried to seduce her in the hallway?"

"Objection!"

"Sustained. Ms. Daley, please confine yourself to questions, not statements."

"Yes, Your Honor. Mr. Hutchings, rather than allowing myself to get carried away, please tell me what happened that night."

Hutchings paused as he looked at his lawyer. Again, the elegantly dressed and coiffed attorney nodded to him. "All right, I didn't want to embarrass Ms. Caissen in public, but you leave me no choice. What happened that night was the reason I was forced to terminate her employment."

While Hutchings spoke, Ann again returned to Ti's side.

"When we reached her apartment, she gave me the

keys and asked me to open the door. When that was done, she stood very close to me, and moved suggestively against me. I asked her to stop, but she just smiled. She said that she was attracted to me, and that if I wanted, she would be *very nice* to me."

Ti stiffened angrily, then relaxed as Ann's hand again pressed her shoulder in reassurance.

"I tried to tell her I was her boss, that I didn't believe in romantic relationships between employees. But she said that certain relationships had certain benefits. If I wanted to have an *understanding* with her, she was very agreeable to it. However, she wanted a raise."

Ann released Ti's shoulder and walked back to the witness stand. "And did you refuse her generous offer?"

"Your Honor!" called Overton.

"Ms. Daley?"

"Sorry, Your Honor, a momentary lapse in light of this incredible story." Ti heard a short laugh behind her and turned to see Julia Ansen, one of the secretaries from Matheson whom she had been friendly with wink at her. She took some measure of warmth from that. Hutchings's reputation was widespread at the company.

"Did you refuse Ms. Caissen's offer of a sexual relationship in exchange for a raise?"

"I most certainly did," Hutchings answered haughtily.

"I see, and then what happened?"

"I left after that, I was embarrassed. The next day I decided it would be best if she were to leave our employ."

"By any chance do you remember meeting someone in the hallway at Ms. Caissen's apartment on the night in question?"

"No."

"Oh, what do you usually drink, Mr. Hutchings? Scotch?"

"Yes," he replied with a puzzled look on his face.

"All right, Mr. Hutchings, I just have one more question. If everything happened as you say, why was Ms. Caissen summarily dismissed without the normal notice or severance pay?"

"Objection, Your Honor," called Overton. "Matheson and Company's termination policies are not at issue here."

"Sustained."

"Your Honor, no more questions for this witness for the present; however, I request that Mr. Hutchings's presence be required for the remainder of the trial as I may have more questions for him."

"It is so directed. Does the defense wish to cross-examine?"

"Not at this time, Your Honor."

"Very well, Ms. Daley, you may call your next witness."

"Thank you. I will now call Ms. Ti Caissen."

Ti released her long-held breath as she stood. She was shaken by the out-and-out lies Hutchings had told, and only hoped that she would be able to rebut them convincingly enough for the judge to believe her story.

She walked across the endless expanse of polished floor until she reached the witness stand. Inside, she turned and faced the clerk. He swore her in quickly, and told her to be seated.

"Ti," Ann said, looking directly into her eyes, "how much did you have to drink when you had dinner with Mr. Hutchings?"

"I had one glass of white wine," Ti answered.

"How can you be so positive?"

"I don't drink a lot, especially hard liquor."

"And how many drinks did Mr. Hutchings have?"

"Objection, Your Honor, Ms. Daley is as—"

"Your Honor!" Ann cut in swiftly, effectively stopping Overton's objection. She walked to the bench and waited.

"Go ahead."

"I submitted the restaurant receipt into evidence, I would like to call it up now. On the second sheet is a listing of drinks served. It shows one glass of white wine, and eight Scotch-and-waters."

The judge inspected the receipt and then nodded. "Objection overruled, you may continue."

"I guess we can go on to the next question. The project you were working on that afternoon and evening had been assigned to you by Mr. Hutchings, is that correct?"

"Yes?"

"When?"

"That morning," Ti replied.

"I see. Can you tell the court about this?"

"When I came to work that day, Mr. Hutchings called me into his office and asked if I thought I'd be able to handle a large project. When he told me what it was, I assured him I could. He said he wanted to meet with me about it, but would be tied up most of the day and asked if I'd mind staying late. I agreed because I thought I was finally being given a chance to utilize my training."

"What happened that evening?"

"When we were working?"

"No, afterward."

Ti took a deep breath and focused her attention on Ann. "It was around seven when we finished. I told Mr. Hutchings that I was calling a cab, and asked if he wanted one also. He said no, and then he told me that the company paid for dinner when we worked late. He asked me to join him, and said we could talk about the project further.

"I agreed because I thought I could gain more insights into my work. But once we were at the restaurant, Mr. Hutchings began to drink, and we never discussed the project. When dinner was over, I tried to go home by myself, but he said he wouldn't hear of it."

"Did you object?" Ann asked.

"I didn't think it wise to alienate my boss, so I let him accompany me."

"And?"

"He took me home, and insisted on taking me to my apartment." Ti paused as the memory of that night flashed through her mind. She shivered slightly before she continued. Ti spoke clearly, and related every detail of what happened that night, recounting the way Hutchings had threatened her with his power in the company, and repeated word for word his threat about her future if she did not give in to him. She did not spare herself, or the court, any of her feelings, and even described Jason's interruption and Tom Hutchings's physical removal to the elevator.

When she finished, she maintained her gaze on Ann's face. Ann smiled and nodded, then turned to the judge. "No further questions, Your Honor."

"Does the defense wish to cross-examine the witness?"

"No, Your Honor, I would prefer to save everyone from any more of Ms. Caissen's obvious fantasy life."

"Mr. Overton!" the judge snapped angrily. "You can save your petty gestures and theatrics for another courtroom. I didn't realize I'd have to remind you that both you and the plaintiff have bestowed your faith in me, and have waived a jury. I have never been one to be amused or swayed by such obvious tactics."

"My apologies to the court," Overton said, but his face held no contrition.

"Accepted. Ms. Daley, are you ready to call your next witness?"

"Ms. Caissen was my last witness, Your Honor."

"Did you wish to recall Tom Hutchings at this time?"

"No, Your Honor, I would still like to have him available for later testimony."

"Fine. Mr. Overton, is the defense ready?"

"We are, Your Honor."

"Proceed."

"We call Alfred Prince to the stand." Ti watched as a middle-aged man stood and walked to the front of the court.

"Do you know him?" Ann asked.

"I saw him a few times. I think he's in accounting."

"Get ready, and don't say a word," Ann cautioned.

"Does it look bad?" Ti asked.

"Too early to tell," Ann whispered in reply. Then Overton was talking and both women listened intently.

"Mr. Prince, what is your position at Matheson?"

"I'm the comptroller."

"Mr. Prince, do you know the plaintiff?" Overton asked.

"Very well."

"Then you've worked with Ms. Caissen on occasion?"

"Never."

"Then, could you explain to the court how you know her."

"I work in the same company with Ms. Caissen, but not in the same department. I guess it was about a month before she was terminated that she came to my office. We had met when she was hired, and had talked several times in the hallways. But this day she came to my office with a proposition.''

"A proposition?" Overton asked with a sneering grin. Several people laughed, and the judge glanced angrily at the spectators.

Ti felt a warning chill race along her spine as she listened to the man. She leaned over and spoke in Ann's ear. "He's lying. I never once spoke to him."

Ann grasped her hand and squeezed it gently. "Hold on," she said.

"Would you tell the court about this *proposition*, please."

"Well," he said as he shifted uncomfortably in the chair. "She came to my office and said she was unhappy where she was. Then she hinted that if I were to help her, give her a position on my staff, she would be more than *grateful*."

"Mr. Prince, I can put several meanings to the phrase 'more than grateful.' Did Ms. Caissen mean she would be loyal and hardworking?"

"Hardly," Prince said with a snort of emphasis.

"Then I think you'll have to be more specific."

"She hinted at sexual favors."

"Hinted?" Overton asked. "I'm afraid you'll have to be a little more specific. A hint carries no weight in these proceedings."

"Well . . . Actually, it was more than a hint," Prince said in a reluctant voice.

Ti tensed, and for a moment she thought the man was going to tell the truth. Then he spoke in a barely audible voice.

"She . . . she said that if I arranged for a position on my staff at a high salary, she would become my mistress."

Ti's gasp cut through the silent courtroom like a shot.

Everyone looked at her, and then Overton, smiling, spoke.

"No further questions, Your Honor."

"Ms. Daley, do you wish to cross-examine?"

Ann stood, her anger written in harsh lines across her face. When she reached the witness stand, she glared into Prince's face.

"Mr. Prince, are you aware you are under oath?"

"Yes," he replied in a low voice.

"Excuse me, could you speak up, I don't think Ms. Caissen heard you."

"Objection!"

"Overruled!"

"Mr. Prince," Ann said again, "are you aware that you are under oath?"

"Yes," he said in a louder voice.

"And will you tell the court, and Ms. Caissen"— Ann's arm shot out and her index finger pointed to Ti—"that everything you've said here today was the truth?"

Prince's eyes held Ann's for only a second before they wavered. "Yes," he said.

"Mr. Overton," Ann called as she turned and faced the defense bench, "have you advised your witness of the penalties for perjury?" Before Overton could object again, Ann turned to the judge. "My apologies, Your Honor, no further questions for this witness."

"You are excused," the judge said. "Mr. Overton, you may call your next witness."

"Your Honor?" called Ann, interrupting Overton before he could speak.

"Yes, Counselor?"

"May I ask the court for a short recess?"

"Objections, Mr. Overton?"

"No, Your Honor."

"Very well, the court calls a fifteen-minute recess."

Everyone stood when the judge left, and Ann walked over to Ti. "Let's get some air."

"You go, I just want to sit here and think. How could they do that? They're all lying."

"I told you this could be a rough battle. Want to back out?"

"I want to win."

"So do I, but right now I'm worried. That's why I asked for the recess. I want them to lose some momentum. You know they're lying, I do, and I think the judge does, also. I want to give her some time to think about the last witness. Is there anyone we can call for your defense against their charges?"

Ti looked around and spotted the secretary she knew. She pointed her out to Ann, telling her that she might make a character witness if she wasn't afraid of losing her job.

Ann nodded knowingly and went to speak with her. Ti watched as the two women left the courtroom. Soon her mind was lost in thought, not about the trial, but about Jason, her grandfather and California.

Chapter 12

"WAKE UP," ANN SAID TO TI AS SHE SAT DOWN.

"I wish I could. Then this would only be a bad dream and when I woke, it would be over," Ti replied without looking at her lawyer.

"It's far from a nightmare."

"Really?" Ti said as she looked at Ann. She stopped her next comment before it formed on her lips as she saw the attorney's smile. "Julia said she'd testify for me?" Ti asked hopefully.

"If we have to use her, but she's not thrilled about it. She's afraid of losing her job, but she doesn't believe a word of what those men said."

"If we need her?"

"If," Ann repeated and smiled again.

"Why are you smiling?"

"You'll see," Ann said mysteriously.

"Ann . . ."

"Be patient," she whispered as the chamber door

opened and the judge entered. Everyone stood until the judge was seated. Then her voice rang out.

"Mr. Overton, are you ready with your next witness?"

The nattily attired lawyer stood and addressed the judge. Although his face was set in serious lines, Ti didn't miss the smugness in his voice. "Your Honor, the defense has several more witnesses, both to attest to the moral character of Mr. Hutchings, and to the lack of same in Ms. Caissen—"

"Objection!" yelled Ann as she stood. "Your Honor, Counselor has no right to make a judgment of my client's moral integrity."

"Sustained. Mr. Overton, please confine your remarks to proper decorum."

"I withdraw the statement. What I was trying to say is simply that we believe we have offered the necessary proof to sustain our contentions, and that to call further witnesses would only serve to humiliate the plaintiff; therefore, with her consideration in mind, we are willing to close our defense at this time."

"That's very noble of you," Ann snapped.

"Ms. Daley," called the judge, "I don't think your sarcasm is proper."

"But it is, Your Honor, it is." Then Ann approached the judge's bench. "Your Honor, I believe a miscarriage of justice, and a violation of my client's rights, has occurred in this courtroom."

"In exactly what way?" the judge asked, her voice suddenly defensive at Ann's charges.

"Excuse me, Your Honor, let me rephrase that. It is not the court that I accuse, but the defense. Your Honor, I charge both defense witnesses with willful perjury in order to slander and besmirch my client and to avoid the proper prosecution of their wrongful act in the violation of Ms. Caissen's civil rights!"

"Your Honor!" called Overton as he, too, strode toward the judge's bench. "I must object most emphatically."

"Of course you must. Mr. Overton, what do you say to the plaintiff's charges?"

"I think my colleague, Ms. Daley, is being overzealous in her client's behalf."

"Ms. Daley?"

"Your Honor, I can not only prove what I've just said, but am prepared to call a witness who will rebut Mr. Hutchings's testimony, prove that he perjured himself, and do the same for Mr. Prince's testimony."

"Your Honor," Overton said in a calm, confident voice. "The plaintiff has already ended her case. Why did she not bring this up before? Or is this some grandstand play for the press?"

"I had no idea at the time that the defense would stoop to the use of perjury to win this case!" Ann snapped.

"How dare you insinuate that I—"

"Just a second, Mr. Overton," said the judge as she interrupted his tirade and looked from one attorney to the other. "Can you prove this perjury conclusively?"

"Yes," Ann replied, not looking at the judge, but straight into Overton's eyes.

"If you fail to do so, I shall have no option but to find for the defendant."

"I understand that," Ann said as a smile appeared on Overton's mouth.

"Very well. Mr. Overton, do you object to the plaintiff calling a new witness?"

"I do."

"Objection overruled. Call your witness, Ms. Daley."

"Thank you, Your Honor," Ann replied as she turned back to the wide-eyed spectators.

Throughout this confrontation, Ti had watched the proceedings carefully. She heard everything that was said, and although she knew Ann was trying her best, it was with a sinking heart that she saw Ann turn. Julia couldn't possibly do what Ann was suggesting.

Then, with everyone else, she waited for Ann to call the secretary.

"I would like to call Mr. Jason Patten to the stand."

Ti's breath caught as she turned. Jason was here! She searched frantically, until she saw him standing in the rear of the courtroom. Then she forced herself to breathe as he walked down the aisle toward her. His face was held in firm lines, and the twin grooves running from his cheeks to his jawline seemed to have deepened. His hair glistened, and his mouth, under the dark mustache, was a tight line.

He wore a gray pin-striped suit, with a white shirt and a solid blue tie. As he passed Ti, she smelled the aftershave she had come to associate him with. She watched him walk to the stand, and willed her heart to slow its beating. It would not listen to her commands. All the love she'd felt for him returned as she stared incredulously at him.

When he was in the witness stand he turned and gazed directly at her. Ti saw his umber eyes search her face, and felt the warmth they projected. Then the clerk swore him in, and her entire body echoed from the deep sound of his voice.

"Mr. Patten, would you tell the court your name and occupation?"

"My name is Jason Patten, and I am the General Manager of Barkley Vineyards of California."

Ti's jaw dropped at his statement. Jason had said he *is* the general manager, not *was*.

"Mr. Patten, what is your connection with this case?"

"I was present in the hallway outside Miss Caissen's apartment when she and Mr. Hutchings were there."

"You mean you were a witness to what happened?"

"Yes, ma'am," Jason said as he turned his head and stared at Tom Hutchings. Ti followed his eyes, and saw her ex-boss turn ashen.

"Objection!" called Overton.

"On what grounds?" the judge demanded. Her eyes hardened as she looked at the attorney.

Overton stared at the judge for a moment then shook his head. "Withdrawn," he muttered as he sat down.

"Mr. Patten," said the judge as her eyes went from Overton to Jason's, "you are instructed to continue."

"Yes, ma'am," he said with a slight smile as he glanced quickly at Ti. "I was in the hallway that night when Miss Caissen and he came out of the elevator. They didn't see me, and before I could make my presence known, they were at her door. Miss Caissen opened her door and thanked the man for dinner, but before she could go into her apartment, he grabbed her.

"She tried to fight him off, but he was pretty persistent. They argued for a minute, and then Hutchings told her she had better be nice to him if she wanted to go places in the company."

A hum of voices erupted in the courtroom at Jason's testimony, and the judge cautioned everyone to be quiet. Then Ann prompted Jason again. "And what happened then?"

"Miss Caissen told him she would not be in the following day because she quit."

"And that was the end of it?" Ann asked.

"No, ma'am. He still wouldn't take no for an answer. That was when I stepped in and . . ."

"And?"

A smile formed on Jason's lips as his eyes caressed

Ti's face. "I escorted Hutchings, by his collar, to the elevator." The entire courtroom exploded with laughter. Then, suddenly, everyone was staring at Tom Hutchings.

Overton whispered into Hutchings's ear for a moment and then looked at Jason.

"Thank you, Mr. Patten, that will be all," Ann said.

The judge looked at Overton, and the anger on her face was visible for all to see. "Did you wish to cross-examine, Mr. Overton?" she asked.

"Not at this time, Your Honor," Overton said in a low voice.

"Then when?" snapped the judge. "Mr. Overton, what I have just heard has greatly disturbed me, and given rise to many questions. How can I now doubt the validity of Ms. Daley's statement that your client has committed perjury? Might I suggest you speak with your client about recanting his testimony?"

"A moment, Your Honor," Overton said as he sat down and whispered earnestly with his associate and Hutchings.

Ti only partially watched what was happening because she couldn't tear her eyes away from Jason. Everything that had happened in the last few days was wiped from her mind as she bathed in the radiance of his presence.

She had missed him terribly, and now knew just how desperately she loved him. She wanted to stand up and run into his arms and feel his strength and warmth against her. She needed him to hold her, to soothe her and to love her.

Overton stood again and Ti drew her eyes from Jason to watch him. "May I have a word with you and Ms. Daley first?" he asked.

"Step forward," the judge said. The two attorneys walked to the bench and stood to face the judge.

Although the lawyers and the judge spoke in low voices, Ti could hear everything that was said, and as she listened a wave of relief washed over her.

"Your Honor, I must apologize for what has happened here today, and I also want to assure you that I had no idea that what my client told me was anything but the truth of the incident between him and Ms. Caissen."

"Very eloquent," the judge replied as she waited for him to continue.

"I would beg the court's permission to have both witnesses' testimonies stricken from the record at this time, and a plea of 'no contest' entered."

"Ms. Daley?" the judge asked with raised eyebrows.

"There is more," Overton interrupted. "I feel certain that Matheson and Company will be more than willing to settle this dispute in a very amicable way."

"According to what we have already asked for in our suit?" Ann asked.

"I can see no problem with that, if the case is dropped," Overton agreed.

Ti heard it all, and felt a number of different things. But above it all was the anger and humiliation which Hutchings and Company had heaped on her today. She glared at Overton and waited. Then she realized that Ann was looking at her with an unvoiced question on her face.

Ti smiled and shook her head.

Ann nodded and her smile matched Ti's. "Your Honor, we'd prefer to allow the wisdom of the court to decide this case. We will not withdraw our petition."

"Very well, Ms. Daley," the judge replied. "Mr. Overton, did you wish to cross-examine the witness?"

"No, Your Honor," he replied stiffly as he turned and went back to his seat.

"Mr. Patten, the court would like to thank you for

coming forward and helping us to ascertain the truths in this case. You are dismissed."

Jason stood and, as he drew himself to his full height, nodded his head to the judge. Then, slowly, he walked from the witness stand toward the aisle. As he passed Ti, he paused momentarily. Then, without further hesitation, he continued on down the aisle. At the last row, he stopped and turned.

Ti watched his back until he stopped, but just before he returned to his seat Ti heard the judge's voice ring out and she forced herself to face forward.

"Bailiff, step forward," the judge ordered. When the man reached the desk, the judge leaned forward and whispered something in his ear. The bailiff nodded his head once, and left the courtroom. "Ladies and gentlemen," called the judge. The courtroom fell silent again as everyone looked expectantly at the woman. "Because of what has happened here today, and because of the importance of this hearing, I will not delay in giving my decision. This case is not just one of local interest. Its roots reach back almost to the beginning of recorded history and reflect accurately what is happening everywhere. The widespread and flagrant practice of sexual harassment against women in the work forces of this country is something every individual should be made aware of. Today, it is the sincere hope of this court to add to that awareness.

"I would like it to be known for the record that the defense has asked the court to withdraw the testimony of its witnesses. However, after careful consideration, I find myself unable to allow that action.

"And, let it be also shown in the records that the Court hereby orders both witnesses, Hutchings and Prince, to be remanded to the custody of the Marshal, in order to be charged with the crime of perjury under oath. Marshal?" called the judge. Walking toward the bench was the bailiff, and the Federal Marshal. They stopped at the defense attorney's bench, and stood to one side, waiting until the proceedings were over before taking the two men into custody.

The Judge then looked from Hutchings to Ti, and spoke again. "It is the opinion of this court that Matheson and Company did, through their agent and through their own collusion, allow the sexual harassment of the plaintiff. And, due to the unusual circumstances of this proceeding, the court has no other choice than to find this case in favor of the plaintiff.

"The court thereby awards to the plaintiff the full and entire amount of justifiable damages asked in the petition—the sum of five hundred twenty-five thousand dollars. Furthermore, the court orders Matheson and Company to rehire Miss Caissen in a position of equal rank and pay, and to cease and desist in any further acts of sexual harassment and civil rights violations. Case dismissed."

The courtroom erupted with noise, but for Ti, the only sound she heard was the judge's words. Ti had won. She had beaten them, and she was glad. Then the sound of the judge's gavel penetrated her ears, and she realized everyone had become silent again.

"There is one more thing I would like to say," said the judge. "Miss Caissen, will you permit me to give you some advice?"

"Yes, Your Honor," Ti replied in surprise.

"Although you have regained the right to return to work for Matheson and Company, I think such a valuable person as yourself could find a better and more ethical employer."

"I think so, too, Your Honor," Ti said as a large

smile spread across her face. "Thank you," she whispered. Ti suddenly found herself enveloped in Ann's arms.

"We did it!" the lawyer cried.

"Thank you, Ann, I mean that."

"I know. And we'd better thank your Mr. Patten," Ann said as both she and Ti turned to find Jason. But they couldn't see him.

Ti's mind was numb as her eyes searched across every face in the room. Where was he? *No,* she cried silently when she realized he was gone. *Not again,* she pleaded. As she tried to push through the milling crowd, Ann's hand gripped her arm.

"Wait," the lawyer cautioned. Ti tried to pull away but couldn't.

"I have to find him," she said.

"You'll have to wait. We've got twenty reporters who want to speak to you. Now, take a deep breath and get ready."

"I can't," Ti said.

"You have to."

And Ti saw that Ann was right. As they walked out of the courtroom they were enveloped by the waiting media. Questions were fired at Ti from every direction as television-camera lights and flashbulbs blinded her. Helplessly, knowing that she could never escape to find Jason now, she began to answer the reporters' questions.

Chapter 13

ENDLESS HOURS LATER, TI STEPPED OUT OF THE CAB AND crossed the sidewalk to her building. A chilled wind swept forlornly along the avenue, and the late fall sky was overcast and threatening. Ti smelled the all-too-identifiable and varied odors of the city, and for the first time in her life she hated the ugliness and filth around her. Although she had won a major battle today, she felt no elation. She was still without the man she loved and needed.

Pushing away the tendrils of despair that had infiltrated her mind since Jason's disappearance from the courtroom, Ti rode the elevator to her floor. There, as her eyes stared at nothing, she walked slowly toward her empty apartment.

She stopped suddenly as she saw a shadowy figure in her doorway. Fear flashed in her mind, but fled quickly as her gaze penetrated the murky shadows and recognized the form within. Her mind swam, and her heart pounded so hard in her chest it hurt. As if her feet were mired in quicksand, Ti walked unsteadily toward him. Then they were together and Jason's lips were on hers.

The kiss lasted for an eternity and stirred Ti's blood heatedly until her mind exploded in relief and longing. They separated and, in the low light of the hallway, Ti gazed into Jason's handsome and angular face.

"I thought you were gone."

"Only once," he said as his hand cupped her chin. "I learned my lesson in California."

"Welcome home," she whispered as she raised herself on her toes and kissed him gently.

Ti drew back from the warmth of his lips, and allowed herself to bathe in the soft glow radiating from the depths of his eyes. They were together now, and she knew that as long as they stayed that way, they would never be lonely again.

Ti dared not speak a word. Instead, she slipped her key in the door and opened it. Taking his hand, she led him inside and, once the door was closed, fell into his arms.

Jason pulled her to him, his lips seeking hers, the hunger within him demanding as the object of his love joined with him.

"We have to talk," Ti murmured as she reluctantly drew her lips from his.

"We have the rest of our lives to talk. I love you, Ti. I need you, now. . . ." Jason said, a deep desire filling his voice.

Ti couldn't think clearly as he pressed her to him. She gazed into his eyes, and was again covered by the warmth and love issuing from them. With her eyes holding his, Ti nodded.

"I need you, too, Jason," Ti whispered, her voice low and far away. "And I . . . I thank you for being here for me."

Slowly, Ti stepped away and removed her jacket. Smiling shyly, she turned and walked across the room. "Give me a minute," she said as she entered her bedroom.

Jason watched her disappear through the doorway as he took off his coat and jacket and loosened his tie. He felt like a schoolboy. His heart beat powerfully in his chest, and his mouth was dry. He knew he would soon be crossing more than the threshold to Ti's bedroom, he would be crossing the threshold into a new life.

But he'd known that from the moment he'd turned his car around and had started back to the winery three days before. On the way back to see Ti and Sam, he'd stopped at the cemetery and found the envelope with his name printed boldly on it. He'd opened it and read the note written in Ti's neat hand.

Dearest Jason,

When you love someone, you must believe in them. There must be a selfishness, and a selflessness to that love. There must also be trust. A person's past is part of that trust and part of that love. When you are ready for the future, I will be there for you.

Ti

"I know," Jason had whispered when he'd finished the note. Then he'd turned from the grave and had gone to his car. The note had not added any fuel to his mission, but it had done one thing; it had told him that he had been right in returning to face Samuel Barkley.

"Jason."

Jason's breath caught as he looked at Ti. She stood framed within the bedroom doorway; her hair fell loosely around her shoulders before dropping down along her back. One coal-black tendril fell across her breasts, showing the contrast between her hair and the white negligee. The low light from the bedroom silhouetted her, and outlined the lush curves within the white satin.

Jason crossed the floor. "You're beautiful," he said as his arms went around her. "I love you," he whispered, just before his lips crushed down on hers.

A lightning bolt of fire scorched downward from Ti's mouth to shoot wildly throughout her body. Suddenly the ground was no longer under her feet, and she was being carried across the room. Ti buried her head on Jason's chest as her hands held on to his wide back.

Jason carried her as if she were as light as a feather. When he reached the bed, he reluctantly placed her upon it. He sat on its edge and as his hand stroked her cheek, his eyes devoured the beautiful contours of her face.

Ti captured his hand within hers, and brought it to her lips. She kissed his palm gently, moving it slowly across her lips as her other hand began to unbutton his shirt.

The next few minutes passed in a blur of love and desire, until Jason was lying naked next to her, slowly removing her negligee.

Ti wanted to say something as she drank in his perfection, but words would not come. Even as she looked into his eyes, she knew words were unnecessary as Jason's face drew close to hers and his lips covered her own. Darting, searing jolts of electricity lanced through her body as he kissed her. A small fire built up within her, and as Jason's mouth left hers and began to travel along her neck, the fire grew stronger. His lips were welcomed as nothing in her life had ever been. Then his hands began to caress her. His strong fingers dug gently into her skin, and the fire within her erupted into a consuming ball of passion. Her breasts exploded each time his lips went across them. His teeth and tongue made her entire body tremble whenever they captured her taut nipples.

Her hands wove through his hair, alternately pressing him harder to her, and then pulling him away. The pain of her desire was so strong she could not control her body.

Then Jason sat up and gazed at her. His eyes washed across her and told her of his need. As she reached up for him, she regained control of her desire. It hadn't abated, but it was no longer commanding her. She smiled slowly at Jason, and he smiled down at her. He moved carefully, his mouth reaching down to hers. They kissed, a slow, tantalizing kiss held by only one thing—love.

Suddenly Ti knew what was happening. The instant desire that had filled her was gone, replaced by a deeper, stronger feeling of love, surpassing the desires that had ruled their lovemaking until now.

And she saw the same thing reflected within Jason's eyes. Ti's breathing slowed as Jason lowered himself to her side. They lay together in silence, just holding each other, content for the moment.

"I never realized that we could have this," Ti said as she stroked Jason's cheek.

"We never let it happen," he responded as his hand began to caress the soft, silken skin of her belly. Then their eyes closed, and their lips met. The heat of their lips was generated throughout their bodies. Ti turned on her side to face him, and pressed her breasts against Jason's chest. She luxuriated in the warmth they shared as their tongues danced and their blood began to run hot again.

Then Ti was on her back and Jason was caressing her with his lips. With her eyes closed, and her hands tracing lazy circles on his back, Ti gave herself up to him, and accepted the love he was offering.

Jason traced a path across her breasts, stopping at each dark-tipped mound to gently kiss and bite the stiffened skin, before continuing his downward journey. His lips skimmed along the soft, glowing skin of her abdomen just as his hands began to stroke her sides. Then his mouth turned to fire as he crossed the downy moss of soft hair, to pause for the barest of seconds as his tongue darted to taste the hidden recesses of her femininity. Ti's back arched, and a low moan floated in the air. Then Jason's lips were on the oversensitive skin of her inner thigh, while his fingers gently kneaded the pliant skin of her hips.

Slowly, his lips and tongue traversed the expanse of warm flesh, and as the floral musk of her womanly aroma sent his senses reeling, his lips and tongue caressed her intimately.

For long, excruciating moments, Ti languished within Jason's power. His hands, fingers, lips and tongue made love to her, and her body responded with abandon until she could no longer stand the heightened pleasure. At that moment she called out to him as her nails dug crescent moons into the tight muscles of his shoulders.

"I need you, Jason, I need you now," she pleaded. He moved, slowly, maddeningly, sliding upward along her body. His lips devoured her even as his tongue rasped along her skin. When he captured her nipple, she cried out.

As her hands cupped the back of his head, she lifted her head and drew him to her mouth. Their lips met in an explosion of desire, and Ti pulled him further along her body. She could feel him at her now-moist entrance, and gently opened her thighs as her hand traced the muscles that flowed along his back. Her fingers glided along the rise of his buttocks, and then guided him into her, absorbing the burning path he made.

Neither moved. Their eyes opened and locked. Blinking, Ti lifted her lips to his. Their mouths touched in a gentle kiss of love, and their hands pulled each closer to the other. They lay like that for endless minutes, each unwilling to move or disturb the peace and love that washed over them in waves of contentment.

When their lips parted, the desire returned, spreading upward and filling Ti with a renewed passion, surmounting anything she'd thought possible. A low moan tore from her throat as his heat fueled the fires, and when he finally moved, her entire body responded to him.

Her breasts swelled against his chest, and her legs wrapped around his hips. Her lips found the sensitive skin on his neck, and she felt the blood rushing through his veins below them. Then they were moving together, and with each of Jason's deep and filling thrusts, Ti moved her hips to meet him.

Under her hands, his muscles rippled powerfully, and with each breath she took, she pulled herself closer and closer to him. Then Jason began to move faster. His muscular body pressed along her length and deep within her, she could feel him grow harder. Suddenly her mind refused to function, and she relinquished control, knowing that her love and trust of him would never again know bounds.

"I love you," she cried as her body tensed, and she climbed to the apex of her physical love. But Jason would not slow, and his long, powerful thrusts drew cries more and more frenzied from her, until at last, he poured his liquid heat within her soft depths.

After many minutes passed, they turned onto their

sides, and Jason wound his fingers gently through her hair. "We'll never be alone again," he whispered, "our love will see to that."

Ti nodded her head slowly, unable to stop her tears from spilling out. "Will it?" she asked in a husky voice.

"Yes. I never thought something like this was possible, but I fell in love with you."

Ti gazed at him. She searched his face, and then traced every line and angle on it with her fingers as his words continued to echo within her mind. Slowly, she nodded. "We'll make it so. But," she added as she looked at him steadily, "what will you do?"

Jason knew she was referring to work, and he smiled warmly at her. "It doesn't really matter anymore, but Barkley Vineyards needs us, and your new winery does, also."

Us, Ti thought wondrously. "My grandfather?"

"Approves. When I spoke to him, I realized I was the one who was wrong, not he. For the moment I'm still the general manager, but . . ." Jason's voice trailed off as he gazed intensely at Ti. He took a deep breath, and as his hand caressed her shoulder, he spoke again. "Ti, I want to go back, but when I boarded the plane in San Francisco, I knew I wouldn't return without you. If you won't, or can't come back—if you feel that too much has happened and you don't want to live in the Valley, or at the vineyards—I won't force you. Wherever we are will be our home."

Ti stared at him. Her love for him, and for the sacrifice he was offering, thundered in her mind. Her heart opened wide, and she knew from that moment on that everything would be right.

"Wherever we are is our home," she repeated as she gazed into his eyes. "And wherever you go, I shall go with you. But my love," she said as she caressed his cheek, "there is only one place for you, and I accept it gladly."

"I love you," he whispered as he turned onto his back and drew her along with him. As her hair fell across his face in soft waves, the tips of her breasts grew stiff and pressed into his chest. She tossed her head, and her hair flipped upward into the air above them before settling fanlike across her back.

"I never knew how strong love could make me feel. I feel loved, possessed, possessing and wanted. Jason, I love you," she whispered as she kissed him again.

Epilogue

SUNLIGHT FLOODED THE HILLS AND BROUGHT OUT THE varied contrasts that filled the earth to present them in an all-encompassing splendor. Stately and majestic trees rose upward toward the sun. Emerald-green grasses offered a soft carpet for the foot and soothed the mind and eye. The winding vines that proliferated in the neatly tilled fields were an unending expanse of beauty to the four people who sat on the lawn.

Birds called to each other, and in the distance the sounds of people relaxing and enjoying this peaceful summer Sunday floated through the air of the Napa Valley.

A little girl, three years old, her raven hair in a ponytail, and her hazel eyes sparkling with life, played with a small golden retriever puppy. Behind her, watching everything she did, were three adults, seated on lawn chairs. A small white wrought-iron table was in front of them, and on it rested a bottle of wine, with the Gentle Winds label, and three partially filled glasses.

"It feels good," Sam Barkley said to Ti and Jason.

"The sun?" Ti asked.

"No, life. And having you, Jase and Jenna living here."

Ti gazed at her grandfather and smiled. He was right, being here with her family did feel good. It had since the day they'd arrived, four years ago, and told Sam they were getting married. And for four years she, Jason and Sam had worked hard to make sure everything would be good for them. The results of their efforts were the rewards they received daily. The rewards of love, peace and happiness that started when they woke and continued through their dreams. For Ti, it was a fairy tale come true.

"Granpa!" cried the little girl as she ran toward them carrying the chubby puppy in her arms. Ti started to stand, but stopped as Jason's restraining hand fell on her arm. When the little girl reached the adults, she stopped in front of Sam Barkley. "Thank you, Granpa, he's booootiful," said three-year-old Jenna Patten.

"Have you given him a name yet?" Sam asked as he smiled at his great-granddaughter. He looked at her, as he had done every day since her birth, and felt love and pride fill him at the sight of her beauty and inner warmth.

"Yes . . ." she said hesitantly as her large eyes looked from her father, to her mother, to her great-grandfather.

"Well?" asked Ti.

Jenna put the golden-haired puppy down, took a deep breath, and faced her mother. "I was named after your mother, right?" Jenna asked, an innocent smile exposing her shiny little teeth.

"Yes," Ti said as she nodded slowly, wondering what her impish daughter was up to now.

"And Granpa said you was named after your ansister Ticonaroga . . ."

"Ancestor, and Ticonderoga," Ti corrected her, unable to hide her smile.

"Yes! Can I name my puppy after someone, too?"

"Of course you can," Sam declared expansively.

"Thank you, Granpa. I want to name him Sam," she said as she released the puppy to the ground.

"Sam?" came the startled cry of all the adults as they stared at Jenna. Suddenly Ti began to laugh, and Jason joined her as they both saw a wide range of expressions flash across Sam Barkley's bearded face. Then they watched as Sam, flushing with pride, scooped up his great-granddaughter in one arm, and the puppy in the other.

"Sam it is," he said as he turned to face Ti and Jason, an open challenge written across his features, defying them to argue with him.

"Thank you, Granpa," Jenna said as she kissed his cheek. "I love you."

"And I love you, too," he said in a choked voice. "All of you," he added as his eyes swept across Ti and Jase.

Coming in October 1983

Janet Dailey

CALDER BORN CALDER BRED

The Calder family story which began so dramatically in <u>This Calder Sky</u> and continued in <u>This Calder Range</u> and <u>Stands A Calder Man</u> now comes to a close in this all-new novel, as powerful, as enthralling as the first three.

If you've thrilled to the first three Calder novels, you will not want to miss Janet Dailey's new novel—on sale in October.

....

Or, use the coupon below to order by mail
Pocket Books, Department 983
1230 Avenue of the Americas, New York, NY 10020 ℙ
Please send me _____ copies of CALDER BORN, CALDER BRED
(83610-2 / $6.95). Please add 75¢ to cover postage and handling.
NYS and NYC residents please add appropriate sales tax. Send
check or money order—no cash, stamps, or CODs, please. Allow six
weeks for delivery.

Name_____

Address_____

City_____ State / ZIP_____

Silhouette
Intimate Moments

more romance, more excitement

———————— $2.25 each ————————

#1 ☐ DREAMS OF EVENING
Kristin James

#2 ☐ ONCE MORE WITH
FEELING Nora Roberts

#3 ☐ EMERALDS IN THE DARK
Beverly Bird

#4 ☐ SWEETHEART CONTRACT
Pat Wallace

#5 ☐ WIND SONG
Parris Afton Bonds

#6 ☐ ISLAND HERITAGE
Monica Barrie

#7 ☐ A DISTANT CASTLE
Sue Ellen Cole

#8 ☐ LOVE EVERLASTING
Moëth Allison

#9 ☐ SERPENT IN PARADISE
Stephanie James

#10 ☐ A SEASON OF
RAINBOWS Jennifer West

#11 ☐ UNTIL THE END OF TIME
June Trevor

#12 ☐ TONIGHT AND ALWAYS
Nora Roberts

#13 ☐ EDGE OF LOVE
Anna James

#14 ☐ RECKLESS SURRENDER
Jeanne Stephens

#15 ☐ SHADOW DANCE
Lorraine Sellers

#16 ☐ THE PROMISE OF
SUMMER Barbara Faith

#17 ☐ THE AMBER SKY
Kristin James

#18 ☐ THE DANVERS TOUCH
Elizabeth Lowell

#19 ☐ ANOTHER KIND OF LOV
Mary Lynn Baxter

#20 ☐ THE GENTLE WINDS
Monica Barrie

- -

SILHOUETTE INTIMATE MOMENTS, Department IM/5
1230 Avenue of the Americas
New York, NY 10020

Please send me the books I have checked above. I am enclosing
$_____ (please add 50¢ to cover postage and handling. NYS
and NYC residents please add appropriate sales tax.) Send check or
money order—no cash or C.O.D.'s please. Allow six weeks for delivery

NAME _____

ADDRESS _____

CITY _____ STATE/ZIP _____

Silhouette Intimate Moments

Coming Next Month

Raven's Prey by Stephanie James

Honor Knight had to convince Judd Raven the two men who
had hired him to find her weren't her father and brother.
Only Honor hadn't realized Judd was holding her prisoner
for his own reason: he was in love.

Against The Rules by Linda Howard

At seventeen Cathryn Ashe had fought Rule Jackson and lost.
Now, more sure of herself and her new-found independence,
she was ready to challenge him again—only this time,
her heart was at stake.

The Fires Of Winter by Beverly Bird

As editor of a small paper, Heather Cavelle tried to write only
of the good in the world. Then David Sullivan took over and
plunged the paper into a search for crime and hidden truths,
and what they discovered was their love for each other.

Fantasies by Pamela Wallace

When Spencer Tait met the new studio president
Devon O'Neill they clashed immediately. Tensions were high
and the future at stake as the cameras rolled—because this
time, the real story was taking place behind the scenes.

Genuine Silhouette sterling silver bookmark for only $15.95!

What a beautiful way to hold your place in your current romance! This genuine sterling silver bookmark, with the distinctive Silhouette symbol in elegant black, measures 1½″ long and 1″ wide. It makes a beautiful gift for yourself, and for every romantic you know! And, at only $15.95 each, including all postage and handling charges, you'll want to order several now, while supplies last.

Send your name and address with check or money order for $15.95 per bookmark ordered to
Simon & Schuster Enterprises
120 Brighton Rd., P.O. Box 5020
Clifton, N.J. 07012
Attn: Bookmark

Bookmarks can be ordered pre-paid only. No charges will be accepted. Please allow 4-6 weeks for delivery.

N.Y. State Residents
Please Add Sales Tax

Dear Reader:

Please take a few moments to fill out this questionnaire. It will help us give you more of the Silhouette Intimate Moments you'd like best.

Mail to: **Karen Solem**
Silhouette Books
1230 Ave. of the Americas, New York, N.Y. 10020

1. How did you obtain **THE GENTLE WINDS?** [9-20]

10-1 ☐ **Bookstore**   -6 ☐ **Newsstand**
  -2 ☐ **Supermarket**   -7 ☐ **Airport**
  -3 ☐ **Variety/discount store**   -8 ☐ **Book Club**
  -4 ☐ **Department store**   -9 ☐ **From a friend**
  -5 ☐ **Drug store**   -0 ☐ **Other:**_____

(write in)

2. How many Silhouette Intimate Moments have you read including this one?

(circle one number) 11- **1 2 3 4 5 6 7 8 9 10 11 12 13 14 15 16**

3. Overall how would you rate this book?

12-1 ☐ **Excellent** -2 ☐ **Very good**
  -3 ☐ **Good** -4 ☐ **Fair** -5 ☐ **Poor**

4. Which elements did you like best about this book?

13-1 ☐ **Heroine** -2 ☐ **Hero** -3 ☐ **Setting** -4 ☐ **Story line**
  -5 ☐ **Love scenes** -6 ☐ **Ending** -7 ☐ **Other Characters**

5. Do you prefer love scenes that are

14-1 ☐ **Less explicit than**   -2 ☐ **More explicit than**
     in this book   **in this book**
         -3 ☐ **About as explicit as in this book**

6. What influenced you most in deciding to buy this book?

15-1 ☐ **Cover** -2 ☐ **Title** -3 ☐ **Back cover copy**
  -4 ☐ **Recommendations** -5 ☐ **You buy all Silhouette Books**

7. How likely would you be to purchase other Silhouette Intimate Moments in the future?

16-1 ☐ **Extremely likely**   -3 ☐ **Not very likely**
  -2 ☐ **Somewhat likely**   -4 ☐ **Not at all likely**

8. Do you prefer books at (check one)

17-1 ☐ **A longer length of 256 pages?** **-3 Other:** _____
  -2 ☐ **A shorter length of 192 pages?** (write in)

9. Will INTIMATE MOMENTS affect your purchasing SILHOUETTE DESIRES? 18-1 ☐ **yes** -2 ☐ **no**

10. Please check the box next to your age group.

19-1 ☐ **Under 18** -3 ☐ **25-34**   -5 ☐ **50-54**
  -2 ☐ **18-24**   -4 ☐ **35-49** -6 ☐ **55+**

11. Would you be interested in receiving a romance newsletter? If so please fill in your name and address.

Name_____

Address_____

City_____ State_____ Zip_____

19___ 20___ 21___ 22___ 23___